A LESSON IN
MURDER

Books by Verity Bright

A LESSON IN MURDER

VERITY BRIGHT

bookouture

Published by Bookouture in 2021

An imprint of Storyfire Ltd.

Carmelite House
50 Victoria Embankment
London EC4Y 0DZ
www.bookouture.com

ISBN: 978-1-80019-571-4
eBook ISBN: 978-1-80019-570-7

*To Hovis, my dog, who is nothing like Gladstone
but every bit as precious.*

It is absurd to divide people into good and bad.
People are either charming or tedious ~ *Oscar Wilde*

CHAPTER 1

It wasn't the early June heatwave that was making Lady Eleanor Swift feel lightheaded, even though it was stifling in the packed hall. She tried to swallow her anxiety but the knot in her stomach tightened again, making her feel more than a little uneasy.

Botheration. Why, oh why, did you say yes, Ellie!

Even choosing her outfit that morning had uncharacteristically turned into something of a drama. Never one to fuss about her appearance, she had nevertheless tried to dress for the occasion, it being Speech Day at St Mary's, her old school. The result had driven her normally propriety-mad butler, Clifford, to suggest she wear whatever she was most comfortable in. *Well, there's a first time for everything, Ellie!*

She glanced at Clifford, who sat at the back of the hall, which was a long, white-painted auditorium, hung with scroll-top boards embossed with decades of head girls' names in gold lettering below the austere, high-vaulted ceiling. He caught her eye and gave her an encouraging nod. Despite Clifford's formal demeanour, since her uncle's death last February he had quietly assumed so much more than his butler's duties entailed and was exactly the rock she needed right now.

She ran an anxious hand through her flame-red curls and implored her brain to ignore that she was seated in the grandiose velvet chair reserved for the guest of honour. On stage! Even the warm smile of her now elderly favourite teacher, Mrs Wadsworth, whom she'd assumed had long since retired, couldn't calm her nerves.

Eleanor had been sent to St Mary's at the age of nine, after the disappearance of her parents, and had struggled to fit in and make friends. Mrs Wadsworth had been a beacon of compassion and comfort, both as Eleanor's English teacher and boarding housemistress. She had gone out of her way to befriend the fiery, but desperately unhappy girl Eleanor had been back then and make her days at St Mary's as tolerable as they could be.

Eleanor tried to avoid looking along the lines of staff perched on fold-out wooden chairs on either side of her, but one teacher in particular, a grim-faced woman with sharp black eyes, dressed in a conservative, grey high-necked suit, caught her eye. Mrs Coulson, the deputy headmistress. They had met briefly. Eleanor shuddered. *Not briefly enough.*

She focused instead on Miss Lonsdale, the headmistress. Standing in front of Eleanor behind a highly polished lectern, she addressed her attentive audience with dignified confidence. Off the stage, expectant parents sat nodding approvingly as she ran through the school's many successes that academic year. There were even a few sporting achievements.

Since Miss Lonsdale had taken over St Mary's Boarding School for Young Ladies, it was rapidly becoming more progressive. Or at least, she'd confided in Eleanor, that was her hope. In her letter inviting Eleanor to be the guest of honour, she'd written effusively about how Eleanor epitomised the progressive woman she saw as the way forward for St Mary's girls. However, glancing at the rows of parents, Eleanor doubted many of them held that view. Their fashionable tailored suits and designer dresses paid testament to St Mary's exclusivity and staggeringly high fees, rather than any progressive tendencies. It struck her as ironic that their daughters would leave as accomplished young ladies destined for nothing more than a society wedding to the most eligible bachelor available.

She groaned quietly. They definitely wouldn't want their daughters to turn out like her; fiercely independent, impetuous, naturally unorthodox and, as a result, unmarried at thirty. Thus, she concluded with another wave of anxiety, neither would they want to hear a word of her speech.

The young ladies in question sat behind the parents, three abreast on wooden gym benches, hands ladylike in their laps, ankles demurely crossed. Their smart navy pinafore dresses with matching ties over white blouses took Eleanor back to her own hideous days at St Mary's. After her parents disappeared in Peru, she'd been wrenched from a bohemian life abroad and forced into the strict regime of an English Victorian girls' school. Her every waking moment from then on had taken the form of a battle of wits, or attrition, depending on how one viewed it, between her and most of the staff.

She tried to distract herself by remembering the feel of that pinafore dress she had hated so much. In the early days she'd railed against the itchy wool that was uncomfortably hot in summer and even more uncomfortably damp in winter. As she'd grown into herself and become more self-aware, she'd also loathed how it hung shapelessly on her long slender frame. Not to mention that the blue clashed with her bright green eyes and head of red curls. From the day she'd left St Mary's, she'd lived almost exclusively in green of any and every shade.

Against Eleanor's better judgement, she let her eyes rove once more along the packed rows of parents but blanched at the sea of attentive faces. *This is ridiculous, Ellie. You've faced charging rhinos and armed assailants and cycled around the world on your own. This should be easy. It's just talking, after all.*

But it wasn't so much the talking as the feeling. The feeling of once again being that confused nine-year-old who had no idea why her parents had suddenly disappeared and why she had been sent to this prison. And why she'd been expected to only speak when spoken to and comply with a thousand more rules designed purely, it seemed, to squash her free spirit.

Three short sharp rings of the school bell rang through the hall. She came back to the present and shook her head. It had seemed to her back then that the school bell had dictated her every waking moment at St Mary's. A movement caught her eye. Behind the teachers the rest of the stage was hidden by a floor-to-ceiling black curtain, used for the end of term productions. Mrs Coulson had risen at the sound of the bell and was holding it open as several other teachers rose and disappeared through it. Miss Lonsdale paused in her speech and glanced at Mrs Coulson, who nodded and closed the curtain behind her.

What was that about, Ellie? I don't remember three short rings when I was here. Maybe it's something Miss Lonsdale has started. But what for?

Shrugging, she returned to listening to the headmistress who had seamlessly resumed her speech. After what seemed like an eternity, but Eleanor knew was only five or ten minutes at most, she heard the words she'd been dreading.

'And now, dear parents and girls, we are honoured to have an alumna or, as we fondly say at St Mary's, "an old girl", as our special guest today. If I might just mention a few of her notable achievements, you will understand why I invited Lady Swift to give this year's speech and present today's well-deserved prizes.'

Eleanor gripped her chair and looked to her butler for help. He took a deep breath in and out and then discreetly pointed at her. Taking his cue, she cursed her jumbled thoughts and took a couple of deep breaths herself.

'So, with no further ado,' Miss Lonsdale said, 'ladies, gentlemen, members of staff and girls, allow me to invite Lady Swift to speak.'

Polite applause followed Eleanor to the lectern. She felt something brush her shoulder and half turned, sensing her mother's presence as she often did in stressful moments. *'Remember, darling girl, nerves just mean you are being braver than you've ever been before.'* She smiled to herself. She'd been especially close to her mother. Even though her parents had always been involved in some important educational project in some far-flung place, her mother particularly had religiously made time for Eleanor. She'd always allowed her daughter to do her own thing and be bold, but she'd also always been there to pick her up, soothe her bruises, and encourage her to try again. They'd been inseparable.

Squaring her shoulders, Eleanor carried on past the lectern to the front of the stage. She didn't have a glib life lesson to deliver, instead she would be herself, as Clifford had assured her she should be. Glancing at him, she couldn't help smiling as he continued the clapping to buy her an extra few seconds.

As the applause subsided, she opened her mouth only to be interrupted by the return of Mrs Coulson. Looking even more grim-faced than when she'd left, she whispered to Miss Lonsdale. The headmistress' hand flew to her chest. She turned and hurried off the stage. Mrs Coulson stepped over to Eleanor.

'I'm sorry, Lady Swift, but would you please be seated a moment?'

As Eleanor sat back down in confusion, Mrs Coulson turned to the equally confused crowd.

'Ladies and gentlemen, please bear with us a moment.'

The second the deputy headmistress had left the stage, the hall erupted into muted conversation. Eleanor looked to catch Clifford's eye with a questioning shrug, but stopped short on seeing his empty seat. *What on earth is going on, Ellie?*

Fifteen minutes passed during which the odd cough among the parents and whispers from the girls turned into shuffling feet and impatient mutterings. Then Mrs Coulson returned and walked to the front of the stage. Eleanor noted her seemingly permanent look of disapproval had been replaced with one of… distress, was it?

Mrs Coulson cleared her throat twice. 'Ladies and gentlemen, please accept our sincere apologies, but this year's Speech Day will have to be rescheduled.'

'Rescheduled?' a self-important voice said from the front row. 'What, for later today? I've a very urgent appointment at—'

Mrs Coulson held up her hand. 'I am sorry, but there will be no further proceedings today. We will have to reschedule for later. I don't know when at present.'

'But why?' a deep voice boomed from the third row.

Mrs Coulson hesitated.

'Because… well, there's been a most unfortunate incident.'

CHAPTER 2

'Lady Swift,' a deep female voice with an Irish lilt said in Eleanor's ear, 'let me take you somewhere a little less… fraught.'

Eleanor looked round to see an athletically built woman in her mid thirties with close-cropped brunette hair. The woman impatiently flapped the white ribbon tie of her sailor-collared burgundy wool dress out of the way and held out her hand.

'Louisa Munn. Head of physical education.'

'Miss Munn, thank you.' Eleanor winced at the strength of the woman's handshake.

Miss Munn lowered her voice. 'Ghastly affairs these Speech Day events, you know.' She snorted a chuckle. 'Probably shouldn't say it to the guest of honour, especially when she's a titled lady, but, if I'm honest, formality brings me out in a rash, it does.'

Eleanor laughed. 'Me too. Head-to-toe and everywhere in between!'

With an amused quirk of one eyebrow, Miss Munn headed off down the short flight of wooden steps at the front of the stage. Eleanor followed her gratefully. As she ducked through a door off to the left, she noted the line of grumbling parents being ushered from the hall by apologetic staff.

Miss Munn led Eleanor along a corridor that had the same heady odour of disinfectant she remembered as a pupil. A moment later they emerged into the smart entrance area where Eleanor had first met the headmistress. Here the disinfectant gave way to the fragrant scent of white gardenias, which bloomed there in ornate pots. On the highly waxed herringbone wood floor stood a full-size porcelain statue of a demure young lady in a deep-set circular window, representing St Mary's 'ideal'. Eleanor had never recognised an ounce of herself in the statue throughout her years there, and still didn't. She cleared her throat.

'Do you know what this "unfortunate incident" Mrs Coulson mentioned can be?' she asked Miss Munn.

'Goodness only knows,' Miss Munn called over her shoulder. 'Between you and me, I wouldn't honestly be surprised if it was something the deputy headmistress deliberately set up, you know. She was her usual vocal self about Miss Lonsdale's err... choice of arrangements and it was her who announced to the parents that Speech Day was cancelled, which probably delighted her.'

Confused as to the choice of which arrangements, Eleanor just nodded.

As they reached the door to the staffroom, Mrs Coulson herself was issuing instructions to the hovering teachers.

'All of you wait here. The bursar is organising the porters in getting the parents off site as quickly as possible. We do not want any of you trying to answer awkward questions. Goodness only knows what you might let slip.'

Miss Munn motioned for Eleanor to step into the staffroom, but Mrs Coulson held up an imperious hand.

'Not in here if you don't mind, Lady Swift. This is the province of teachers. It would be more appropriate if Miss Munn would show you to the headmistress' study to await her return.' She broke off to glare at the head of PE before turning back to Eleanor with a hint of disdain to her tone. 'Although, perhaps you might remember where that is?'

'Only too well, Mrs Coulson,' Eleanor said brightly and spun on her heel.

Alone in Miss Lonsdale's study, Eleanor found her feet rooted to the spot in front of the desk. That lost-nine-year-old feeling washed over her again. *How many times did you stand here waiting for the previous headmistress' wrath, Ellie? Trying to bite your tongue and invariably failing because of the injustice of yet another sanction over some stupid school rule you'd broken?* She ran a hand down the sleeve of her jacket. *Definitely not wearing an itchy wool pinafore now, Ellie. You're grown up! You're not nine any more.*

She sighed. St Mary's had been an anathema from day one. And so it had remained, until, aged sixteen, she'd sprinted down the front steps of the boarding house for the last time, rushing out to leap into the waiting Rolls. Not that Henley Hall, her uncle's country estate, inevitably devoid of her ever-travelling uncle, had felt much more like home.

Clifford had caught her trying to burn her school uniform in the garden incinerator later that evening. To her amazement, rather than admonish her, he had simply slid open the grate to better fan the flames before turning silently back to the house. The memory made her smile. And frown. Even though she'd finally understood why her uncle hadn't been able to look after her at Henley Hall, she'd never fathomed why he'd concluded that St Mary's was the best place to send her. *Surely, a real prison would have been kinder, Ellie!*

To shake off those thoughts, she stared around the room. The stark grey walls she remembered were now light ochre with a colourful matching cushion on each of the armchairs adding a further touch of warmth. The bookcase previously filled with didactic tomes housed five rows of literature classics peppered with framed photographs of pupils receiving a variety of honours and awards. And where the wooden rack housing an array of birch canes had presided, a watercolour of the main building signed by a fifth-form pupil brightened the previously menacing corner.

Above the fireplace, though, the age-old sampler bearing the school motto still spanned the chimney breast.

'Vincit Omnia Veritas,' Eleanor muttered. 'Truth conquers all things. How come I remember that after all this time?'

She frowned as she gazed at the oil portrait of her former headmistress, whose well-captured punitive stare seemed directed at her. She took two steps to the left but was sure those cold judging eyes followed her. Behind the desk, the long run of internal floor-to-ceiling windows gave a bird's eye view to the ground floor, and specifically the part of school referred to in her day as 'Long Passage'. The corridor connecting the east and west ends of the school had been reserved for staff only and thus declared a forbidden zone for girls.

Ellie subconsciously rubbed her wrist, looking down at the scar she'd earned in that very passageway. Late for lessons yet again, and with a raft of detentions already to her name, she'd dared to do the unthinkable and run down Long Passage. It would not only save time, but also avoid the risk of running into the headmistress in the quadrangle, the very person who had summoned her only an hour previously for another unspeakable infraction of the rules. But, as she'd jumped down the three steps halfway along the passageway, her heart had stopped as a voice bellowed behind her.

'Girl! You are out of bounds! Come here at once!'

Instead of turning back, however, she'd ducked her head down and sprinted for safety. Hurriedly reaching for the science-room door handle, she'd put her hand through one of the door's small panes of glass instead. Even Matron's insistence that both the cut and embedded glass were alarmingly deep hadn't diminished the protracted lecture she'd been subjected to in this very room.

'This is your thirteenth offence so far this term. This term, Swift!' The old headmistress' harsh voice had rang round Eleanor's head. 'You're supposed to be a young lady, not an insurgent! I dread to think how you will turn out.'

That was eighteen years ago, Ellie. She shook her head but smiled at the same time as she addressed the portrait. 'Actually, it seems, the epitome of the progressive woman your successor believes St Mary's girls deserve the chance to become. So there!' She stuck her tongue out at the portrait of the woman who had made so much of her childhood a misery.

Then she jumped as a cough came from behind her. 'Miss Lonsdale.' She smiled weakly, wondering if the present headmistress had seen or heard her. If she had, she didn't mention it.

'Lady Swift, please forgive the terrible interruption to your speech. I am so sorry to have invited you all the way here only to become caught up in this... unfortunate matter.'

Eleanor tried to avoid frowning, thinking she hadn't known she was caught up in an unfortunate matter.

'Please don't apologise. Is there anything I can do?'

Miss Lonsdale shook her head with a quiet sniff. 'In one way, no. Regrettably it is too late. But in another...' She shrugged. 'Perhaps you would be good enough to accompany me to the library?'

What's this all about, Ellie?

'Yes, of course. Would you mind, though, if I sent word to my butler first? Wherever he is, he's probably wondering where on earth I've got to.'

'Mr Clifford? He is already in the library. It was he who asked if I would take you there.'

'Really? Gracious.'

Miss Lonsdale nodded. 'He has a remarkably compelling manner. He said you would understand and' – Miss Lonsdale's hand strayed to her chest just as it had on the stage – 'that you would cope admirably.'

Eleanor felt the icy prickle of apprehension form in her stomach as Miss Lonsdale ushered her out of the office. She followed her back past the staffroom and down the stairs. They bypassed the entrance hall and skirted round the music rooms to emerge at the southern side of the quadrangle. The very route the head girl had led Eleanor and Clifford on the whistle-stop tour she had proudly given them before Speech Day had started.

They turned the final corner, and she saw her smart-suited butler waiting outside the library.

'Clifford. There you are. I was wondering where you'd disappeared to.'

He gave his customary half bow from the shoulders. 'My lady. Please forgive my brief absence.'

She flapped a conciliatory hand. 'I trust your reasons as always, whatever they are. But do tell me, please, what is going on?'

'Miss Lonsdale, if I may?'

She gestured that he had the floor.

He stared back at Eleanor, his ever-inscrutable expression faltering momentarily as he gestured behind him at the library door. 'It's Mrs Wadsworth. Most regrettably, my lady, she is no longer with us.'

'No longer with us?' Eleanor tried to comprehend his statement. 'What do you mean? I... oh no! You mean she's...?'

He nodded. 'Yes. Unfortunately, the lady is dead.'

She shook her head. 'But how? She was so full of life when I spoke to her before Speech Day started. And on stage.' She swallowed hard. 'She was my favourite teacher all those years ago. The... only teacher I liked, in truth. And my boarding housemistress. She... she was so kind to me.'

'I know, my lady. During the rare summers you spent at Henley Hall, hers was the only name you ever mentioned with affection. My abject apologies for not being able to break the news another way, but more so, for suggesting you need to see for yourself.'

'See for myself? Why would you possibly want me to see for myself?'

'It is my firm conviction that we need your first impression of the regrettable scene.'

She nodded slowly. 'I can't fathom why, but I trust your judgement, as I said.'

As Clifford pushed open the door and stepped aside, her heart faltered. Between two of the long wooden bookcases was the sprawled form of Mrs Wadsworth lying at an awkward angle on her front, her snow-white head framing lifeless eyes.

Stopping a few feet short of the tragic spot itself, Eleanor covered her mouth as she took in the rest of the scene. The hardback book splayed open, the cover uppermost on the floor by the woman's motionless hand and then the tall A-frame wooden steps facing the bookshelves nearest her.

She frowned as something tugged at her brain, but shock whipped any clear thinking from her faculties. Finally finding her voice, she turned to Miss Lonsdale.

'When you left the stage and arrived here, was Mrs Wadsworth already—'

'Dead.' Miss Lonsdale nodded. 'I was too late. We all were. Matron confirmed the worst before Mrs Coulson fetched me. It is such a heartbreaking accident to have occurred.'

Eleanor looked at Clifford. 'I know you are part wizard, but how on earth did you know what had happened?'

'When Mrs Coulson appeared on the stage in such a state of agitation, I was concerned something was about to throw you off delivering the speech you have worked so hard on.'

'But that doesn't answer the question.'

He coughed. 'No, my lady.' He glanced at the headmistress. 'Scandalously I, ahem, used my lip-reading skills to garner what Mrs Coulson said to Miss Lonsdale. "Accident", "library", and "Mrs Wadsworth" were sufficient to instinctively propel me from my seat.' He turned back to Eleanor. 'Given that the lady was such a positive part of your time at St Mary's, I wished to ensure that whatever the situation I was abreast of it to mitigate any possible distress to you.'

She smiled weakly. 'Thank you. Although I now doubly don't understand why you wanted me to see—'

The steps, Ellie! She stared at them in horror and swallowed hard again.

Clifford followed her gaze and nodded. 'I sincerely hoped you would insist I was wrong, my lady.'

They shared a look and both shook their heads.

'Miss Lonsdale,' Eleanor said to the obviously confused headmistress. 'I'm afraid we need to lock the library and retire to your study immediately.'

'But why, pray, Lady Swift?'

Eleanor glanced back at the body lying on the floor and then at the steps. 'Because you need to place an urgent telephone call through to the police.'

CHAPTER 3

'My lady, are you sure there is nothing I can get you?'

'A magic wand, so I could make this awful business disappear?'

She watched as with a magician's flourish from his pockets her butler pulled a bag of mint humbugs, a copper-plate handwritten copy of the speech she was originally going to give, his pince-nez, a pocket edition of Voltaire's *Dictionnaire Philosophique*, a folding clothes brush, two pristine handkerchiefs, a miniature mending kit, a pocketknife and a pair of shoelaces.

'Ah, regrettably, my lady, the one item I did not anticipate the need to pack this morning.'

Appreciating his attempt to bring a glimmer of lightness to her mood, she marvelled as the long list of items disappeared back into his form-fitting jacket.

'Tsk, very disappointing. It's unlike you to be unprepared.' She wandered over to the bookcase and pulled out *Little Women*. 'Mrs Wadsworth gave me a copy of this. I used to sneak out of the dorm after lights out to read it by candlelight in the Holly House linen cupboard and imagine I had sisters and parents.' She smiled. 'I remember Mrs Wadsworth saying, had I been born twenty or so years earlier, I would certainly have been Louisa May Alcott's muse for one of the March sisters.'

'Josephine, perchance?'

She peered up at him. 'You terror! You mean because she was a tomboy and most unladylike?'

'I really couldn't say, my lady.' He gave her a rare smile. 'But not entirely. Perhaps, for certain other more… resolute qualities. However, once the police have taken our statements, I shall whisk you back to Henley Hall as expediently as safety permits.' His tone softened. 'I know that neither a mischievous bulldog, early house pyjamas or a fortifying warmed brandy will change anything but, collectively, they have proven to be something of a restorative for you previously.'

'Thank you, they sound absolutely perfect. There's just one thing missing, though. Can we add in a distracting game of chess or draughts, if I might impose upon my butler's wonderfully calming company?'

He bowed. 'With sincere pleasure, my lady.'

She looked out the window for the hundredth time.

'How long can it take for the local police to get here? Surely Bedfordshire can't operate along lines too dissimilar to our own county of Buckinghamshire? They share a border, after all!' She glanced at him. 'Don't they?'

'Indeed they do, my lady. I wonder though, if it is the local police who will attend?'

She looked at him quizzically, but her reply was cut short by the long-awaited return of Miss Lonsdale.

'Any news?' Eleanor said, darting forward eagerly.

Miss Lonsdale held up her hands. 'I do apologise for keeping you waiting, Lady Swift. And, yes, Miss Rice, our school secretary, has just informed me the police have arrived.'

'Thank goodness.' Eleanor glanced over the headmistress' shoulder. 'But well, where are they?'

Miss Lonsdale frowned. 'Why, being shown up when the coast is clear, naturally.'

'Naturally.' Eleanor was mystified but noted Clifford's knowing nod out of the corner of her eye.

A few minutes later there was a demure rat-a-tat on the study door. A perfect English rose in her mid twenties popped her finger-waved blonde head around with a nervous smile. 'The policeman, Headmistress.'

Miss Lonsdale nodded. 'Thank you, Miss Rice.'

The school secretary had met Eleanor and Clifford on their arrival and also escorted them to the headmistress' study. Now her cornflower-blue dress rustled against her shapely curves as she gestured at the tall, suited form behind her.

'Please step in. Headmistress, this is Detective Chief Inspector Seldon.'

Hugh! Eleanor managed to stop herself from saying the name out loud. 'Inspector, how… unexpected.'

Detective Chief Inspector Seldon stopped and stared at her. 'Good… afternoon, Lady Swift.' He raised his eyebrows. 'As you say, unexpected.'

Her heart sank. How could it be that they were destined to only ever meet when there was a dead body? *Actually, you don't mean 'meet', Ellie, you mean 'lock horns with'!* Once she'd dreamed of her and Seldon being an item. However, their whole association had been an unmitigated disaster except for one deliciously unexpected evening of dinner and dancing on her last birthday.

Seldon turned to Miss Lonsdale and presented what looked like a short letter. The headmistress took the proffered paper and read it carefully. She looked up and removed her pince-nez.

'Chief Inspector, thank you for coming, but tell me, how is it that you know Lady Swift already?'

Seldon adjusted the collar of his smart charcoal-grey suit.

'Our paths have… crossed on occasion.'

'Quite unorthodox. Please excuse me just a moment.' Miss Lonsdale hastened over to Miss Rice and, taking her arm, ducked out into the corridor, pulling the door to behind her.

Seldon frowned, his chestnut curls falling forward as he leaned in to whisper, 'Eleanor, for Pete's sake, what on earth are you doing here?'

'Likewise,' she hissed back. 'We're miles from Oxford and London, where you're based. Why are you the one to have answered a call so far away? More budget cuts?'

He shrugged. 'Orders. From the top. Your turn.'

Eleanor pulled a face, trying to defeat the familiar butterflies his strong frame and soft brown eyes always set aflutter in her stomach. 'I'm an old girl of St Mary's. And even though I have no idea why they would ever have wanted me back on the premises, Miss Lonsdale invited me to be the guest of honour at today's Speech Day.'

He frowned. 'I see, but that doesn't explain why—'

Clifford coughed discreetly. 'Chief Inspector, my apologies for interrupting, but it was at our joint insistence that the police were called.'

He laughed. 'That is quite a terrifying idea.'

At that moment, Miss Lonsdale reappeared. Clifford pulled over two chairs, then stood discreetly to one side. Seldon waited for the headmistress to sit at her desk and Ellie to sit on one of the chairs before he sat on the other, trying and failing to fit his long legs underneath. With a sigh, he turned sideways towards Ellie and crossed one leg over the other. From his inside pocket, he produced a flip-top leather notebook.

'Miss Lonsdale, I believe it was you who reported the incident?'

'Yes, Chief Inspector. Poor Mrs Wadsworth. It's unthinkable.'

'A tragedy, I'm sure.' He regarded his notes. 'So, when you went to the library, where I believe Mrs Wadsworth was found?' Miss Lonsdale nodded. 'You asked Lady Swift and her butler… to accompany you?'

She shook her head. 'No. I left Lady Swift on stage, ready to project her words of inspiration to the furthest reaches of the school hall on my return. Unfortunately, that was not to be.'

Seldon addressed Eleanor without making eye contact. 'So, Lady Swift, you took it upon yourself to go and investigate, perhaps?'

'No, Chief Inspector, I was summoned,' she said more tartly than she'd intended.

A faint smile appeared on Seldon's lips. 'The lady of the manor summoned? By whom?'

'Clifford, actually.'

Seldon rubbed his forehead and spun round to stare at Clifford, who nodded.

'It is true, Chief Inspector. Although one might have chosen the term, "requested the presence of" as being more respectful and' – he peered at Eleanor – 'accurate.'

Seldon waved his hand dismissively. 'Semantics aside, why were you in the library at all?'

'Because I had sensed trouble and wanted to make sure if Lady Swift had to become involved, she was forewarned. Unfortunately, what I observed on arriving immediately caused me to be alarmed. And more unfortunately, I was forced to ask her ladyship to view the regrettable scene to confirm or otherwise my assessment of the situation.'

'It took me a minute to see what Clifford had so shrewdly spotted,' Eleanor said. 'And I drew the same conclusion independently. Hence our suggestion to Miss Lonsdale that the police be called in. But how to explain succinctly?'

Clifford's deferential cough turned all heads towards him.

'If I might perhaps be permitted to demonstrate?'

CHAPTER 4

At the library door Miss Lonsdale produced a key. 'I have kept the door locked since the incident, Chief Inspector. No one else has been in except your men.'

Seldon nodded. 'Good thinking, Miss Lonsdale.'

Eleanor was relieved to find that Mrs Wadsworth's body had already been removed. From Seldon's lack of surprise, she deduced he'd arranged it. Between the four of them they agreed the lines marking where the body had lain were correct. Having done that, Clifford stepped over to the wooden A-frame steps and cleared his throat.

'If you would observe that they are securely fastened in the fully open position by the hooked brass struts spanning each pair of the ladder's legs. The wheels too' – he pointed to each corner – 'are also locked by a small foot pedal.' The others watched as he climbed up to the top step. 'On first arriving at the scene, I noted Mrs Wadsworth was a lady of relatively average stature. Roughly five foot four and a half, I would guess.'

Miss Lonsdale nodded agreement to Seldon, who wrote this down without taking his eyes off the demonstration.

'Ergo,' Clifford continued, 'that would signify on a woman, an arm length of twenty-eight to thirty inches.' He indicated the measurement with his left forefinger two thirds of the way along his jacket sleeve. Then he pointed to a book. 'Mrs Wadsworth need only have stretched five inches to reach this volume which, according to the Dewey library cataloguing system employed here by the lady herself' – he tapped the neatly glued set of numbers on the spine of the book – 'would have been the neighbour of the one lying beside her when she was found. Five inches is not an excessive distance to stretch safely, even for a lady of advanced years.'

'So,' the headmistress said, 'you're saying Mrs Wadsworth likely didn't fall because she overstretched?'

He nodded. 'Indeed, madam. But that is not the most significant element. Because, if we suppose I am wrong in that assessment, watch!' With that, he leaned precariously forward and then fell.

Miss Lonsdale jumped backwards as his body rushed towards her, then gasped as he landed nimbly on his feet, crouched like a cat. The steps hit the oak parquet floor with a loud thwack behind him.

'Mr Clifford! Really, that was… extraordinary.'

'Thank you, madam, and my sincere apologies for the minor drama. But as you can clearly see—'

Seldon stepped forward and nodded. 'The steps fell when you reached over, but they were still upright when Mrs Wadsworth's body was found. If she had overstretched, they would have fallen with her.' He stared at the spot where the body had been lying.

'Precisely!' Eleanor said.

Seldon tapped his pen on his chin. 'But what if she fainted? Mr Clifford, could you?' He indicated the fallen steps.

'Of course, Chief Inspector.' Clifford picked them up and placed them carefully back where they had been standing. Repeating his pretend fall, he landed squarely by the side of the ladder. 'As you can see, again Mrs Wadsworth could not have come to rest where her body was found if she had lost consciousness.'

'Hmm.' Seldon's pen worked furiously across his notebook.

'And,' Eleanor said, 'Uncle Byron used to have several pairs of these exact steps in the library at Henley Hall. But, after years of too many tumbles from overreaching and a broken ankle, so Clifford informed me, he swapped them for a system of sliding rails with fixed ladders.' She shook her head. 'No matter what, Mrs Wadsworth's body was in the wrong place for it to have been an accident.'

Clifford cleared his throat. 'Regrettably, Miss Lonsdale, it means that someone either climbed up behind Mrs Wadsworth and knocked her off—'

'Or,' Eleanor said, 'that they were at the bottom of the ladder and simply shook it sufficiently that the poor woman was flung off.'

Seldon nodded. 'All more than plausible. And thank you for the demonstrations, Clifford.' He turned back to Miss Lonsdale. 'In your own words, please tell me what happened leading up to the discovery of Mrs Wadsworth's body.'

The headmistress gathered her thoughts for a moment.

'We were all in the hall. The staff, girls and, of course, parents for Speech Day. I had just introduced Lady Swift when my deputy headmistress, Mrs Coulson, came to my side and told me that there had been a terrible accident in the library.'

Seldon looked up from his notes. 'Who found the deceased?'

'Miss Small, our head of art.'

'Thank you. So, on hearing the news, you?'

'I left Speech Day in the hands of Mrs Coulson and ran as fast as I could to the library.' She shook her head. 'I'm always the one calling girls back for running in the corridors. But I couldn't believe it. Not until I saw it for myself. And to think I'd reminded her only yesterday of my instruction not to climb those steps, but to find another member of staff to do it for her.'

'For what reason?'

'Because she was sixty-eight.'

Seldon's brows rose. 'Isn't that a little old to still be in post as a teacher?'

Miss Lonsdale glared at him. 'Age alone, Chief Inspector, like gender, need never be a barrier but for the prejudice of others.'

'Quite so.' He cleared his throat. 'My apologies, I meant no offence to the lady.'

Eleanor watched this exchange with a mixture of mild amusement and sympathy for Seldon. In his own way, he could be as unwittingly flat-footed over sensitive topics as she could.

'That said,' Miss Lonsdale continued, 'I reduced Mrs Wadsworth's teaching timetable soon after I took up my post here. I felt she had many other talents which could serve the school just as well, if not better.'

'Is that why she was head of the library?' Eleanor said.

'Yes, since she had been head of English for nineteen years previously, it was a very neat and beneficial fit for us all. That, and her characteristic quirk, of course.'

Seldon's mouth opened, but he seemed to hesitate over how to probe further without causing more offence. He glanced sideways at Eleanor who hid a smile.

'Unless Mrs Wadsworth had a complete personality change since I was here, I think Miss Lonsdale is alluding to her compulsion for painstaking order. It made Clifford's meticulousness look like the work of a hair-brained chimpanzee after too much sugar in comparison.' She turned to her butler. 'No offence, Clifford.'

He nodded. 'None taken. I am merely sorry not to have met the lady. I'm sure we would have got on famously.'

Eleanor noted Seldon needed a second to control the twitch at the corner of his lips.

'Was that still the case, Miss Lonsdale? The, erm, deceased's compulsion, not the rest of Lady Swift's rather vivid description, I mean?'

'And beyond, Chief Inspector. We all subconsciously set our watches by Mrs Wadsworth. She was rigid in her habits to the extreme.'

'I see.' Seldon made a lengthy note and then looked up. 'Unfortunately, given the height of the ladder, the hardness of the floor and the' – he avoided Miss Lonsdale's gaze – 'age of the victim, I find myself agreeing again with Lady Swift and Clifford. This is most definitely a murder investigation.'

Miss Lonsdale nodded resignedly. 'It would seem so, Chief Inspector.' She sighed. 'Can you tell me some good news? Anything at all?'

Eleanor watched Seldon take a deep breath. 'I believe from the, admittedly scant, evidence Mrs Wadsworth's death was likely premeditated. Why, as yet, I obviously have not had any chance to determine. But it would suggest that this was a one-off attack.'

Miss Lonsdale raised an eyebrow. 'And how is any of that good news?'

'Because it means the killer had an objective, which was Mrs Wadsworth's death. With that, unfortunately, achieved, it seems unlikely they would have cause to kill again. In consequence, I believe your girls are in no danger.'

'Thank heavens. And the staff?'

'Likewise.' He paused. 'Although obviously I can't be one hundred per cent sure.'

Eleanor's head shot up. 'Which means—'

Seldon sighed. 'We need to catch whoever murdered Mrs Wadsworth before they prove me wrong.'

CHAPTER 5

Back in the headmistress' study, Eleanor looked for some way to comfort Miss Lonsdale.

'How fortuitous that the inspector was sent to deal with this matter, Miss Lonsdale. I can assure you there is no finer detective in England's police force. He will undertake the investigation with unparalleled vigour.'

Seldon shot her a grateful glance and ran a hand through his curls. 'Kind words, Lady Swift, but actually,' he grimaced, 'not entirely accurate.'

'What? You mean you won't conduct the investigation yourself?'

Miss Lonsdale replied before Seldon could. 'Lady Swift, the chief inspector certainly cannot conduct this investigation given the sensitive circumstances.'

What sensitive circumstances, Ellie?

The difficulty of the situation showed all too clearly in Seldon's furrowed brow. 'I am still working on that. It is not an easy situation, thus there is no easy solution.'

Miss Lonsdale rose. 'Indeed, however, I'm afraid your presence here cannot continue.' She looked around the assembled company. 'Now, if you will please excuse me for a moment.'

Once the headmistress had departed, Eleanor turned to Seldon.

'Why do I feel like I'm the only one in the dark?'

Clifford cleared his throat. 'My lady, if I may assist. I believe the issue is that, like his lordship, your late uncle, the fathers of many girls here hold diplomatic or government posts. Ergo, a police presence needs to be avoided at all costs for fear of the press learning of the affair and the inevitable media circus that would ensue. Miss Goldsworthy, the head girl who greeted us is, for instance, the daughter of Sir Oswald Goldsworthy, Private Secretary to His Majesty.'

'Oh,' she said, feeling foolish. 'I didn't know any of that.'

'There is no reason why you should have. Succinctly, his lordship was anxious for you to attend St Mary's due to the school's sterling reputation for understanding the delicacy required for gentlemen in his… position.'

Ah! Of course, Ellie! She nodded. After she'd inherited Henley Hall on her uncle's death the year before, Clifford had hinted she'd been sent to St Mary's for her own safety, something he'd never confessed to her as a child.

It seemed her uncle, Lord Henley, had resigned his military command over his support for home rule in India but had still continued to publicly voice his unpopular opinions, earning him dangerous enemies. His habit, inherited by Eleanor, of also helping those the police wouldn't or couldn't, had equally caused him to fall foul of several criminal organisations around the area. Now she understood.

Clifford seemed uncomfortable. 'My sincere apologies for not enlightening you earlier, my lady. I should have—'

She flapped a hand. 'It's fine. You both did everything for the best for me. And you still do. I know that. Besides, none of us expected this to happen.'

The room lapsed into silence, punctuated only by Seldon drumming his fingers against his closed notebook, deep in thought.

'Drat it!' he murmured. 'Why did it have to be St Mary's?'

Miss Lonsdale returned a few minutes later and took her seat, looking as though the weight of the world was hers to bear alone.

'Are you alright?' Eleanor said.

'Yes, thank you. At least I will be when this is all over. I went to telephone my contact in Whitehall since I am duty-bound to keep him abreast of any potential issues. As it happens, he had already been informed by the chief inspector's superiors. My contact made it abundantly clear ,as I expected, that this "situation", as he called it, must be dealt with extremely swiftly and with no publicity whatsoever. He would not countenance Chief Inspector Seldon's presence in the school for long.'

Seldon nodded. 'Exactly the instruction I received on being dispatched here. I was told if some of the girls' fathers got wind of myself, or any other inspector, conducting an investigation in their daughters' school there would be hell to pay. I don't know how I'm supposed to magic up the impossible though.' He looked at the headmistress and shrugged.

Eleanor clicked her fingers. 'A female police officer, that would work! She could pose as a temporary teacher, here to replace poor Mrs Wadsworth. No one would think—'

Seldon held up a hand. 'A good suggestion, Lady Swift. However, there are no women on the force except those in the Metropolitan ranks and they can only perform very limited duties. Even if one could be seconded, she would not be competent to deal with anything beyond...' He tailed off at the look on Eleanor and the headmistress' faces.

Miss Lonsdale let out an exasperated snort. 'With the tragic loss of so many young men to the war, to say nothing of Spanish flu, the country should be crying out for competent individuals irrespective of their gender. Thank goodness, at least, we have someone who is unquestionably capable of acting in place of an undercover policewoman.'

'You do?' Eleanor said. 'That's amazing. But... well, will she be willing to undertake such a difficult task?'

'I will leave that up to the chief inspector to persuade the young lady. But I'm hopeful it won't require too much exhortation.'

Seldon rubbed his brow, oblivious to the mussed curls that fell back against his forehead.

'Miss Lonsdale, please do not think I'm not grateful for any suggestion you make, but I cannot allow civilians to take part in a murder investigation.'

Eleanor tutted. 'How can you say that when you don't even know who it is yet?'

The room held its breath as all three of them stared back at her. 'What? *Me?*'

'And why not?' said Miss Lonsdale.

Eleanor took one look at Seldon's disapproving face and shook her head.

'I'm sorry, even if I wanted to, it would be unlikely to work.'

'Unlikely is a far better option than any other I am facing,' said Miss Lonsdale. 'It would be eminently plausible that you offered to stay and cover Mrs Wadsworth's boarding duties temporarily.'

'I—'

Miss Lonsdale held up a hand. 'If you won't do it for me, or the chief inspector when he realises that he has no other choice' – she glared at Seldon – 'please do it for Mrs Wadsworth.'

Eleanor let out a quiet moan. 'She was so very good to me. Without her instilling a love of stories in me, I would never have read all those magical tales of foreign lands that made me burn to see faraway places. She lit a fire inside me.' She smiled wistfully. 'Along with my parents' rather bohemian outlook, she is responsible for me having dusted off my bicycle that day and set off across the world. In fact, she was the only person who turned up to see me off.' She glanced at Seldon again and sighed. 'Perhaps… perhaps I could repay her by helping bring her killer to justice?'

Seldon shook his head. 'I simply can't allow it.'

The headmistress sat back in her chair. 'Then rather than repeat yourself like a stuck record, Chief Inspector, please enlighten us on just how exactly you intend to catch Mrs Wadsworth's killer before, as you put it, he or she proves you wrong and… kills again?'

Seldon looked from one to the other and then stared at the ceiling. Finally, he let out a deep breath.

'Alright. In the absence of any other workable solution. But on two conditions.'

'Which are?' Miss Lonsdale said.

'That Mr Clifford is able to stay on site. I can only allow this if I'm certain of his protective presence and also' – he gave Eleanor a pointed stare – 'his restraining influence.'

Clifford nodded. 'I would not countenance her ladyship staying in any other circumstances, Chief Inspector.'

'Thank you, Clifford,' Eleanor said.

Miss Lonsdale waved her hand. 'That is not a problem at all. Mr Clifford, you may stay in the spare groundsman's cottage. In your role as Lady Swift's butler and chauffeur, that will not pose any matters of impropriety, nor raise any other awkward questions.'

Eleanor nodded. 'Clifford can be my eyes and ears in the grounds. He will need a cover that allows him access to areas and people I can't, though.'

'Perhaps I could also assist as a temporary handyman, Miss Lonsdale?' Clifford said. 'If you have a spare cottage, your grounds team must be a man down. I could legitimately help ease their workload before the long list of summer works I imagine will commence after the end of term?'

'Perfect,' Miss Lonsdale said. 'And very thoughtful too, thank you.' She looked at Seldon. 'And your second condition, Chief Inspector?'

His eyes flicked to Eleanor. 'That Lady Swift agrees to be entirely under my command. She will report to me anything she finds out and not act without my explicit instructions.'

Eleanor rolled her eyes. 'Inspector, I have no more desire to be involved in this than you have to involve me. I am perfectly happy with those conditions if Miss Lonsdale is?' She looked to the headmistress who nodded. 'Then count me in.'

Miss Lonsdale clapped her hands. 'Well, that seems settled.'

'Against my better judgement,' Seldon muttered.

Miss Lonsdale seemed not to have heard. 'So, to immediate business. Lady Swift, you will obviously be here for several days at the minimum. You will need some things from Henley Hall, I imagine?'

'Gracious, I hadn't thought of that.'

Clifford held up his leather-covered pocketbook, open at a meticulously handwritten list. Eleanor frowned. *When on earth did he put that together?*

'Miss Lonsdale?' He rose and gestured towards the door. 'Might I trouble you for one thing?' They left together, shutting the door.

Alone with Seldon, Eleanor felt awkward. It wasn't that she didn't want to do everything she could to find justice for Mrs Wadsworth. The very thought of the killer going free stabbed at her insides. Nor was it that she didn't want to help loosen the shackles Whitehall had slapped on Seldon's wrists. It was that she simply wished Seldon might break the rules just once and reach out to take her hands in his. To run his fingers over hers and stutter out something tender like that one delicious time on her birthday when she'd felt every inch the giddy schoolgirl.

Seldon broke the silence. 'I wonder what Clifford is asking the headmistress for?'

'Nothing.'

He stared at her quizzically.

She sighed. 'In his usual inimitable way, I imagine he was making sure we were alone for a few minutes.'

Seldon grimaced. 'Do you really think you can do this, Eleanor? Bow down to my authority on this investigation, I mean?'

She stood up and went over to the window. 'Hugh, do you remember our last telephone conversation? The one where we actually managed not to end on a row?'

'Yes. It was glorious.' The corner of his mouth twitched. 'Go on.'

'You said if this ridiculous situation ever arose again, you'd make me swear an oath to you.' She turned back to him. 'Well, I swear to do my very best to respect everything you say. I can't do any more than that.'

Her heart skipped as his handsome face broke into a warm smile.

'And I would be an absolute fool to expect otherwise.'

CHAPTER 6

'Coffee in my private room, please, Miss Rice.' Miss Lonsdale's voice came from the corridor. A moment later she strode back into the study with Clifford following and threw open a door at the far end of the room. She gestured for Eleanor, Seldon and Clifford to follow her. The space they emerged into was a sitting room, filled with two long settees, upholstered in a velvet stripe of peacock green and blue. A low walnut table separated them, set on a pale cream-and-silver rug that matched the delicate print of the wallpaper.

A collection of pupils' artwork hung on the walls, with several architectural designs dotted among them, one being of St Mary's itself. Eleanor marvelled at the intricacy of every stair, bannister rail and window frame drawn in fine pencil lines. Even the gables along the many roofs and the chapel's enormous stained-glass window had been faithfully reproduced. On a white-painted pedestal, a plasterwork sculpture of what appeared to be two staircases artfully twisted into one dominated a corner. Clifford traced the swirling balustrading.

'A particularly fine example of a double helix, madam, if you will forgive my offering an opinion.'

'Thank you, Mr Clifford,' Miss Lonsdale said, her pride evident.

He cocked his head. 'Based perhaps on Leonardo da Vinci's staircase at the Château de Chambord?'

She nodded. 'I'm impressed, Mr Clifford, it is indeed. Two long but enjoyable years in the making. All, however, for it to end up tucked away in my little haven of solace.'

'A criminal shame, if I might be so bold.'

'Gracious!' Eleanor said. 'You made that incredible piece of art? And these architectural drawings are yours too?'

'Yes.' Miss Lonsdale waved for them to sit.

Eleanor slid onto the opposite settee, joined after by Seldon. Clifford remained standing.

'Yet you chose to teach?' said Seldon.

Miss Lonsdale sighed. 'Architecture has fascinated me since I was a little girl. However, indulging my passion was deemed unseemly for a young lady. Begrudgingly, I was elbowed over to the more acceptable world of teaching with the supposedly generous allowance of being able to specialise in fine art.'

Eleanor shook her head. 'How unjust that you were denied your dream. I feel quite the spoiled girl now after having had the opportunity to indulge in my passion for travel.'

Miss Lonsdale shook her head. 'It is one thing to be given the opportunity, but very much another to defy convention and seize it as you did, Lady Swift. I didn't have the courage to fight for my dreams back then. And that is why I have placed such emphasis on character education throughout my teaching career and particularly since joining St Mary's. The standard curriculum is fine and necessary, but our girls need so much more. They must have conviction in themselves, fortitude, tenacity. And, dare I say, even a healthy measure of audacity sprinkled with a sense of adventure to live the life they deserve.'

Scanning through his notes, Seldon muttered, 'Watch out world, a generation of little Lady Swifts in the making!'

'Which,' Miss Lonsdale said sharply, 'will be a significant bonus for the world, Chief Inspector!'

Eleanor hid a smile as Seldon kept his eyes on his notebook.

The secretary appeared with a tray, which Clifford stepped forward and took from her.

'Thank you, Miss Rice. So kind.'

Setting it down on the central coffee table, he set about arranging cups, saucers and plates for the accompanying shortbread biscuits and rich sultana and cherry cake. With everyone served, he retired to one corner and stood, hands behind his back. Miss Lonsdale threw Eleanor a look of appeal.

'You try,' Eleanor said. 'He's delightfully, but impossibly, respectful.'

The headmistress patted the end of her settee. 'Mr Clifford, this room is a haven away from the stricture of the harshest of rules and formality. Which have their place, do not misunderstand me. But along with Lady Swift, you have been a great help in all this. Please, join us.'

With reluctance, he bowed and came round to perch on the edge of the very end of the settee. Pouring himself a small coffee, he turned the handle to line up with the pattern of the saucer and sat back up poker straight.

Seldon had received the coffee and cake like a man who had missed breakfast and lunch and had no prospect of an evening meal. Clearly impatient to press on, however, he started in, trying to cover up the ungentlemanly gurgles from his stomach.

'Miss Lonsdale, I shall secure the key facts before we get to how the investigation might be conducted.'

'Discreetly, Chief Inspector, that is precisely how.'

'Without question. Although that has already posed a problem. My men found several sets of fingerprints on the ladder Miss Wadsworth fell from. Unfortunately, all except two sets are too smudged to use. I expect we'll find one set belonging to the deceased, the other I'll put through our records. We only have some known criminals fingerprinted, however, and the system is in its infancy. Really, there isn't even a proper nationwide database. And besides, it's highly unlikely any of St Mary's staff would be on it if there were. We need to get all the staff fingerprinted, but how to do so discreetly...' He threw his hands up. 'Anyway, we'll leave that problem for the moment. Now, who was the last person to see Mrs Wadsworth alive?'

'Well, all and any of the staff, girls and parents would have seen her seated on stage. And most would probably have seen her leave the stage when the burglar alarm rang.'

He stiffened. 'That hasn't been mentioned before. When and why did the burglar alarm ring?'

'It rang at approximately two twenty because one of Mr Hepple's team – he is our head groundsman – thought he had seen someone creeping about in one of the art rooms. But it turned out to be a false alarm.'

'One moment. That extra incident has raised a raft of questions. Please can you go back to how he would have sounded the alarm?'

'Of course. I instigated a simple system last year after a brief spate of thefts by a group of youths from the village. My deputy headmistress assured me it was the first occurrence in many years. So, rather than waste time and money on something rarely needed, I instructed the staff to simply make use of the school bell. There is a manual push button in the office.'

'So Mr Hepple would have gone up to the school office?'

'Goodness, no. For the duration of Speech Day, he had been assigned to the main rear door in case of fire and to keep a general vigilance. He would have instructed his staff to use the internal telephone nearby to call.'

Seldon frowned. 'But who responded to the call asking for the alarm to be rung then?'

'The bursar was in the school office and took the call from one of Mr Hepple's grounds team in the porter's lodge. He then rang the bell. A continuous ring means "fire" and three short rings mean "unwelcome visitor". So, having heard the bell, each head of department left the stage and went to their area. And those with an office, such as the deputy headmistress, checked that as well as the surrounding corridors. If they had apprehended a miscreant, which they didn't in this case, they would have taken him to the school office where the bursar would have kept him until I arrived. The bursar himself has a twisted ankle, so was unable to check anywhere except the corridor immediately outside his office.'

Eleanor swallowed her mouthful of cake. 'I wondered what that bell was signifying, as there was nothing like that when I was here. Some of the staff rose immediately on hearing it and disappeared through the stage's wings. Mrs Wadsworth being one of them, I noticed. Then they returned and slid back into their seats.'

Seldon made a hasty note. 'So Mrs Wadsworth would have gone to her area, which was no longer English, if I remember correctly? Hence her being in the library?'

'Quite,' Miss Lonsdale said. 'However, as English is a core subject and thus, like mathematics, has more than one classroom, she was still assigned to check the three rooms adjacent to the library.'

'At sixty-eight?' He held up a placatory hand as the headmistress pursed her lips. 'I am merely ensuring I understand the procedures you have here. A lady of advanced years chasing after intruders is not something I had anticipated being part of those.'

'Chief Inspector,' Miss Lonsdale said testily, 'the staff are all instructed to act in line with their capabilities. There is not, and never has been, any expectation of heroics. You might be more accustomed to violent criminals, but we are talking here about one or two young boys from the village. Boys merely looking to see what petty spoils they can grab and flee with.'

Seldon let out a grunt. 'Except that on this occasion, it seems there was, in fact, a violent criminal at large.'

Miss Lonsdale's tone was as stern as the look she threw him. 'Chief Inspector, none of us could have predicted the presence of one with such malicious intent. As I said, we are barely used to petty thieves. And had any of those been in Mrs Wadsworth's area, she could have easily "arrested" them by jumping into authoritative teacher mode. They would have frozen in their tracks, despite her "advanced years", as you insist on repeatedly alluding to. You might be surprised to learn a teacher's voice can be a powerful weapon, capable of subduing a couple of young scallywags with ease. And I repeat, it was a mistake. There was no intruder.'

'You said Mr Hepple was stationed on the main rear door. What about all the other doors? St Mary's must have a great many entry and exit points.'

Miss Lonsdale nodded. 'However, as it was Speech Day, from one forty-five precisely, no one could get in or leave school except through the door Mr Hepple guarded, or through the one our head girl was manning as some parents were still being seated. As for Mr Hepple, he is extremely diligent and I have absolute confidence he would have followed my instruction to ensure all external doors and windows were locked by that time. Hence the alarm being a false call.'

Seldon frowned. 'What was the last door to remain open?'

'The last one would have been the door into the hall our head girl manned, as I said. All parents were seated by one fifty-five and that then was closed, although not locked. Speech Day commenced at two o'clock sharp.'

'What about latecomers? Surely some of your parents would have travelled a fair distance to get here?'

'Quite so, Chief Inspector. However, when one is dealing with parents of St Mary's calibre, I'm afraid one needs as many artful tactics to engender the desired behaviour in them as for our pupils. Thus, a reference to the high regard we place on punctuality in the girls was underwritten into the invitation each set of parents received.'

Eleanor laughed. 'It never occurred to me that you would need to keep the parents in line.'

After a long swig of coffee, Seldon forged on. 'And, if I'm correct, Miss Small found Mrs Wadsworth's body at around two twenty-five?'

'That's correct. Miss Small is our head of art, as I believe I said.'

'And how did she come to find the body?'

The headmistress paused as if running over a conversation. 'She had left the stage at the bell like the other heads of departments and checked her art rooms. She was rushing to take her seat back in the hall for Lady Swift's speech when she thought she heard a cry from the library. Initially, she ignored it, but said as she hurried away, it tugged at her so she returned to check. I—'

'One moment, please. What reason did she give you for being in such a rush?'

'Miss Small is always rushing, Chief Inspector. That need not ring any alarm bells with you. She is a brilliant art teacher but utterly and hopelessly disorganised. Really, I find myself admonishing her as often as the girls for running in the corridors.'

'So Miss Small turned back to where she heard the cry from the library. And then?'

'She entered the library and saw Mrs Wadsworth lying motionless and screamed. That drew the attention of Mrs Coulson, my deputy headmistress, whom you've met. She sent for Matron. Then, as I said before, Matron pronounced Mrs Wadsworth to be' – she swallowed hard – 'no longer with us, and Mrs Coulson came to fetch me from the hall.'

'Thank you. I understand this must be difficult for you.'

As Miss Lonsdale accepted a top-up to her coffee from Clifford, Eleanor nodded discreetly at Seldon. Whoever had found the body would be high on their suspect list.

'So, Miss Lonsdale, to recap, Mr Hepple was guarding the only unlocked door into St Mary's at the time of the murder, except for the one your head girl was in charge of?'

Miss Lonsdale nodded. 'Yes. Lydia Goldsworthy, our head girl, was posted on the other, the main door to the hall, charged with meeting and greeting parents and ticking off names. In the event of a fire, I would lead the staff and pupils out of the door guarded by Mr Hepple, and Lydia would lead the parents out of the other. Perhaps you would like to speak to her?'

'Thank you. But what about discretion?'

'Not a problem. Lydia Goldsworthy is eminently trustworthy and will not tittle-tattle with the other girls. You just need a plausible reason for your questions, and it would also help' – she tilted her head – 'if you could just try to look and sound a little less like a policeman!'

CHAPTER 7

Lydia Goldsworthy must have been the tallest girl in her class. In fact, in any class. Eleanor marvelled at her height for the second time that day. They had decamped back into Miss Lonsdale's study and the head girl stood in front of them with her fair hair tamed in a neat plait running across her confidently held head.

'Goldsworthy,' Eleanor said. She hated having to call the girl by her surname, but remembered all too well it was the convention. 'I wanted to thank you for the tour you gave Mr Clifford and myself. It was most interesting to see St Mary's again after such a time away.'

'Oh, it was my absolute pleasure, Lady Swift.'

'Your parents must be very proud that you've been made head girl. Let me guess, they were the first to arrive today?'

Lydia beamed. 'Oh yes. They arrived early, so we had a moment before the other parents needed attending to.'

Eleanor laughed. 'And I bet some of the parents were late. Or tried to leave while the headmistress was talking?'

'Oh no, Lady Swift. No one was late or left early. I had all their names ticked off my sheet by one fifty-five, so I knew when to close the door. And no one left until the deputy headmistress told everyone Speech Day was cancelled.'

'How can you be so sure?'

'As head girl, I made sure to stay at my post until the deputy headmistress told me to let the parents out.'

'Thank you, Goldsworthy. That will be all,' said Miss Lonsdale.

As Lydia closed the door behind her, Seldon reached for his notebook.

'So the murderer had to be someone who was in the building by one fifty-five, when Miss Goldsworthy closed the door into the hall. But not a parent, as they had no way to leave without being spotted because Miss Goldsworthy and a host of others would certainly have seen them. Which means then, it could have been any of the staff who left the stage when the burglar alarm rang.'

Eleanor caught Seldon's eye.

'But what about any staff who *weren't* on stage?' She turned to Miss Lonsdale. 'It didn't seem quite the number of people on stage I would have expected had your entire staff been there.'

Miss Lonsdale nodded. 'Another shrewd observation, Lady Swift. There were a few not on the stage for various reasons. I shall arrange for my deputy headmistress to draw up a list, although she will be even more resistant than I am to the idea. She is still convinced it was an accident.'

'Miss Lonsdale,' Eleanor said gently. 'Your confidence in your staff is wonderful to hear. It's no consolation I know, but I've learned that a wrongdoer never gives one a reason to mistrust them until they seize the opportunity they've been waiting for. I'd like to imagine it was an outsider who snuck in and then somehow escaped in the melee of parents leaving after the event was cancelled. But as the windows were secured and all the doors locked, except the two guarded by Miss Goldsworthy and Mr Hepple, it seems—'

'Highly unlikely,' Seldon said. 'Unless any windows or other doors *were* left open or there are signs of a break-in?'

Miss Lonsdale shook her head. 'I already asked the staff to double-check. All the windows and other doors were still secured.' She put her hands in her lap. 'It really does seem like it was someone from… within St Mary's who carried out this horrible crime. But… well, I still find it hard to believe.'

Seldon cleared his throat. 'Perhaps we might talk to the head groundsman now? Again, discreetly, obviously.'

Miss Lonsdale agreed and sent Miss Rice to fetch him. A few moments later there was a nervous tap on the door. Looking every inch the fish out of water, Mr Hepple stood on the threshold, tapping his cap against his leg, and smoothing a calloused hand over his shock of grey hair. At Miss Lonsdale's insistence, he shuffled in and closed the door behind him.

Eleanor threw him a genuine smile. 'I was admiring the grounds earlier, Mr Hepple. You and your team do an outstanding job. When I was a pupil here, the field and the little wooded area beyond used to be my favourite places.'

He seemed unmoved by her praise. 'Woods has always been out of bounds, madam.'

'Ah! Perhaps they were.'

'Mr Hepple,' Seldon said. 'Miss Lonsdale was explaining about the burglar alarm system you have in place. It sounds an excellent arrangement, although I would have thought you might experience more break-ins than you do?'

'My lads work hard on maintaining all the walls and fences, sir. Can't see a reason why you might think otherwise.'

'Oh no, that's not what I meant. More that there must be a lot of valuable equipment around the school. Inside and out. It was lucky that today's little scare was a false alarm, what with all the parents here.'

Mr Hepple turned to Miss Lonsdale, his cheeks colouring. 'Apologies again for having got the bell a-ringing, Headmistress.'

'No harm done,' she said. 'It is always better to be safe than sorry.'

'What was it in fact that your assistant saw?' Eleanor said.

'Summat in one of the art rooms,' said Hepple. 'I was guarding the rear door as is my duty, like. So I tells young John to walk the perimeter and check everything's alright. Truth is, young John is not the sharpest tool in the box, if you get my drift. Though the lad's a good worker when he's a mind to.' He glanced up at Seldon and then lowered his gaze again. 'Thing is, them girls had been making paper model statues. Dratted thing made a shadow just like a person moving. Or so John thought. Anyway, he comes running up to me telling me there's an intruder in the art room. So I tells him to go to ring the office, while I stays on the door so the blighter don't escape. Course, no one did, 'cos there weren't no one, anyhows.'

Clifford nodded. 'A natural assumption, Mr Hepple. It can be quite the trial to manage security when numerous visitors are on site, is it not? People do tend to wander around at will, I find.'

Hepple frowned. 'Nobody wandered off anywhere. I had all the doors and windows locked, same as always for Speech Day. And I had my lads working on different areas round the near grounds so they could be looking out too. 'Twas no chance anyone could think of taking any liberties in mooching wherever they fancied. Though none of 'em tried, like I said. Never saw a soul once all the parents was in the hall.'

Miss Lonsdale rose. 'Mr Hepple, please thank your team personally for me. You have all done a splendid job today, as always.'

'Headmistress.' He nodded, before glancing round the others. 'Folks.' And with that, he was gone.

CHAPTER 8

'Perhaps something to eat would suit?' said Miss Lonsdale once Clifford had taken his leave to drive back to Henley Hall for Eleanor's things.

Eleanor looked at her gratefully. 'Actually, I'd forgotten about food. What with poor Mrs Wadsworth and everything. But now that you've mentioned it, I'm suddenly famished. I imagine the inspector might be too.'

'Our wonderful kitchen porters will serve us in the staffroom since all the staff are busy supervising the girls. I have arranged for supper to be brought up for the four of us.'

'The four of us?' said Seldon.

'Yes, Mrs Coulson will be joining us. Please, this way.' Miss Lonsdale gestured for both of them to follow her.

After she had shown Seldon in, Miss Lonsdale turned to Eleanor.

'I wonder if this hallowed sanctuary might be more familiar to you than your previous headmistress intended it to be?'

Eleanor winced at Miss Lonsdale's shrewd assessment. 'To borrow one of Clifford's diplomatically evasive phrases, I really couldn't say.'

'Ah! A particularly high-stakes game of dares, I imagine?'

Eleanor laughed and nodded. 'Fifth form, autumn term. I was never caught because—' she hesitated. It was a long time ago and probably no longer used, but her nine-year-old self refused to give away one of the girls' most closely guarded secrets. 'But I really shouldn't be telling you that. I was always falling foul of the fact sanctions could be backdated. Maybe they still can?'

Miss Lonsdale smiled. 'Oh, absolutely. But I'll consider setting the limit at ten years. Everyone deserves a little leniency.'

'Gracious! I think I might actually have flourished under your influence.'

Miss Lonsdale arched a brow. 'Perhaps you flourished anyway, Lady Swift? Has it never occurred to you that forever railing against St Mary's rules and constraints gave you something invaluable? Perhaps take a moment one day to consider that. I think you'll find it an enlightening exercise. Ah! The clank of covered plates at the bottom of the stairs. Supper is arriving.'

The staffroom had the air of a space that had just been bustling with activity and was trying to catch its breath. Twelve mismatched chairs were set in a haphazard horseshoe, while four others made a smaller circle. Three wicker baskets nearby spilled over with old newspapers, dog-eared magazines and well-thumbed books. On the left were two wooden dining tables and on the right an oak counter with an enamel sink set at one end and a gas stove at the other. On each burner, stood an enamel kettle. Stacks of teacups, saucers and cake plates nestled amongst a throng of biscuit tins, three enormous tea caddies and a smaller grey tin marked 'Mrs Coulson's coffee'.

'Gracious, it was nothing like this when I broke in,' Eleanor said in a hushed tone.

The headmistress walked to the middle of the room and gestured round the space. 'On joining St Mary's, with the governors' agreement, I set aside a budget to improve the staffroom.'

'What a wonderful idea! I can tell how much you value your staff.'

This drew a snort from Mrs Coulson who had appeared in the doorway. She turned to the four porters bearing inviting trays, all hovering behind her.

'On the table. And they'd better still be hot!'

Eleanor groaned inwardly. *Whatever else happens while you're at St Mary's, Ellie, something tells me you're going to have trouble with that woman!*

As Eleanor stepped past Seldon, he whispered, 'Looks like supper comes with a serving of tart horseradish, whatever it is we're actually eating.'

'Fish, of course,' she whispered back with a roll of her eyes. 'It's Friday. Keep up!'

'I fail to see how that could be necessary, Chief Inspector,' Mrs Coulson said as they ate. 'The poor woman merely fell from the bookshelf steps. Why on earth do you need a list of those who were on stage when the bell rang and those who weren't?'

'No doubt she did,' Seldon replied noncommittally from his seat across the dining table. 'However, in the event of an accidental death, it is common protocol to record some pertinent details.' He accepted a second round of bread and butter with a grateful nod. 'For the certificate.'

Mrs Coulson frowned. 'I still don't see—'

'No doubt,' Seldon repeated and turned back to his pilchard pie.

Peeping sideways at the hard expression this had brought on in the woman beside her, Eleanor wrinkled her nose. That dismissive approach would not work for her in dealing with Mrs Coulson, she was sure of that. Especially as, Eleanor realised with a jolt, the deputy headmistress was a suspect as she'd left the stage with the other teachers at the sound of the bell.

A phrase of her mother's came back to her. *Everyone may not be good, but there's good in everyone.* Clifford had informed her recently it was actually a quote from Oscar Wilde. She sighed to herself. After all this time, she still missed her mother and a small part of her still expected her to walk in the door of Henley Hall, looking just as she did the last time she'd seen her, twenty-one long years before.

She shook her head. *So, Ellie, all you need to do is find out what is good in Mrs Coulson and you'll get along famously. Unless, of course, she's the murderer!*

She tuned back into Mrs Coulson talking.

'Headmistress, how do you plan to cover Mrs Wadsworth's Holly House boarding duties? As head of boarding, Mrs Jupe asked Miss Rice to step into the breach this evening but that has only left other duties uncovered.'

Miss Lonsdale nodded in Eleanor's direction. 'Fortunately, Lady Swift has very kindly offered to stay on and assist us for a few days.'

'What? Lady Swift as boarding housemistress? But really, I mean surely—'

'Surely, like myself, you are extremely grateful?'

'But' – Mrs Coulson looked Eleanor over disdainfully – 'without experience, it will be one mishap after another just waiting to happen.'

Miss Lonsdale tilted her head. 'Personally, I can think of no better experience than actually having been a boarder at St Mary's.'

'But this year's Holly House girls are a handful already. They will take the opportunity to get up to goodness only knows what.'

Eleanor took a long sip of her water. 'I shouldn't worry, Mrs Coulson. I can't imagine flouting the rules looks very different now to when I was here. The girls will be disappointed to find I am one step ahead of them no matter what they try.'

Mrs Coulson snorted. 'Headmistress! Think what the parents would say!'

'A heartfelt thank you, if they had any sense. Or manners,' Miss Lonsdale said with such finality that the deputy headmistress dropped her knife and fork with a clatter.

She pushed back her chair. 'Well, excuse me while I rush to go and do the inspector's bidding and put together that list, then.' She marched out, head in the air.

'Coffee for three, please,' Miss Lonsdale said to the porter who had returned to clear away their supper things.

Eleanor rose and patted her stomach.

'Please thank everyone in the kitchens. I had forgotten how good school dinner tastes when you're hungry. And I remember always being absolutely ravenous. But that plate of heads and tails totally hit the spot. It was delicious.'

'Heads and tails?' Seldon said.

She laughed. 'Every meal had a nickname when I was a pupil here. "Heads and Tails" is pilchard pie. "Grey Coats" is fried mullet. And' – she gave a small shudder – '"Whitey Frighty" is boiled cod with soggy cauliflower. Really, were you never at boarding school?'

He stared at her for a second. 'No, Lady Swift, like most of the country, I wasn't.'

Miss Lonsdale smiled. 'We try to make sure our vegetables aren't too soggy these days. Now, please take a seat wherever you will be most comfortable.'

Eleanor walked over to the other side of the room, but as she went to sit down, her breath caught. She ran her hand along the arm of the chair next to the one she'd chosen. 'Oh gracious. Mrs Wadsworth's seat.'

Miss Lonsdale joined her and patted the chair. 'This has affectionately been known as Wadsworth Corner for many years, I was informed on my first day here. But how could you know that?'

'I recognise her old blue cardigan with the big square pockets hanging on the back.' She swallowed down the lump that had sprung into her throat. 'She used to start our English literature lessons by pulling a book of short stories out of the left side one and her glasses from the right. Each time she would read a different tale and spin the room off on an instant adventure.' She smiled at the memory. 'All too soon the end-of-the-lesson bell would ring. She really was an incredible teacher.'

Miss Lonsdale reached into the left-hand pocket and pulled out a small, well-worn book, its original blue cloth covered in a map of the world, folded and glued at the corners to form an additional dust jacket. She ran her finger over the bookplate inside, beautifully inscribed in calligraphy.

'"Enchant. Enrapture. Embolden." Her personal teaching mantra.'

Not trusting herself to speak, Eleanor perched on the edge of a chair, staring at her hands. Seldon took the one beside her, throwing her a quick look of concern. Clearly ill at ease being alone with two emotional women, he became engrossed in watching the porter make a steaming pot of coffee in the kitchen area.

The cups had just been filled, and the porter sent on his way, when Mrs Coulson returned. Putting two sheets of paper down on the table, she waited until Miss Lonsdale joined her before launching into what looked like a controlled tirade. Eleanor turned her head as if staring out the nearest window, but it was really to allow her sharp hearing to catch the deputy headmistress' words.

'Of course, I defer to your seniority, Headmistress, but I feel I must put on record that calling anyone other than the local police was a lapse of judgement. Our duty is to the girls and their parents and bringing in this... this over-officious inspector can only create unnecessary drama. Mrs Wadsworth died by accident. It happens, tragic though that is. And as for Lady Swift staying on, well really!'

'Feel better?' Miss Lonsdale asked genially.

Mrs Coulson looked at her coldly. 'Is there anything else, or shall I continue taking responsibility for all the staff while you are busy with your *guests*?'

'*Our* guests, Mrs Coulson. St Mary's is a family, as I'm sure you remember.'

Once the three of them were alone again, Eleanor shook her head.

'You should swap notes with Clifford. He shares your amazing ability to chide in the most calmly respectful manner and yet leave you feeling like a reprimanded nine-year-old.'

'Interesting,' said Miss Lonsdale. 'But how does that fit into his duties of chauffeuring and butlering?'

Eleanor shrugged. 'Honestly, I'm not sure. But he manages to juggle them all effortlessly. Especially the telling me off side of things. He's particularly proficient at that. Between you and me, this lady of the manor thing hasn't turned out to be quite as I imagined. Certainly nothing like the languid days of the elegantly refined creatures Mrs Wadsworth painted in the regency classics.'

'Well, however unorthodox your methods, I am sincerely grateful for your joint assistance in this ghastly matter. And to you too, Chief Inspector, for agreeing to pull whatever strings you will need to, to allow Lady Swift to be your second in command.'

'To be *under* my command.' He pointedly caught Eleanor's eye. 'As agreed.'

She gave him a smart salute in return.

Miss Lonsdale held out the two sheets of paper she had brought over from the table. 'These are the lists Mrs Coulson has prepared.'

'Could you check you agree with them?' said Seldon. 'To the best of your knowledge, of course. I appreciate you were entirely caught up with, what I imagine is, the most important day in the school's annual calendar.'

They worked through the list. Eleanor tapped the paper. 'What about this "young John" who raised the initial alarm?'

Miss Lonsdale shook her head. 'He is, as his name suggests, a young lad who does whatever manual labour is needed in the grounds, under Mr Hepple's guidance. He's been here since he was thirteen and is only sixteen now. He has never even, to my knowledge, been inside the main school building, let alone met Mrs Wadsworth.'

'What about Mr Hepple, then?'

Miss Lonsdale took in a sharp breath. 'Mr Hepple is an institution at St Mary's. He came here at fourteen and has proudly devoted himself to keeping the school's grounds and buildings in pristine condition for the last thirty or more years. He is also our resident handyman. What that man cannot fix isn't worth fixing. His work ethic and demeanour has never diminished, even when his wife died twelve years ago.'

Eleanor bit her lip and snuck a look at Seldon, fearful that this might be too painful a reminder of his own loss five years earlier. Reassured that he did not look too troubled, she turned back to Miss Lonsdale.

'But that means Mr Hepple was here when I was a pupil. I don't remember him.'

'As you shouldn't, Lady Swift. Our parents – and uncles – are not paying handsomely to have their charges fraternising with the ground staff. Not now and not then either.'

While Miss Lonsdale was talking, Seldon quietly added two stars to Mr Hepple's name. He then rewrote the list, cleared his throat and read out the names.

<u>Staff who left the stage when bell rang</u>
Mrs Coulson, Deputy Head
Miss Small, Head of Art (found the body)
Mrs Jupe, Head of Music
Miss Munn, Head of Physical Education

Mrs Wadsworth, Head of Library (deceased)
Miss Rice, School Secretary

<u>Staff not on stage when bell rang</u>
Bursar
Chaplain
Matron
Mr Hepple, Head Groundsman

<u>Unlocked doors</u>
Guarded by Miss Lydia Goldsworthy, head girl and Mr Hepple

Other grounds staff had no access to building

'Well, there it is.' He leaned back. 'In black and white. So, unless we find out that Mr Hepple's young John was actually right and there was an intruder—'

'Which seems highly unlikely,' said Eleanor.

Seldon nodded. 'Which, I agree, seems highly unlikely, then, excluding Miss Goldsworthy, of course, one of the people on that list is our murderer!'

CHAPTER 9

Miss Lonsdale shook her head. 'I can't believe it. I simply can't. Chief Inspector, are you sure?'

'As sure as I can be at this early stage.' He ran his hand round the back of his neck. 'Do you feel up to giving me your statement? It's best to do so as soon as possible but I understand if—'

She gave a wan smile. 'No, please, help me get it out of the way. I need to return to running the school. Mrs Coulson does an admirable job, but we are not always on the same page.' She sighed. 'Or even in the same book.'

'I have the impression she is rather more of the old guard?' said Seldon.

'She is adamant it is the only way. And there are so many elements of that original approach with great merit. But the world is changing and our educational approaches must follow suit. This is 1921 and I will not have our girls disadvantaged by those adhering to obsolete methods out of misplaced loyalty and fear.'

'Fear?' said Eleanor.

'Fear of change, Lady Swift. That is the greatest paralyser of rational thought and threat to progress throughout history. And, as I mentioned, Chief Inspector, I am anticipating resistance from Mrs Coulson as she is clinging to the belief that Mrs Wadsworth's death was no more than a tragic accident.'

Seldon nodded. 'And at this stage it is important that she continue to do so. Moreover, that she believes we too think that is the case. But I shall need to question her. She, after all, was the next at the murder scene after Miss Small and she was the most senior teacher and organised the other teachers who left the stage. But how to question her without arousing her suspicions?'

'Mmm. How would it be if you asked her to check my statement and add anything she feels needs to be recorded?'

Seldon nodded slowly. 'I suppose it's the best we can do.'

Miss Lonsdale asked Miss Rice to fetch the deputy headmistress. Once Mrs Coulson arrived she wasted no time in reading Miss Lonsdale's account of that afternoon's events and putting her right.

'Well, of course, we were both on stage. The entire parent body was eagerly awaiting the ceremony and' – she gave Eleanor a cool look – 'words of wisdom.' She carried on down the page. 'No, wait. That is not correct. I checked my office first and then I heard Miss Small scream.'

Seldon gestured for her to continue reading while he noted her amendment in his notebook.

'Mmm, yes, you and I did both rush back to the library once I had informed you on stage about the accident, Headmistress. But' – she tutted – 'I told you that I dispatched *Miss Small* to go and find Matron. Once she had stopped screaming, of course. I had hoped for more from her, although she has always been highly strung.'

'An artistic temperament often appears so to those of a more practical nature,' said Miss Lonsdale evenly.

Seldon added Mrs Coulson's remarks and took a sip of his coffee as she continued through the remaining paragraphs, which referred to Mrs Wadsworth herself.

'Professionally, I'd agree with your comments, Headmistress, although you have been rather generous in my opinion. In terms of Mrs Wadsworth personally, I have nothing to add. As a senior member of staff here, I make it my business to keep my distance from the others as you know.' She looked at Seldon with a thin smile. 'One cannot command authority and be everyone's best friend.'

He nodded. 'I am sure, however, you will be of great assistance to Miss Lonsdale in being able to predict who will suffer most over Mrs Wadsworth's death? In my experience, bereavement tends to affect people quite differently, and sometimes belatedly.'

Miss Lonsdale seemed to catch his drift. 'Actually, that would be such a help. You and I will need to begin securing a replacement for Mrs Wadsworth all too soon, which will take our combined efforts. I'd hate to lose you to having to suddenly mop up a raft of staff incapacitated with grief. Whom would you say might we need to keep an eye on because they were particularly… close to Mrs Wadsworth?'

Mrs Coulson closed her eyes momentarily. 'No one particular springs to mind. She was almost universally popular.' She sniffed. 'So much so that it was hard to appraise her work, as I mentioned to you on several occasions. I believe, in truth, most of the staff were covering for her inadequacies on and off.'

'Only most? What a shame,' Miss Lonsdale murmured. She cleared her throat. 'So who would you say was not a fan of hers?'

'Miss Munn. And the bursar, for sure.'

'Well, there we are. They must have very different reasons, however, given the nature of their roles here. Any thoughts?'

'I overheard Miss Munn on several occasions complaining that the girls were often discharged late from English, which impacted on their games lessons.' She sniffed again. 'All good teachers dismiss their class on time.'

'And the bursar? I always find him a most amiable person.'

'That is because you do not perpetually harangue him for figures and balances and argue that you have not in fact spent your allocated budget when you have. As I said, Mrs Wadsworth had some… inadequacies which made the job of other staff harder.'

Seldon seemed to be trying to find the right words. Eleanor jumped in. 'Mrs Coulson, I am sorry, by the way. Heartily so. I should have offered you my condolences so much earlier. I'm sure you must have had a soft spot for Mrs Wadsworth after all your years here together.'

'We pursued a professional relationship, Lady Swift. I do not hold inappropriate "soft spots" for any colleagues, as I thought I had made clear. I am thoroughly neutral in my relationship with staff members.'

Out of the corner of her eye she spotted Seldon had also noted the slight flush that passed over the deputy headmistress' cheek.

After the deputy headmistress had left, followed by Miss Lonsdale, who had to attend to school matters, Seldon glanced at his watch.

'I'm sorry, Eleanor, but I need to be going.' He took her notebook – which she had brought with her as an aide-memoire for the speech that she had sadly never given – and deftly copied the list of suspects into it and then handed it back.

Eleanor shook her head. 'It's no good, Hugh, I know what you're doing. You hope that by writing out the list in my notebook in your perfectly neat handwriting, I won't scrawl all over the page with my untidy spider's hand.'

He laughed and placed the original list in a small holdall he'd brought with him. 'Tomorrow morning first thing I shall begin a background check on all the staff on the list.'

'And I'll get going in sussing them out,' said Eleanor, waving her notebook. At his pointed look she held up her hands. 'With Clifford's guiding and restraining assistance, I promise.'

Seldon nodded. 'I know I don't need to tell you how to suck eggs, Eleanor. You've investigated enough murders, Lord knows. But do try and be discreet about it this time.'

She went to reply, but caught his eye. 'What?'

'Nothing. I'm sure you can be discreet if the need arises.' He shook his head. 'Actually, I doubt it, but miracles do happen. We'll have a catch-up call tomorrow.' He sighed. 'All we've learned so far is that the headmistress has a soft spot for the head groundsman and the deputy headmistress has a soft spot for no one.'

And with that, he was gone.

Eleanor frowned. *Maybe Mrs Coulson didn't have a soft spot for any of the staff, Ellie, just a murderous spot for one in particular?*

CHAPTER 10

Eleanor was decidedly itchy. The school routine was continuing as if nothing had happened, which meant everyone was busy except her, and Clifford would be at least another hour or more. And although Miss Lonsdale chatted while working through the pile of papers on her desk, she kept peeping at the clock, clearly feeling the pull of her many other duties.

Finally, the scuff and thud of footsteps on the stairs wafted in through the open door. 'Homework and evening assembly are finished, it seems,' said Miss Lonsdale with evident relief.

She escorted Eleanor to the staffroom, and introduced her to the new faces. Explaining Eleanor had kindly offered to cover Mrs Wadsworth's boarding duties, she left with the coded message she would be just along the corridor in her study if anything was needed.

Of the three teachers, only one piqued Eleanor's interest since neither of the other two were on Seldon's suspect list. The two not on the list were discussing Mrs Wadsworth's demise in hushed tones, but left a few minutes later after pointedly wishing Eleanor good luck with her temporary duties. *Maybe Mrs Coulson was right, Ellie, and you've taken on more than you realise?* She shook the thought from her mind. *There's a job to do, Ellie. No time like the present.*

Over by the kettles she smiled at the tall slender woman with the most beautiful dark skin and deep black eyes she'd ever seen. It seemed Miss Lonsdale's progressive outlook was more than just talk.

The woman adjusted the silver-threaded violet scarf framing her face in a valiant effort to keep her mass of glossy black spirals in order. She ran her eyes over Eleanor's own fiery-red curls appraisingly before smiling back.

'Lady Swift, how lovely to meet you properly. Tea?'

Eleanor's stomach baulked at the idea of swishing more liquid on top of the coffee and pilchard pie, but it would give her an excuse to continue chatting.

'Lovely, thank you.'

Mrs Jupe busied herself spooning tea leaves into a brown-and-mustard striped teapot.

'And one for the pot, as the bursar always insists, ad nauseam.' She rolled her eyes as she added the extra scoop. 'His imbecilic expressions resolutely lodge in my brain. I think he believes it adds to his charm, which, trust me, it does not because he has none. At. All!' The last part was delivered with such force that Eleanor blinked. Mrs Jupe poured the boiling water into the pot. 'I must say though, Lady Swift, it's an exceptional offer of yours to stay on and assist us in our hours of need.'

'It just felt the right thing to do.' Eleanor was unsure if there had been an edge to the woman's tone. 'Wouldn't any old girl of St Mary's want to help out?'

Mrs Jupe laughed, a soft musical tinkling sound. 'Not if that meant staying on to deal with the current Holly House. I imagine they would, what is the expression? Run a mile? And faster than any of the Sports Day races they would have competed in when they were here.'

'Gracious! I'd forgotten about Sports Day. All that running and jumping, endless hockey and so forth! All of us hoarse through bellowing encouragement to anyone in our house.' She rubbed the furrow that had sprung to her forehead. 'It always incensed me that you were allowed to scream as loud as you liked then, but any other time it was considered unladylike.'

Mrs Jupe poured two cups of tea, staring intently at the stream of amber liquid.

'St Mary's is, as we are constantly reminded by our beloved headmistress, a family. But it's a grand, extended family of plentiful backgrounds thrown together in one hectic, often stifling house. No one can do anything in isolation. Or in private.'

'I imagine the girls still delight in finding out snippets of their teachers' private lives?'

Mrs Jupe stared at her for a second. 'Of course they do. I repeat, it is almost impossible to get any privacy in this place. People are always trying to find out your secrets.'

The last remark was said so pointedly that Eleanor wondered if Mrs Jupe was referring to their conversation. She mentally shrugged. *If you're going to help Seldon catch Mrs Wadsworth's killer, Ellie, you'll have to ride roughshod over a few finer feelings now and then.*

'But everyone needs a secret of some sort. Even someone like Mrs Wadsworth, surely?'

Mrs Jupe shrugged. 'I've no idea. The only thing I ever saw her doing of late, outside of reading her beloved books of course, was replying to her post and discussing art with Miss Small.'

Eleanor sighed. 'You've just reminded me of the absolute highlight when I was here. Not that it happened very often, but getting something in the post felt like your birthday and Christmas all at once. It proved there was life outside St Mary's.'

Mrs Jupe gave her a sideways glance. 'It sounds as if your days at St Mary's were rather lonely, Lady Swift.'

Eleanor shifted uncomfortably at the woman's sharp perception. 'Perhaps a little. So Mrs Wadsworth shared a love of art with Miss Small?' *If only of late, Ellie?*

'Again, I don't know. We didn't tittle-tattle over such things. I just saw them often talking together in a corner and assumed it was about the art and not books. As far as I know, Miss Small has never read a book in her life unless it was about her beloved art.'

'How do you know that?'

'I don't. But every time I saw her going in or coming out of the library in the last few weeks she was carrying an art book, so I assumed that was all she read.'

'So do you know why Mrs Wadsworth was suddenly so interested in her correspondence and art?'

Mrs Jupe shrugged. 'She suddenly had a lot of free time on her hands as she was relieved of many of her teaching duties.'

Eleanor remembered Miss Lonsdale mentioning something similar.

Mrs Jupe waved a dismissive hand. 'Enough of that, let's talk about you. Haven't you had to cancel a great deal of engagements to stay on so unexpectedly? Or' – she avoided Eleanor's gaze – 'left a husband in a temper at your having deserted him at such brief notice?'

Sadly no to both, Ellie. Although a husband? Really, is that what you want again? She'd been married once, six, no, seven years ago now. A whirlwind romance with a dashing officer in South Africa who'd actually turned out to be a gunrunner. She shrugged, more at her thoughts than the woman's question.

'Actually, I happen to be free of both. This week, anyway.'

'Hmm. Surprising,' Mrs Jupe muttered. 'But then again, maybe not.'

Gosh, I'm all for straight-talking, but this is going a bit far, Ellie!

'Is there any particular reason you think I'm not married?' she said, her voice not quite as even as she intended.

Mrs Jupe smiled. 'Perhaps because men fear you, Lady Swift?'

Eleanor blinked. 'Fear?'

Mrs Jupe nodded. 'I know a little about you.' At Eleanor's surprised look, she shrugged. 'When you are a pioneer, you seek out other pioneers to give you fortitude. You and I are both pioneers, are we not? Women do not cycle around the world on their own and women from Mauritius, or anywhere else non-European, do not work in the British education system. Although, like you, I am not the first.' She laughed. 'Well, perhaps the first woman, I'm not sure.'

'Ah! That's it! You know, I've been trying to place your wonderful accent. I've never visited Mauritius, but I hear it's beautiful.'

Mrs Jupe smiled thinly. 'Not everyone at St Mary's approves of my accent... or face.' She shrugged. 'But then again, the feeling is mutual.'

I know you want to find out more about how someone from Mauritius came to be teaching at St Mary's, Ellie, but you need to focus on tracking down your old English teacher's murderer.

Mrs Jupe waved a hand over to the chairs. 'Sitting on the stage this afternoon is the only time I haven't been on my feet. Do you mind if we take a seat?'

'Of course.'

She slid into a seat while Mrs Jupe folded her long form neatly into the opposite chair.

'This... this feels much better than squirming under the scrutiny of a full hall up on stage, if I'm honest. Not that I wish the tragedy of today happened so I could be saved from stumbling through my speech, of course. I hope it didn't come out like that?'

'Yes. To some degree.'

Eleanor winced again at the woman's candour.

'Gracious, how insensitive of me. Perhaps you were close to Mrs Wadsworth?'

The woman shrugged. 'As I said, not so much. We were colleagues. No more.'

Mrs Jupe picked up her cup and gestured she was going for a top-up, just as Eleanor's stomach let out an unhappy gurgle.

'No more, thank you.' She racked her brain for a way to ask about Mrs Jupe's movements during the afternoon. 'Aren't you also head of boarding?'

A faint smile played around Mrs Jupe's lips. 'You have been doing your homework on me as I have on you, I see.'

'Actually, when that bell rang, I noticed you left the stage with some of the other teachers. Where did you go?'

Mrs Jupe looked at her sharply. 'To look for the intruder. Pointlessly, as you probably know. Mr Hepple made a schoolboy error in not checking on what he'd been told. It took me ages to check my department since I could not detour across the quadrangle with all the doors being locked for Speech Day.'

'Now, let me see if my geography of St Mary's is intact after all these years.' Eleanor closed her eyes. 'If the music rooms are still in the same place, furthest from the main teaching classrooms to keep the noise from distracting other lessons, you must have had to go round to the front of school.' She tapped her temple. 'Am I right?'

'Quite right. You've an excellent memory,' Mrs Jupe said drily.

Eleanor tried to cast her mind back to the flurry of staff as they had returned to the stage. Had Mrs Jupe been among the main group? *Dash it, Ellie! Why didn't you notice details like that? Probably because you had no idea a woman was going to be murdered!*

She chose her next words carefully, watching closely for the woman's reaction.

'At least, you would have been in too much of a hurry to call in at the library to see if Mrs Wadsworth needed a hand, I guess? It would have been quite the shock to find her.'

'Indeed it would have.' Mrs Jupe pursed her lips. 'Our headmistress had warned her about using those ridiculous steps. I can't imagine what she was doing up there instead of returning in haste to the stage like the rest of us. Still, if a person will not take good advice.' She shrugged. 'A harsh lesson learned, one might say.'

Eleanor faltered. 'I rather think the lesson went unlearned since it would have been too late.'

'Speaking of late, I have something I need to catch up on.'

'Yes, of course, I hope I haven't kept you chatting here too long?'

'No, it is just a hiccup over the Speech Day programme which fell to me to sort out when I should have been doing my own work.'

'I said at the time I was sorry, Mrs Jupe,' a soft voice said.

Spinning round in her seat, Eleanor smiled at Miss Rice, noting that her flawless complexion was in fact rather pale. Those earlier rosy cheeks had clearly been the addition of masterfully applied rouge. Her big blue eyes almost seemed to swim in the perfect heart shape of her face. With her pronounced curves she would doubtlessly turn a fair number of heads.

Miss Rice shook her blonde curls. 'I'm sorry, I didn't mean to eavesdrop. Mrs Jupe, the headmistress asks that you pop into her study briefly before you return to your evening work.'

The head of music let out a quiet moan but nodded. Miss Rice smiled at Eleanor.

'And, Lady Swift, sorry to keep you hanging around. I have something to finish, but I'll be back soon.' She walked off, her shapely hips making the soft blue skirt of her dress swing with each step.

Eleanor turned back to Mrs Jupe. 'Such a pretty thing. She reminds me of an exquisite renaissance muse.'

'Well, she certainly doesn't see herself that way. Men these days want women to have the boyish figure of a pencil, like yours and mine. It is the fashion. Now, please excuse me, I've been summoned it seems.'

Pencil, Ellie! She sat back in her seat and ran a hand over her shoulder and down her side. There wasn't much that curved, that was true, but boyish? A blush ran up her neck. *Well, from the way Hugh held you that night on the dance floor, maybe chief inspectors are taken with the elegance of "pencils"!*

CHAPTER 11

A few minutes later Miss Rice returned and escorted Eleanor to the sanatorium, before leaving to 'do some more of the bursar's work for him' as she put it. The smell of the school's sick room immediately transported Eleanor back to the rare occasions she had been confined to it. The heady mix of vinegar, borax and carbolic soap lashed her nostrils like an irate asp's tongue. She scrunched her eyes shut against the stinging sensation.

'It certainly takes a while to get used to,' said a hearty female voice.

Eleanor forced her eyes open to take in a comfortably proportioned, middle-aged woman whose thick brown curls defied the many pins of her starched cap. Eleanor stood a good six inches above the woman, who was dressed in a navy and white uniform, reminiscent of the one Eleanor had worn as an auxiliary nurse during the war.

'Luckily, I can't smell it at all any more,' said the woman. 'Unlike Miss Small who makes a royal fuss if she ever visits. But it's all just been scrubbed down since my last little patient left an hour ago, so it is a bit raw.' She gestured to the two rows of empty metal-framed beds. 'Amazingly, none of the girls are unwell at the moment.'

It wasn't just the floor and tiny bedside stand in each cubicle that appeared to have been scoured, the walls were blindingly white, being tiled to head height and painted beyond. The blue curtains pulled halfway across the short run of narrow windows were also spotless, although so faded they had to be those she herself had peeped through years ago.

Eleanor held out her hand. 'Hello. You must be Matron.' *And a suspect in a murder investigation, Ellie! She wasn't on the stage when the burglar bell rang.* 'Lovely to meet you.'

Matron took her hand but as she shook it, frowned and turned it over. With a gentle tug, she pulled Eleanor's jacket sleeve further up. 'Goodness to St Elizabeth, you're close to the undrownable cat, aren't you?'

Eleanor stared at her blankly. 'Sorry?'

Matron tapped the long scar running down the underside of Eleanor's wrist. 'A quarter of an inch to the left and you would have been in serious medical trouble from having punctured your radial artery.'

'Instead, I was in a lot more serious trouble with the headmistress for having acquired it running down Long Passage,' said Eleanor ruefully. 'A permanent souvenir of my time at St Mary's. I used to think of it as having been branded, like cows are sometimes.'

'Then Holly House are in for a surprise. And Miss Lonsdale, perhaps.' At Eleanor's look, she tutted. 'Lady Swift, I have been a matron in girls', and occasionally boys', schools for over twenty-six years. Do you imagine I can't instantly spot the mischievous spirits, even when they have long outgrown their uniform?'

Eleanor tried not to smile. 'I have no idea what you mean, but the current Holly House girls can't really be the wild bunch the staff have repeatedly hinted at?'

'Wild, no. Well, not so far.' Matron dropped her voice. 'Between you and me, I confess to having a soft spot for girls who have the courage to bend a few rules. And not only because they're the ones to rarely need my sanatorium.'

Eleanor was intrigued. 'Do you think there's actually a link?'

'I do. I've seen it in too many pupils over the years, especially in girls. The ones who wake up with a head full of pranks, always dash out of bed and charge at the day. They don't even register they have a sniffle, ache or pain.' She consulted the fob watch pinned to her chest. 'Well, we'd best get along now. I must show you where the records of your girls are kept and the basic medical supplies.'

'Oh, yes, of course.'

Eleanor felt an unexpected wash of panic. After years of living and travelling alone, she was used to having only herself to worry about. What if something went horribly wrong? And as her soon-to-be charges were the youngest of all the pupils, likely they would be missing home and their parents. Just as she had so desperately. She tried to swallow down her anxiety. *Ellie, you're thirty, for goodness' sake. Lots of women have children of their own by now. And you're flapping at the idea of minding a handful of other people's. Get a grip!*

Matron seemed to read her mind. She reached up and patted her shoulder. 'Don't worry, I'm always on call. As boarding housemistress, you only need to do the basics. It's just a treat if I'm not repeatedly called out of bed at three in the morning to administer a headache powder or check a temperature.'

'Of course. No problem at all.' Eleanor nodded, her head swimming with memories of the emotional rollercoaster her first year of boarding had been.

'Bandages. Powders. Antiseptic ointment. Thermometers,' Matron said, tapping each of the cupboard doors in front of her in turn. 'Spare towels. Sanitary items.' They shared a sympathetic look in the wide mirror hanging above the two long ceramic sinks. 'And then in the drawer over there behind you, are the medical records of the girls in Holly House. But they're a healthy litter of kittens in the main, so you probably won't need to check anything. But such is the way of protocol and process that I'm required to give you the full tour.'

Eleanor smiled at the woman's fond description of her new charges. 'Thank you for making the time. I always love a bit of protocol and process.'

Matron cocked her head. 'Somehow I sincerely doubt that.' She tapped on the last cupboard door. 'And this I keep stocked up for staff. It is locked, of course, a couple of the teachers have certain… medicines that must be kept safe. But should you need anything, the key is hidden up here.'

Eleanor watched as Matron pulled a wooden stool out from under one of the sinks and heaved herself up onto it. Reaching behind the mirror on tiptoe, she produced a small key on a length of green ribbon and waved it at Eleanor before replacing it. She stepped heavily back down and straightened the skirt of her uniform.

'I imagine Mrs Wadsworth might have had trouble scrambling up on that stool?'

Matron stared at her momentarily before looking away. 'Poor Agnes.' Her hand strayed to her mouth. 'It was so awful seeing her lying there.'

'Gracious, I'm sorry to have been so insensitive. I should have realised that you would have been called to check on her.'

'I thought I'd seen everything, but never a… a death. Not in a school. In the field hospital, obviously.' Matron turned away from Eleanor. Reaching into her pocket, she pulled out a handkerchief and blew her nose loudly.

Eleanor waited until she'd finished. 'I am sorry. It must have been a terrible shock. You must have known Mrs Wadsworth very well?'

'Well indeed. If only that wretched burglar alarm hadn't rung, she might be with us still.'

'Possibly. Although, she was obviously still the very determined lady I remember if she was ignoring Miss Lonsdale's request to ask a colleague to climb the library steps for her.'

Matron's shoulders stiffened. 'Headmistress told you about that? How… strange.' She stepped sideways to the nearest sink and turned on the tap. After splashing her face several times, she reached for the towel hanging on a small brass hook. 'It was a terrible accident, Lady Swift. Let us speak no more of it, please.'

'Of course. I noticed you weren't on stage during Speech Day?'

Matron looked up quickly, still dabbing at her eyes with the towel. 'I was on call. I only had one patient, but I couldn't keep leaving the stage to check on her. It would have disturbed everyone. So I kept an eye on her in the sanatorium. Now, we'd better get going. They'll be driving Miss Rice up the wall.'

Eleanor nodded, thinking she wanted to find out more about Matron's movements at the time of Mrs Wadsworth's death, but the woman had made it clear she didn't want to discuss anything to do with her former colleague.

Out in the corridor, Matron closed the sanatorium door behind them and started down the passage. As they stepped outside, someone bumped Eleanor's shoulder, knocking her sideways.

'Sorry,' a male voice panted. 'Wasn't looking where I was going.'

'Have you met the chaplain?' said Matron.

Eleanor took in a thick-spectacled, sallow-faced young man whose rounded shoulders and complexion suggested a man of older years.

'I think I have now, although rather more forcefully than intended, I'm sure.'

He ran a hand over his tousled mousy hair, which looked as if he had trimmed it himself in front of an inadequately lit mirror. In peculiar contrast, his loose-fitting black jumper and trousers seemed freshly laundered.

'Chaplain, this is Lady Swift.' Matron nodded at Eleanor.

'What? Oh yes, hello, I'm sure. And, well, my apologies again. In a rush. Got to get on with things, you see.'

'Of course,' Eleanor said, not moving out of his way, eager to quiz at least one more of the names who hadn't been on the stage at Speech Day. 'I imagine quite a few of the girls might be seeking you out after the news of poor Mrs Wadsworth? And the staff too?'

Out of the corner of her eye, she noted Matron's lips purse. A fleeting look of apprehension crossed the chaplain's face as he busied himself rolling and unrolling one of the cuffs of his jumper. 'Yes, precisely. I need to be on hand in the chapel to offer words. Words of comfort as necessary, that is.'

'Yet Mrs Wadsworth was a colleague of yours too. My condolences.'

The chaplain gave only a curt nod of acknowledgement in reply.

Eleanor tilted her head. 'I'm an old girl of St Mary's in case you hadn't realised. Father Christopher was here then. We called him Father Christmas because he had such a bushy white beard.' She laughed. 'You know, Chaplain, I always wondered when I was younger who chaplains turned to when they needed help.'

The chaplain stared at her. 'Obviously, Lady Swift, I would turn to Our Lord. Now, excuse me.' Stepping around her, he marched inside.

Eleanor pulled an apologetic face. 'I hope I didn't offend him, Matron? He seemed a bit off at the end there. I just wanted to lighten the mood.'

Matron tore her eyes off the chaplain's receding figure. 'Oh, I shouldn't worry. He's been distracted lately.' She shook her head. 'A man as young as him should be full of life.' She suddenly seemed to register that Eleanor was there. She clapped her hands brightly. 'Now, speaking of full of life, you have a houseful of unladylike tom cats waiting for you!'

CHAPTER 12

Holly House, with its brick frontage and low, navy front door flanked by two bay windows, looked smaller than Eleanor remembered as she walked up its hopscotch stone path. So small that Eleanor wondered how the staff had ever fitted the girls' trunks in the tiny attic room. Pausing beside Matron on the worn front step, Eleanor couldn't help running her finger over the iron door knocker in the shape of a woodpecker. Lifting its tail caused its sharp beak to rap on a dented circular plaque.

'So Woodster still lives at Holly House then,' she muttered.

Matron cocked her head. 'I thought you might remember his name.'

She nodded, not wishing to explain that she did but had always hated how cold he was to touch. And how the noise of him rapping on the door made her jump every time. Not that teachers ever knocked. She remembered Mrs Jupe's remark about lack of privacy for the staff. It cut both ways. Her thoughts flew back to standing on that step on her first night at St Mary's, staring at Woodster's beady black eye and unforgiving beak. It had been halfway through the term, and she'd known the other girls would be settled and would have sorted out their friendships long before. She was the latecomer; unexpected, unwelcome and unwillingly thrust into a new world in a country she'd only visited four, maybe five times before. In that long moment of waiting for the door to open, Woodster had symbolised everything she detested about her young life at that point.

'Roll call!' Matron sang out as she ushered Eleanor inside. The flurry of chatter drifting down the hall ceased. Miss Rice appeared at the head of the white-painted wood staircase.

'Ah, wonderful. You're here.' Miss Rice walked elegantly down the stairs and beamed at Eleanor. 'Matron will introduce you. I need to be elsewhere. Best of luck!'

Three short crocodiles of girls aged nine to eleven, wearing blue blazers, lined the hallway as Miss Rice shut the door behind her.

Eleanor raised a hand. 'Right. Well, good evening, everyone. I've been looking forward to meeting you all.'

Each head turned to its nearest neighbour at this, a few brows raised, some shoulders shrugged. Matron tutted.

'Girls! Where are your manners?'

'Good evening, Lady Swift,' a dozen voices chorused without enthusiasm. But then they had just lost their boarding housemistress, who Eleanor knew first-hand had most likely been very popular.

Matron folded her arms. 'I expect to hear nothing but positive reports of your behaviour from Lady Swift in the morning. Do we understand each other, girls?'

'Yes, Matron.' This time, the chorus rang back off the white-washed walls.

'Good. Then I shall leave you to each introduce yourselves and give Lady Swift a proper St Mary's welcome.' She patted Eleanor's arm. 'You know where I am if you need me.' She looked at the girls expectantly.

The tallest of them left her spot at the head of the line and walked to the front door, which she opened before standing to languid attention.

'Good evening, Matron,' she said demurely as she closed it behind the woman's plump frame.

Spinning round, she stared at Eleanor, her eyes seeming to size her up. An uncomfortable silence hung in the air. *Oh crumbs, Ellie, you're the new girl all over again. The unexpected latecomer thrust on everyone without warning.*

'Welcome to Holly House, Lady Swift,' the girl said primly.

Eleanor smiled at her. 'Thank you.' She looked along the line of expectant faces. 'Er, how about you start off by telling me your names next door.'

'As you wish.'

Another pregnant pause followed. *No girls before adults, Ellie, remember! You fell foul of that so many times. How could you forget St Mary's golden rule?* Frustrated that this already felt like the stiff formality Clifford valiantly fought to keep between her and her staff at Henley Hall, she took a deep breath.

'Ah, yes, of course.' She turned and led the way under the arch.

Three long settees, covered in a hard-wearing blue canvas material, were arranged in a fan shape. They were dotted with red-and-white gingham cushions that must have been an early project in a needlework class, given their less-than-square corners and wonky fringing. Along the opposite wall, two untidy bookcases stood either side of a wide stone fireplace. A jumble of cardigans were strewn across the arms of the settees and among the half-drunk glasses of milk on the low tables pushed together in the centre of the room. The only sense of any order was the ring of upholstered chapel stools by the empty fire grate. A dropped notebook or writing pad and pencil lay in front of each.

Eleanor smiled as the last of the girls filed in hesitantly. She gestured to the stools.

'It looks as though I've interrupted a house meeting?'

All faces turned to the tall girl with a look of alarm.

'We were just, erm… thinking about things to do in the remaining days of term.'

Eleanor's new charges shot over and grabbed the notebooks and pads, causing two bumped heads in the general rush.

'I see,' Eleanor said, not believing a word of it. She recognised a hastily called war council when she saw one. The disconcerting thing was, by the way they had snapped their notebooks shut, she had the distinct impression she may have been the only item on their agenda. 'Let's start with names then. You all know mine.'

The girls shuffled back into line.

'Elsbury.'

Surnames only, of course, Ellie!

'Morton.'

'Harrison.'

'Finsmore.'

'Weston.'

Those last three almost look identical, Ellie.

'Duffy,' the tall girl said.

And, despite her best efforts, the last six she'd forgotten by the time they'd said them.

Concluding it was way too early days to venture into breaking the boundaries and even asking for first names, Eleanor waved an arm towards the settees. 'Fancy telling me what you enjoy about boarding?'

The girls dutifully squashed together, half of them ending up with their legs stuck out in front of them, being too short to reach the floor. Again it was Duffy who led the group.

'The end of prep so we can actually talk.'

This brought a flurry of enthusiastic replies.

'Tuck box time!'

'Breakfast!'

'Swapping dressing gowns!'

'Cake at half past three!'

'Saturday evening extra free time!'

'Apple pie beds!' Morton said with a grin. 'They catch everyone out, every time.'

Eleanor remembered having the trick played on her. You folded the top sheet back on itself halfway up the bed so that when the occupant dived in, they wouldn't fit because they couldn't stretch out their legs. And Eleanor had had longer legs for a nine-year-old than most.

'I'd say all of those were my favourite bits too when I was here. Along with midnight feasts, of course.'

A collective gasp filled the room.

'Oops!' Eleanor shrugged exaggeratedly. 'I probably shouldn't have said that. But I remember always being hungry.'

'Like you, Piggy Pigerton,' Duffy said, digging a quiet-looking girl in the ribs.

Eleanor racked her brain as she scanned the girl's flushed face. 'Elsbury, isn't it?'

Her 'Yes, miss,' was said almost inaudibly.

'I say lucky you for having a hearty appetite. Food is a wonderful thing, I find. It's close to a hobby of mine. Best stick with me at cake time, since we're the only ones who'll really appreciate it.' She looked up to see the other girls staring at her open-mouthed. She hid a smile. 'Now, girls, do you know what would be a real treat for me?'

'A tour?' Duffy said, standing up. 'It's tricky when you're old, I imagine. To remember things, I mean.'

Two hours later, Eleanor stared at the heap on the bed that she had pulled out of the suitcases she'd found waiting in her bedroom upstairs in the boarding house. Feeling uncharacteristically overwhelmed, she glared at the muddle of things with no enthusiasm for putting any of them away in the tall cedar wardrobe or the matching chest of drawers. In one corner, a soft green velvet armchair called to her instead, bringing home how exhausted she truly felt. And how mixed up her emotions were.

Thrust back into a raft of uncomfortable childhood memories, while trying to focus on solving the murder of her favourite teacher, made for a dizzying set of thoughts and feelings. And how she ever hoped to toe the official line and still give the girls in her care the fun and love she believed they needed remained a mystery.

They'd lost Mrs Wadsworth, just as the staff had. Suddenly, sadly, and without the chance to say goodbye. The resilience of youth no doubt accounted for the lack of tears or questions at bedtime as the girls braided each other's hair. And as they kneeled beside their beds saying prayers before snuggling down, tugging on the edge of their blankets or scooping a doll or teddy bear under the covers. That had been her once.

In the dormitory, she'd run her hand along the metal frame of the bed she'd slept in all those years ago. Last on the right under the slope of the ceiling where she had glued a photograph of her parents, the only one she had to remember them by. Only there had been no teddy, no doll – her uncle, never having had children, had missed how much comfort that would have brought her in those first weeks. As she'd turned off the lights in the dormitory, there had been a lump in her throat.

With a sigh, she gathered the muddle of her clothes into her arms, trailing stockings, and a multitude of blouses and cardigans across the rug, and dumped it all unceremoniously on the window seat. With a wistful glance out towards the cottage where her bulldog would now be curled up in his bed and her butler would be lost in Voltaire, or some similar highbrow literature, she yanked the curtains shut.

Something caught her eye, a note fallen from one of the suitcases. She picked it up and read it.

'Thank you, Clifford,' she said with a fond smile, sliding into the armchair, suddenly feeling cheered enough to tackle tomorrow.

CHAPTER 13

Not usually one to rise early, Eleanor found herself surprisingly awake as she hurried in the weak dawn sun towards her butler's temporary residence.

'Morning, Clifford!' She waved as she stepped up the stone path to the slate-grey door of the tiny cottage. 'And morning, Gladstone!' She kneeled down as her bulldog lumbered out with a soggy leather slipper in his mouth as a greeting present. 'Hello, boy. My two favourite companions are both here. Thank goodness.' She gave the bulldog's ears a good ruffle and stood up.

'What the—?' She swallowed a laugh. Her normally suited butler was wearing a bottle-green jumper, chocolate-brown corduroy trousers and workaday leather boots.

'Did you burgle someone's washing line, Clifford? I've never seen you out of your butlering togs before.'

Clifford bowed. 'Please forgive my distressingly informal appearance, my lady, which is not, in fact, the result of misappropriation from a washing line. If I am to blend in whilst assisting Mr Hepple and his team, that will not work if I parade around in morning-suit tails, carrying a silver tray.'

She chuckled. 'True. Although I'm sure if you did, you wouldn't get so much as a speck of dirt on your impeccable togs. I've only walked from Holly House and, look, somehow I've managed to rip my sage skirt. I don't know how you do it, really.'

'Likewise, my lady.'

She arched her brow. 'I don't do it on purpose.' She sniffed the air. 'I say, something smells amazing even though' – she pulled her late uncle's pocket watch from her wool jacket and glanced at it – 'it's only just six thirty in the morning.' She shook her head. 'It's a long time since I've seen six thirty in the morning.'

'If ever,' he muttered.

Her sharp ears caught his words, but she pretended not to have heard.

'Now look, your note specifically said to be here before chapel so, as it is my first morning, I cheekily asked Matron to finish getting the girls ready for morning service.'

'If you will forgive my presumption, I conjectured that you would not have had the opportunity last evening to dine in the, ahem, robust style you favour at home. And since breakfast does not commence until after chapel, I—'

'Don't remind me! I've woken up starving this morning.' Her stomach gave a loud and unladylike grumble.

'As I thought. Which is why I assumed you might wish to partake with myself and Master Gladstone?'

'I'd say so! I simply can't think straight until I've had a proper breakfast.'

'As Oscar Wilde said, my lady, "Only dull people are brilliant at breakfast."' He stood aside to let her pass into the cottage with Gladstone hot on her heels.

Having done so, she took in her butler's new surroundings. A simple dining-cum-sitting room, with a door at the far end that led into what smelt tantalisingly like the kitchen. A narrow ladder-style staircase gave access via an elongated hatch in the ceiling into what she imagined was a very low-roofed bedroom nestled in the eaves.

Against the right wall, a small pine table sat with a serviceable wooden classroom chair on either side, ready laid for breakfast and covered with a gingham tablecloth. Opposite, a pair of patched armchairs were turned towards each other, one a deep holly green, the other a restful print of mint and grey.

On two sides, curtainless windows looked out over the boarding houses on one side and the main building and swimming pool on the other. She smiled fondly at his neat row of books arranged in perfect height order between improvised candlestick bookends: Voltaire and Tolstoy mingling with science and engineering tomes.

Gladstone sprawled on the rug in front of the green-and-white tiled unlit fireplace, even at this early hour, the weak morning light bathing him and the whitewashed walls in sunshine.

'Well, Clifford, it's cosy, if a far cry from your rooms at Henley Hall. Oops!' Her cheeks coloured. 'Not that I've seen them more than once.'

'Heartening news, my lady.' He glanced at her mischievously. 'Should I, however, arrange to have the locks changed to ward off any further invasion?'

'Absolutely not, you terror! I wouldn't dream of intruding in your personal space, ever. Well, not now. At the time, I had good reason, as you know. I'd literally just arrived at Henley Hall and I thought…' She shrugged.

'That I was trying to kill you?'

'True. But we didn't know each other at all then. Now I've learned that you would do anything to keep me safe, including diving in front of a bullet as you have done on occasion. For which, by the way, I'm still as equally horrified as I am eternally grateful.'

'My pleasure, my lady. I hope there was nothing you needed missing from your luggage?'

She shook her head. 'No. Everything was there, meticulously organised in your usual fashion, thank you.'

His inscrutable expression turned to one of horror.

'My lady, Mrs Butters packed all of your cases and dealt with all your… private things, as was entirely appropriate with her being your housekeeper.' He ran a finger around his collar. 'I would never—'

She laughed. 'Relax. I was teasing. So now we're even.'

'Touché, my lady.'

'Although, Clifford, it seems that another of my staff also knows me too well. Tucked inside my overnight bag, almost as if the closure had been opened just enough to slide it in, there was a disgraceful penny dreadful novel winking at me.'

'I shall have stern words with the perpetrator, my lady.'

'I'd rather you let him know I was very grateful for his thoughtfulness, as he also correctly conjectured, I would struggle to sleep.'

'Consider him thanked. Are you ready to join your breakfast companion, my lady?'

'You're going to eat with me for once? What an absolute treat!'

'Actually, I was referring to Master Gladstone, but I shall join you if you insist.'

She nodded. 'I do. No one but you and I shall ever know, so don't worry.'

He bowed. 'Very good, my lady. Master Gladstone. Sausages!'

The bulldog woofed loudly, eyeing Clifford with a beady, and greedy, stare.

In the kitchen, Eleanor hid a smile as Clifford tied a flowered pinny around his waist. She clapped her hands.

'Right. Breakfast first, and then we must discuss—'

Clifford held a finger to his lips, pointing with the other at the large window, which was open to dissipate the cooking smells. 'Mr Hepple,' he mouthed. At normal volume, he said, 'A fortifying breakfast to help you deal with Holly House, who, I have heard, can be quite the handful, my lady.'

At the table, she laid waste to the mountain of sausages, while Clifford sat with a coffee and a slice of buttered toast. The sausages were drizzled in her cook's finest paprika and onion relish and accompanied by grilled tomatoes, crisp scalloped potatoes and the fluffiest mini cheese and bacon pancakes she'd ever eaten. Breakfast was her favourite meal of the day, although lunch and dinner were close seconds. Oh, and tea and supper, of course. She ate the last morsel on her plate and put down her fork.

'Are you sure you didn't hide Mrs Trotman in your suitcase, Clifford?' Mrs Trotman was her Henley Hall cook. 'That was just too delicious! If you really did cook this, you've given her a serious run for her money in the breakfast stakes.'

'Thank you, my lady. Perhaps, however, you might be discreet enough not to mention so on your return home?' He gave an involuntary shudder. 'Mrs Trotman can be quite sensitive in that regard.'

She laughed. 'Point taken.' She lowered her voice. 'Can we talk safely now?'

As he cleared her empty plate away, he nodded through the window at the distant form of Mr Hepple striding towards the long run of outbuildings. The head groundsman stopped at the first and looked around surreptitiously. Seemingly content he was unobserved, he slipped inside.

Eleanor shrugged at Clifford. *Probably just going for a sneaky cigarette break, Ellie.*

'Right, now we can talk without fear of being overheard. I have some concerns. This investigating lark will be dashedly tricky. I'm used to you invariably being in on every conversation with suspects, but this time it'll be necessary to split up. And I'm not always as consistent as you in note-taking.'

'Consistency, my lady, is the last refuge of the unimaginative, as Oscar Wilde also noted. We will, however, have to be imaginative and adapt to circumstances.'

Eleanor pulled her notebook out of her pocket, followed by her late uncle's favourite fountain pen. She flicked to the page where

Seldon had written out the suspect list the day before. She paused at the last name: Mr Hepple, Head Groundsman. She glanced out the window toward the outbuildings again and then back at Clifford.

'On second thoughts, maybe we should find out exactly what Mr Hepple keeps in that outbuilding, Clifford.'

He nodded. 'Absolutely, my lady. Perhaps, however, for the sake of all that is good and logical, I might respectfully request we start at the top of the list!'

CHAPTER 14

Suitably chastised, Eleanor picked up the pen and hovered over the first name.

'Mrs Coulson!' She bit back a laugh. 'Seldon aptly described her as a jar of tart horseradish.'

Clifford gave a deferential cough. 'Perhaps given our restricted time this morning, my lady, you might save the pleasure of character assassinations for later?'

'It wasn't me who called her that! Anyway, I haven't had a chance to talk to her properly yet, so let's move on.' *What you mean, Ellie, is that you've avoided talking to her. Be honest!* 'Nor have I spoken to Miss Small. But I have spoken to Mrs Jupe, Head of Music, and Matron. First up, Matron.' She peeked at her butler, whose lips were twitching. 'Sorry, I meant Mrs Jupe, as she is next on the list and we wouldn't want to do them out of order, would we?' Clifford rolled his eyes. She hurried on. 'Now, Mrs Jupe's a peculiar fish.'

'How so, my lady?'

'Well, she was rather cold about poor Mrs Wadsworth. She was also distinctly reticent to answer some of my questions.'

'Interesting, but not incriminating, my lady.'

'Agreed. But more interestingly, she doesn't like the bursar, at all.'

'Is that relevant to Mrs Wadsworth's demise, do you think?'

'I don't know, but she was quite clear that she finds him an oily tick. As he's a suspect, I'll have to tackle him, regardless.'

'Let's hope the gentleman is less of a libertine than Mrs Jupe has suggested.'

'Let's hope so, indeed.' Her eyes narrowed. 'He'd better not be like that with me or I might forget I'm a lady.'

'Again,' Clifford muttered.

She pretended not to have heard him a second time.

'Anyway, I've also added that Mrs Jupe said she took the long route to check the music rooms before reporting to the office. With all the external doors locked on account of Speech Day, that makes sense, I think.'

'Did you notice her being later than the other staff returning to the stage? Not having met the lady, I cannot call on my own memory on that score.'

'No, I didn't notice. Anyway, what else? Oh, yes, she did mention that Mrs Wadsworth and Miss Small seemed to have a common interest in art. And she was very interested to know about me. Mrs Jupe, that is.' She shrugged. 'She might just be nosy and wants to stick her trunk into my personal affairs. She asked me if I was married.'

'Ah!'

She looked at him questioningly.

'My lady, surely that is quite a normal reaction for someone who is not part of the aristocracy. If you will forgive the directness of my observation, you are a titled lady, with an air of the unorthodox and an adventurous history to match. I imagine every member of staff will be intrigued as to the details of your personal life.'

She sighed. 'Perhaps you're right, but moving on to Matron, she seemed unwilling to talk about Mrs Wadsworth's death. And a little on edge overall.'

'Do you think, perhaps, it is a natural reaction to events?'

She thought for a moment. 'Honestly, I don't know. It's just that… well, I was a nurse in the war, as you know, and I imagine she was as well as she made a remark about field hospitals. Hugh can always check that.' *It still seems odd calling Seldon 'Hugh', Ellie. No, not odd, you've known him for some time, but just…* She glanced at Clifford who was waiting patiently for her to get to the point. 'What I mean is, her reaction seemed surprising for a trained nurse who's seen the horrors of war first-hand. I know Mrs Wadsworth was a colleague, but I don't think they were that close.'

She looked up from her hastily scribbled notes as she was presented with a rich-roasted cup of creamy coffee.

'Ooh, thank you, Clifford.' She looked back down at her notebook. 'In fact, I did detect a fair deal of friction among the staff in general.'

'Possibly to be expected, my lady. This is a highly respected educational establishment, which has not long ago experienced a change of headship. Two things that might result in the staff feeling under considerable pressure to perform to the maximum of their capabilities. Or beyond, perhaps.'

'You're right. And yet, Miss Lonsdale gave me the impression that she sees the staff as being very cohesive. Maybe it's just wishful thinking.' She closed her notebook. 'And that's about all there is for the moment. Not much.'

'No matter, my lady. It is early days and you have gleaned a host of useful information. My sincere commendations.'

She shrugged. 'Maybe, but all this information isn't going to be much use if we can't communicate it to Hugh. When was he going to ring?'

Clifford cleared her breakfast things onto a tray.

'This afternoon, I believe, my lady. And I passed a particularly fine-looking set of tea rooms in the village of Dunningswade, seven miles south-west of here. I suspect it will soon become a firm favourite of a certain chief inspector who shares your love of fruit cake.'

'Brilliant, Clifford, you clever bean!'

She cuddled Gladstone on the rug while the sounds of washing-up filtered out to her. Clifford returned a few minutes later, his open pocket watch in one hand, a green tweed cloth cap in the other.

'My lady, perhaps it is time to settle Master Gladstone in his bed for the morning. I believe the girls will soon be in the dining hall for breakfast and the grounds team in the main hut to be given their list of tasks for the day, whom I should join.'

As Clifford checked Gladstone was snoring happily before locking the cottage's door behind them, Eleanor caught a movement at the end of the hedge.

'Mr Hepple,' she whispered.

'Shall we then, my lady?'

'Good morning,' she called out as Clifford held the gate open for her. 'Isn't it a beautiful day?'

''Tis alright enough, m'lady.' The head groundsman slid off his cap. 'Been too busy working since first light to notice, mind.'

Clifford stepped forward. 'I'm here to help wherever I can, as Miss Lonsdale informed you I believe, Mr Hepple.'

The head groundsman's watery eyes narrowed.

'We'll see.'

Gracious, Ellie, hardly the warm welcome or thank you one might expect! Confident, however, that her butler's infallible knack of getting on with almost anyone in almost any situation would prevail, she simply smiled.

'I'm sure all the arrangements for Speech Day placed quite the burden on your team, Mr Hepple. It was a treat to appreciate it all from an adult point of view yesterday. I'm afraid as a pupil I was more interested in finding an outlet for my energy rather than sitting quietly in the hall.'

'Like swinging from the rope store in the furthest barn, I seems to remember.'

She was momentarily speechless that he'd recognised and remembered her.

'Erm, well as I said, you're probably quite busy having lost the best part of half a day yesterday making sure the parents didn't wander off wherever they fancied. Of course, being the head of your team, you would also have been called away to sort out any hitches?'

He frowned and pushed his forelock of unruly grey hair out of his eyes.

'There was no hitches on Speech Day. My men are well trained. Been here a goodly while too.' He glanced at Clifford. 'Not a newcomer among them.'

She noted one of Clifford's brows twitch.

'No hitches, you say? Except for the false burglar alarm, of course.'

He scowled. 'Told Miss Lonsdale it were a mistake.' He eyed her sceptically for a moment before changing the subject. 'Holly House girls'll keep you busy alright, m'lady, if I've heard right that you'll be taking over as boarding mistress?'

'You have indeed, but only temporarily. Until a replacement is found for poor Mrs Wadsworth.'

Clifford reached into his pocket and pulled out a bag of mint humbugs, offering one to Eleanor first. He then held it out to Hepple, who shook his head curtly.

'Perhaps, Mr Hepple, following the lady's sad demise, you are now the longest-serving member of staff?'

'That I am. Mrs Wadsworth and me actually started on the same day. September twenty-third, 1873 it was. She was new to teaching, barely over twenty years old. And I was just a lad, hardly out of short trousers.'

Clifford nodded. 'Time does fly, Mr Hepple. Speaking of which, we are taking up *your* valuable time. Perhaps you'd like to set me to task now with a member of your team?'

'We'll see.' Jerking a thumb towards the outbuildings, he spun on his heel and strode away.

'Crumbs, good luck cracking that nut,' Eleanor whispered.

'Likewise with Mrs Coulson.' Clifford winked and set off after Mr Hepple.

'Clifford!' she hissed. He stopped and half turned. 'Remember to find out what's in that first outbuilding!'

CHAPTER 15

A familiar hearty Irish voice hailed Eleanor from the doorway.

'Lady Swift, I've just heard, you know.' Miss Munn bounded over, her sailor-collared burgundy wool dress from yesterday replaced with the white cotton sports top and navy flared calf-length skirt of a typical head of PE. Her tennis shoes squeaked against the wooden flooring.

'Heard what, Miss Munn? Whatever it is, it seems to have you quite animated.'

'The most welcome news. That you have offered to stay on and cover Holly House boarding duties! Beyond the call of duty, I must say. I thought last night was a one-off, so I did, and felt I had to come up and thank you. I'm boarding mistress for Beech House so if I can help in any way give me a shout.'

'Thank you, I think.' Eleanor smiled. Remembering that Miss Munn's was another of the starred names on their suspect list, Eleanor nodded towards the kitchen area. 'Do you have time for a quick break?'

'Certainly for a handful of biscuits, I do.' The head of PE laughed. 'Actually, better still, let's hope there's some of the bursar's birthday cake left. Should be. He ordered heaps, as always, in an attempt to impress the ladies, you know.'

Eleanor's stomach rumbled. Despite just having devoured Clifford's amazing breakfast, cake could never be refused.

'Then it must at least have chocolate sprinkles?'

'Oh no. Far better than that. Three layers of chocolate sponge with walnut and cherry cream between each. I so missed proper cake when they rationed everything. Come on.'

A hasty trawl through the tins up on the oak counter ended in a triumphant howl from Miss Munn. 'Just as I thought. Heaps left.' She turned to the two other teachers in the room. 'Cake, chaps?'

'After breakfast! No thanks,' the first female voice called back.

'We haven't all spent the early hours charging up and down the pitches like you,' said the second.

Miss Munn slapped her hands together. 'Just you and me then, Lady Swift. And I am famished.' She set two generous slices on a plate each, then with a grin added a third. She peered cheekily at Eleanor. 'Perhaps I ought to try and find you a delicate fork and a linen napkin?'

Eleanor laughed. 'Since my butler isn't here to sniff disapprovingly and miraculously produce both out of nowhere, I shall be delighted if you don't. I'll pretend I'm a forever-starving nine-year-old again and I'm raiding my tuck box out of hours.'

'Perfect. Do you mind if we stand though, I'm not one for lounging in padded chairs, you know.'

'Not at all. I'm not one for lolling about either.'

Miss Munn's face lit up with admiration. 'That was never in question. I think what you did was incredible.'

'Erm, thank you. But what did I do?'

'Cycled round the world! And unaccompanied too.'

Eleanor shrugged modestly. 'How did you know?'

'Miss Lonsdale. She told me because she knew I'm the only one who would truly understand just how much of a physical achievement that is.'

'Well, that's very kind. But really, I was just indulging my love of exploring and my rather, err, let's say restless nature. I was also incredibly privileged in being able to do so.'

'Aye, well, there have to be some benefits to having little to no family.'

Eleanor blinked. 'Did Miss Lonsdale tell you that as well?'

'No, of course not.' Miss Munn wrinkled her nose. 'I haven't offended you, have I?'

'Not a bit. I'm just curious as to how you know.'

She shrugged. 'I'm curious too. Curious as a cat, my mother always used to say, but it wasn't a compliment.' She rolled her eyes. 'No, it simply seemed likely since you came with your butler. The few old girls I've seen visiting before tend to come draped over the arm of some devilishly handsome male or toting a set of aged parents.'

Eleanor chuckled. 'And I thought Mrs Jupe was the one to speak her mind.'

Miss Munn pulled a face. 'Myrtle's her first name, you know. I don't think it's her real name. She's from some tropical island, I can never remember which. I think Myrtle is like an adopted name because no one can pronounce her real name. Either way, there's no need to look at the weathervane on the roof of the chapel to see which way the wind is blowing. Just slide past the main music room, that'll tell you.'

Seems a tad harsh, Ellie?

'Bit prickly sometimes, is she?'

Miss Munn shrugged. 'Can't seem to get the measure of her, even though we're both immigrants. Or maybe not.' Miss Munn scrutinised her now empty plate. 'I'm never sure if I'm supposed to be Irish or British. I guess I'm Northern Irish now.'

Eleanor caught on. 'Of course. I thought your accent was from the north. And for the last few weeks it's officially been a state in its own right, hasn't it? *Northern* Ireland. I can see that it would be very confusing deciding what to call yourself.'

Miss Munn shrugged again. 'Aye, but home is always home, whatever politicians call it. And may it be too small to hold all of your friends, as we always say.'

Eleanor nodded. 'I think I have some ancestral Irish connection, you know. You've inspired me to find out more about it and go visit my roots.'

'Well, be sure to make time in your cycling schedule for talking endlessly to everyone you see. You'll get a mile a day if you're lucky.'

Eleanor savoured another mouthful of the delectable cake and sighed. 'You know, being here really is bringing back lots of memories.'

'Happy ones?'

'Some.' Eleanor's smile faded. 'Unless my thoughts run back to poor Mrs Wadsworth. But it must be so much more of a shock for you?'

'Silly old stick,' Miss Munn said with a shake of her head. 'She knew I'd always sprint up and down those wretched steps for her. I'd told her to heap the top shelf books on her desk and I'd put them in their proper place when I had time.'

'But I bet she rarely took you up on that.'

'Never, actually. She just had to put them away neatly immediately. But now I'm curious. How could you have worked that out?'

'Worked it out?' Eleanor hesitated. 'I'm not here to work anything out. It's just that I remember Mrs Jupe saying some staff offered to help Mrs Wadsworth and she didn't take them up on it.'

Miss Munn laughed. 'Of course you aren't here to work anything out. Simply to wade into the fray and help.' She avoided Eleanor's gaze. 'Well, at the risk of trumping Mrs Jupe in the forthright stakes, I hope you don't mind me saying you're not quite what I expected, you know.'

Eleanor snorted a laugh. 'Not at all. I get that a lot. The problem is, becoming the lady of the manor doesn't come with an instruction manual. So' – she threw out her arms– 'I'm left having to make it up as I go along.'

'Sounds much more fun.'

Eleanor couldn't fail to notice the gusto with which the head of PE attacked another plate of cake. *She seems peculiarly upbeat given that a colleague of hers has just died, Ellie.*

Miss Munn caught her staring.

'Don't misunderstand my demeanour, Lady Swift. I was very fond of Mrs Wadsworth, even though we had nothing in common.'

'Of course. And then when the burglar alarm rang, you must have needed to check the games areas?' Even as she said it, Eleanor thought that sounded a peculiar place for a would-be thief to think they might find some worthwhile spoils.

Miss Munn shook her head. 'No one's going to steal a bunch of hockey sticks. Mind you, if they knew the price of the tennis racquets, they would probably pinch the lot. No, it's my job to check the boarding houses.' She grinned. 'Being the fittest, in fact the only fit, member of staff, it makes sense that I'm the one to check the largest and furthest part of the school.'

'Impressive nonetheless.' Eleanor frowned, trying to picture the various routes to the boarding houses. 'You probably passed some of the other staff checking out their areas, then?'

Miss Munn paused in her demolition of the second round of cake. 'A strange question, but I have no idea. Oh hang on, now I think of it, aye, I did pass Miss Small dashing down Long Passage. And as I spun back out of the office, someone was belting either up or down the main staircase. At least, it sounded as if they were.' She gestured outside the staffroom door. 'But I didn't bother to see who it was or which way they were going. Too keen to get back and hear your speech, you know.' She glanced up at the clock. 'Oops, I need to go.'

'Well, thank you for the sublime cake, but please don't let me keep you. And, Miss Munn,' Eleanor called as the head of PE turned to go, 'perhaps we can raid the staffroom tuck box together another time?'

Miss Munn beamed. 'Aye, sounds great. Catch you later.'

CHAPTER 16

'I have?' Eleanor tried hard not to frown.

'Absolutely!' Miss Small's soft breathy voice drew out the word dramatically as she hugged her waif-like chest.

'Erm, if you say so.'

Eleanor was having tea in the staffroom with the Head of Art, but she was finding it a little tricky to follow the lady's train of thought.

Miss Small sighed. 'It's such an honour to meet someone who appreciates true art. Living at Henley Hall must be like living in an exquisite gallery.'

Actually, Ellie, she's right about that. The walls are hung with what must be fine art.

Eleanor decided she needed to take control of the conversation. 'Miss Small, unfortunately, I think I'm going to disappoint you a little. I inherited Henley Hall fairly recently and honestly have no real idea about the many paintings hanging everywhere. Not having had time, you see. To be frank, I've only ever looked at my late uncle's portraits. And then out of sentimentality.'

Miss Small's eyes widened. 'But surely you—'

'Perhaps I need to introduce you to Clifford, my butler. He will certainly be able to mentally give you a tour of every painting at Henley Hall, in the minutest of detail.'

'Oh, if you could!' Miss Small leaned back on her hands and swung her ivory-stockinged legs, a dreamy look in her eyes. 'I can't wait.'

They passed another ten minutes in amiable and aimless chatter. Eleanor's next move in the investigation rested on the most witless member of her team but she needed her wizard too. She nodded at Miss Small, keeping the conversation going.

Finally, Clifford appeared by the ornate scrollwork arch in the rose bed to her right, deadheading those blooms that had withered. Miss Small was too busy expounding on the merits of the neoclassical period to notice his presence.

'Fascinating,' Eleanor said. 'Not to change the subject, but last night the Holly House girls were telling me how much they enjoy your classes.'

Miss Small smiled. 'The younger ones usually do. There is one in Holly House who has an extraordinary innate talent. The dear one's just too shy to let it show yet.'

'Well, I have to confess to trying to remember all the details of the art rooms as the girls made me shamelessly nostalgic for my own days here.'

Miss Small laughed, a delicate percussive trill. 'Oh, Lady Swift, I have the most wonderful idea. Come! You'll love it. A tour of my little world. The one you used to inhabit on a Monday and Wednesday, between two and three in the afternoon?'

'Gracious, is the timetable really still the same? And did I really manage to create that level of mess in just an hour?'

Eleanor allowed herself to be wafted off the bench and across the lawns leading to the main block of St Mary's. Not, however, before she'd discreetly nodded at Clifford, who gave a discreet finger wave in return without pausing his deep conversation with Gladstone over the intricacies of pruning techniques.

'Oh, gracious!' Eleanor said as Miss Small stood back proudly against the door to the first of the art rooms. 'It's exactly that eye-watering smell of the paints that I remember so clearly. And these drying racks too.' She ran her hand along the thin metal grilles under the long bank of windows.

'It's the vermillion.' Miss Small wafted a tube of paint under Eleanor's nose, making it wrinkle. 'It's jolly whiffy, but a simply divine colour. I actually have a highly developed sense of smell, so it smells even stronger to me.'

Through the window, Eleanor glimpsed Clifford turning the corner with a very excited bulldog alongside. 'Ooh, but we never had adjustable-height stools.' She pointed away from the window. 'These look great fun.'

Miss Small grimaced. 'Hmm, far too much fun for the Holly House girls. I only have to turn my back to know they will be egging each other on to spin as many times as possible before I catch the little dears.'

Desperately keen to try it out for herself, Eleanor resisted the urge. Scanning the rest of the room, she spotted what she'd really come to see.

'I say, tell me about those marvellous models against the wall.'

'What?' A frown flickered across her face. 'Ah, yes. A study of form and proportion. Combined with perfecting the mediums of wire moulding and papier mâché. As you can see, some misunderstood the "perfecting" part of the lessons.'

Eleanor laughed while glancing discreetly out the window where Gladstone now stood shoulder-deep in a hole he was gleefully digging while Clifford remonstrated with him. He caught her eye and gave a single nod.

'Tell me, Miss Small, why do the models all have their feet attached to a piece of flat wood stuck on a square lump of clay?'

'The wood stops them toppling by keeping their feet firmly planted, but it also lets you turn them on the clay block so they can be examined from every angle. That way, the girls can see how each different plane affects one's view of a person's form.'

Eleanor pointed to one particular model.

'Then it seems this poor fellow was the most popular. His wood has come away from his block completely.'

Miss Small let out an exasperated breath that had no more force than a butterfly taking off. 'I know. Holly House again, I'll bet. What is with them and things that turn, the dears!'

'May I pick it up?'

Miss Small stared at her. 'Pick it up? Whatever for?'

Eleanor shrugged. 'I just wanted to hold it.'

Miss Small hesitated. 'They are rather delicate, but… alright. After all, every piece of art is for everyone to enjoy.'

'Thank you. I'll be careful.'

As Eleanor picked up the model, which was almost her height, she conceded it was indeed surprisingly light. 'Golly, I can carry him with one arm.' She nonchalantly scooped up the clay block, noting the hole the short length of copper pipe sticking from the wood had fitted into.

Miss Small nodded. 'That's the beauty of papier mâché. And it's cheap, which pleases the bursar. Ignorantly, he believes that art materials should cost pennies, not pounds!'

'Come along, Patrick Papier, I need to admire you properly in the light.' To the art teacher's delight, Eleanor danced the model over to the window. 'He's quite the fellow, isn't he? If I met him at a ball, I'd definitely be hoping for the first waltz.'

'Well, he would be totally enraptured by your emerald-green silk gown and matching headband as he twirled you round the ballroom, Lady Swift, I'm absolutely sure.'

Eleanor paused a moment in trying to slide the copper pipe back into the clay block. 'How could you possibly know my favourite gown is emerald green?'

Miss Small waved her arms around the room.

'Because I am an artist, as well as an art teacher, dear one. I pictured myself painting your portrait when you were sitting on stage yesterday, and I was itching to mix the most vivid emerald imaginable for you. With your exquisite Titian red curls, green eyes and' – she pointed to Eleanor's sage jacket and skirt – 'your evident love of green, and your immaculate style, there could be no other colour for you.'

Risking another glance out the window, Eleanor caught sight of Clifford as he picked up his trug, looped a lead onto Gladstone's collar, gently pulled him out of the hole and strode off with a very earthy bulldog in tow.

Eleanor returned the model to its block, happy that he'd obviously seen all he needed to.

'I'm sure I've taken up enough of your time, Miss Small. I'll let you get on. But before I go, I don't mean to pry, but are you alright? You know, after yesterday?'

The art teacher's already pale complexion lost the last of its colour.

'Death is a strangely beautiful thing,' she said in an ethereal voice. *What, Ellie!?*

Miss Small registered the shock on Eleanor's face and hurried on.

'I didn't mean it like that. I meant in paintings when the artist portrays a subject's last breath and beyond. That finality, encapsulated in oils, by expert brushstrokes. It allows us to almost experience our own final moments. To stare and savour the feeling of… of having no feeling any more.'

Eleanor fought to keep her eyebrows from disappearing into her red curls. 'I'm pleased you've managed to find a way to deal with the shock. Why do you suppose Mrs Wadsworth went up the ladder, though? It was right in the middle of Speech Day.'

Miss Small threw up her hands. 'Because she was odd, Lady Swift. And I don't mean to speak badly of the deceased but she was obsessed with neatness and everything being perfectly in order, which I cannot comprehend. It was a common trick among a few of the less pleasant, spiteful girls to purposefully take books off the shelves and leave them on the tables in the library. Or even place them on the shelves in the wrong place. They knew Mrs Wadsworth wouldn't be able to rest until every book was back in its rightful place, the poor dear. I imagine when she checked for that non-existent burglar, she couldn't return to the stage until she'd returned the book to its shelf.'

'Which book?' Eleanor said casually.

'I don't know. Whichever one was on the floor beside her.'

I wonder if it was an art book, Ellie?

Miss Small sighed. 'I just turned and ran for help. Fortunately, straight into Mrs Coulson. Literally. We bumped heads. Then she sent me off to get Matron. Although' – she frowned – 'Matron didn't even seem to have heard the bell.' She shrugged. 'Perhaps she was elsewhere. She seemed flustered.'

That tallies with what Mrs Coulson told Seldon, Ellie. Except Matron not hearing the bell.

'Let's not dwell any more on the image you're trying to forget.' She patted Miss Small's frail arm. 'I imagine Miss Lonsdale is very supportive of all your creative efforts with the girls.'

'I have no idea. She's never said. We didn't mix that much, actually. Mrs Wadsworth and I. Although, ironically, I ended up spending most of yesterday morning with her. Firstly, helping out with the Holly House girls who were too excited about Speech Day to be at all controllable. Then Mrs Jupe caught us both as we were leaving breakfast and tasked us with overseeing the setting up of the hall and the multitude of floral arrangements.'

'Did you expect to be called for those duties?'

'Not a bit. Normally I have little to do on Speech Day except make sure there is a display of the girls' art in the main hall. This year, however, the florist wasn't the usual one, and I have to agree that the last-minute people Miss Rice found had done a terrible job. We had to unpick every arrangement in the flower room and start again. It took us almost until lunchtime. It's a shame you never got your bouquet. I made it especially beautiful.'

'Thank you. But where's the flower room? That sounds new.'

'Oh, it was probably known as the fern room when you were here.'

'Ah, yes.'

The previous headmistress had been obsessed with ferns, even naming the four schoolhouses after them – Beech, Holly, Marsh and Royal. Eleanor pictured the indulgent glasshouse that had housed the headmistress' prized collection. The size of a large sitting room, the smell of peat filled the air even when the roof vents were open in summer.

'Anyway, how did Mrs Wadsworth seem yesterday?'

Miss Small frowned. 'Seem? A strange question. Like me, she was frantically trying to make the best out of a morass of flowers which had been poorly handled and then transported with a disgraceful lack of water.'

'So you didn't chat much then?'

'Only to disagree over the names of the flowers. She got huffy, insisting she knew better, so I let it drop.'

'Perhaps she was distracted about something?'

Miss Small seemed to consider this. 'Now that you mention it, she did seem rather preoccupied with more than just the task we'd been thrown. But she'd been like that for some weeks.'

'Really? Preoccupied with what?'

The art teacher shrugged. 'Who knows? Poor dear. Whatever it was, we'll never know now, will we?'

CHAPTER 17

Dunningswade turned out to be not only a pleasant drive away but also an exceptionally pretty market town that had politely declined to modernise since the death of Queen Elizabeth I.

'Just look at these beautiful black-timbered buildings, Clifford. And their enormous three-sided lattice windows.' She leaned her top half out of the Rolls. 'They're suspended miles out from the buildings themselves, like tall, enclosed balconies. And look at the rows of carved black horses beneath on that one there. How odd!'

'They are called "oriel" windows, my lady. The horses are in fact supports, or "corbels", as is the official term. I believe, however, that they can be equally appreciated from the ladylike position of remaining in one's seat, rather than teetering precariously outside one's moving vehicle.'

'I don't. That suspended covered-over walkway connecting those two tall buildings looks like it's going to collapse any moment!'

'The correct term is a "pentice", my lady.'

She pulled her head back in.

'I really don't know how you fit your colossal brain under your bowler hat. Surely, Mrs Butters must have needed to let the seams out?'

'Bowlers are seamless, my lady, being moulded from a single piece of felt.'

She couldn't hide her smile. 'Touché. Seriously though, Clifford, why are you wearing it? It's the hottest day I can remember for ages and quite unbearably sticky.'

'Or oppressive, as I believe ladies refer to it.' He drove on slowly, staring forward, the corners of his mouth twitching.

As the Rolls turned onto the high street, Eleanor jerked up straighter and pointed at the tall, charcoal-grey-suited figure striding along the opposite pavement, a scowl darkening his handsome face.

'It's Hugh. Why on earth is he walking? He must have driven here, surely.' With one hand on the dashboard, she leaned across Clifford's view and called out of the driver's window. 'Hugh!'

But the inspector was too distracted mopping his brow to hear her.

Clifford ducked down to see through the bottom of the windscreen.

'My lady, if you wish to switch seats, might I request that I am allowed to halt the car first?'

She flopped back into her seat and groaned.

'He doesn't seem very happy. Oh, Clifford, it's too hot to squabble today. Well, maybe not with you, but definitely with Hugh. We'll end up having one of those hideously fractious meetings and then he'll leave in a huff.'

Clifford eased the car to a stop outside a quaint tea room. He gestured to its welcoming mint-and-white striped awning.

'Perhaps the congenial atmosphere inside will soothe the chief inspector's savage brow. Shall we?'

'There you are!' Seldon's deep voice tickled her ears as he crossed the street to meet them. That combined with his tousled chestnut curls awoke the familiar flutter in her chest.

'Hi, Hugh. Fancied a walk, did you?'

He gave her a withering look. 'On the hottest day of the year when I need to be in two different places at once? Hardly. My infernal car decided to give up the ghost at the beginning of town, if you can call this a town! Let's get this over with and then I'll have to sort it out somehow.'

Keen to hide her disappointment at his obvious, if not unjustified, ill mood, she slapped on a smile.

'Perhaps their famous fruit cake will sweeten your temper?'

'Who's in a temper, blast it!'

'I think your quietest table and three speciality afternoon teas, please,' Clifford said to the young waitress who was wearing an elaborate lace apron.

At the table they were shown to, Eleanor looked around at the exposed black beams running across the low ceiling. It was charming, but along with the dark oak furniture they added to the already oppressive atmosphere.

'Golly, it's no cooler in here than outside.' She fanned her face with the linen napkin from her side plate.

Seldon dropped his notebook on the table and pulled out the chair opposite hers, waiting for her to get comfortable before sitting down. He bent down to retrieve his pen, which had rolled onto the floor.

'My lady,' Clifford whispered as he perched on the edge of his seat. 'Propriety always, but perhaps—' His hand went to the knot of his tie and gave it a short wiggle.

'Oh gracious, of course.' She smiled apologetically at Seldon as he sat back up. 'Boys, please remove your jackets and loosen your ties or whatever you need to do to stay sane in this heat.'

Seldon thumbed the two buttons of his jacket open and shrugged out of it with a heartfelt, 'Thank you.' Loosening his tie a quarter of an inch, he pulled on the bottom of his waistcoat and returned her smile. 'Now I might be able to think straight.'

She didn't need to peep sideways at Clifford to know he would not have taken up her offer, despite being the one to have asked. He broke the awkward silence by pouring them each a cup of tea.

'My lady, Chief Inspector, would you excuse me just a moment?'

After he'd gone, Seldon turned to Eleanor. 'Where's he off to?'

She shrugged. 'No idea, but knowing him it's got something to do with trying to help me not argue with you.'

Seldon threw his head back and roared a deep rich laugh, making her jump.

'That's hilarious. I'm sorry, Eleanor, but it is.' He held her gaze for a second, then shifted in his chair. 'You two seem to understand each other so well. It's a little... disconcerting sometimes.' The colour in his cheeks deepened. 'And, if I'm honest, it's refreshing to see I'm not the only one who gets it wrong with you on occasion.'

Her heart skipped at how handsome he looked when he smiled.

'Well, shall we start again?' she said.

'I'd really like that. And apologies for my grumpy mood at my car breaking down.'

'No apology needed. Now, let's sample some of these delicious sandwiches.'

As they munched through the delectable assortment on their plates, she opened her notebook at the two facing pages where he had listed their suspects. She waved a potted shrimp and cucumber triangle at Seldon.

'I've quizzed quite a few of the people on the initial suspect list, and I've got ideas on how to coerce answers out of those left.'

A smile played around his lips. 'You do understand that coercion is frowned on, mostly because it's illegal?'

'Dash it, Hugh. You know what I mean.' She gave him a cheeky salute. 'Thank you for the reminder, Chief Inspector.'

Seldon shuffled his tall frame into Clifford's chair at her suggestion that they could better go through her notes together. However, she hadn't anticipated the extra cloud of butterflies his proximity would release in her stomach. Willing herself to stare at her notebook rather than the dashing inspector's long strong arms under his white shirt with its muted pebble-grey stripe, she grabbed her cup and took a gulp, scalding her tongue.

In the meantime, Seldon seemed to have similar problems, choking on a mouthful of tea. Once they'd both recovered, he nodded at her notebook.

'May I?'

'Mmm.' She mumbled through a roast beef and field mushroom triangle. 'Go ahead.'

He thumbed through the pages, alternately wincing and chuckling as he ran a finger down her entries.

Staff who left the stage when bell rang
Mrs Coulson, Deputy Head – *Checked her office then heard Miss Small scream in library. Found Miss Small standing over body. Sent Miss Small away to fetch Matron. When Matron declared Mrs Wadsworth dead went back on stage and told Miss Lonsdale. Insists Mrs Wadsworth's death was just an accident.*

Miss Small, Head of Art – *Checked art rooms and then was returning to hall when heard scream. Went to library, found Mrs Wadsworth. Miss Munn says she bumped into Miss Small at some point. Miss Small also said she didn't spend much time with Mrs Wadsworth but Mrs Jupe said she often saw them chatting in corners?*

Mrs Jupe, Head of Music – *Couldn't cut across the quadrangle with all the doors being locked for Speech Day. Had to go round to the front of school to check music rooms.*

Miss Munn, Head of Physical Education – *Checked boarding houses, which are the furthest buildings from the school office. Passed Miss Small, Head of Art dashing down Long Passage. And heard someone belting either up or down the main staircase after leaving school office.*

Miss Rice, School Secretary – *Not spoken to yet.*

<u>Staff not on stage when the bell rang</u>
Bursar – *Not spoken to yet but not on stage as 'twisted ankle'. Answered call in school office and rang the bell.*

Chaplain – *Not talked to yet. Did bump into him. Something about his face reminded me of something, but can't think what?*

Matron – *Looking after pupil in sanatorium. Miss Small said she fetched Matron, but she seemed confused and hadn't heard the bell??*

Mr Hepple, Head Groundsman – *Was on duty guarding rear door. Says his assistant saw an intruder and got him to ring the school office. Miss Lonsdale asked young lad herself and he confirmed what Hepple said. Checked out model with Clifford but Clifford said the model didn't look anything like a real person from outside. Also Clifford and I saw Hepple clandestinely enter outbuilding he keeps locked?*

'Terrifying, Eleanor. Quite terrifying.'

'What is?'

'That you have solved six murder cases with this level of... please don't take this the wrong way, chaotic analysis. But I suppose I should have expected nothing less. Peculiarly, it's as reassuring as it is troubling.'

'How so? My brain simply works like this. It drives Clifford potty. In fact' – she stared down at the pages, which were also covered in scribbles and scratchy sketches – 'I did try to be neat. Initially.'

Seldon leaned over and stared at the page she was pointing to. 'I'll believe you. What is that you've drawn for Mrs Coulson, by the way?'

She turned back the edge of her beef sandwich. 'Horseradish.'

He tutted and held his hand out for her pen. Eleanor gasped and then laughed as he added a scowling face to the jar she had doodled.

'I'm sorry, but you hadn't made that woman nearly tart enough.'

'So much for objectivity!'

He leaned back. 'Anyway, thank you. This is very comprehensive. Chaotically comprehensive, naturally, but somewhere in all of this' – he indicated the pages of notes – 'are the clues, or at least the first clues, we need. You've done very well.'

His praise was so unexpected she blushed. Under each suspect, he added a follow up action for her and Clifford in short efficient strokes. He passed the notebook back to her.

'Well, that will certainly keep us busy.'

Seldon frowned. 'Speaking of busy.' He pulled out his pocket watch. 'Blast it! I'm going to be late and I still have to sort my wretched car somehow. But this town looks to be only of use to tourists or someone looking to relive the middle ages. Not anyone blighted with a broken vehicle. How am I supposed—'

CHAPTER 18

Seldon clutched his chest as Clifford coughed beside his elbow.

'You could give someone a heart attack sneaking up on them like that!'

'My sincere apologies, Chief Inspector. Your keys.' He dropped a silver ring with two keys into the hand Seldon held out in confusion.

'But—' Seldon ruffled the pockets of the jacket he had removed. 'Clifford, what the dickens?'

'If you will forgive my intention of trying to avoid you losing more time over a protracted discussion of how it might be achieved, the Crossley is fixed, Chief Inspector. She won't give you any more trouble. She is also parked immediately outside.'

'What? Really!' Seldon stood up, looked out the window to confirm his car was there, and then shook his head. 'I'm eternally grateful, Clifford. You've saved me from a very fraught afternoon I've been dreading.' He lowered his voice, but Eleanor's sharp ears caught his words. 'In more ways than one.'

'Most heartening news, Chief Inspector.'

Eleanor laughed. 'Hugh, aren't you going to officially caution him for picking your pockets? Underneath his immaculate butlering togs, he's obviously a complete scoundrel.'

'Actually,' Seldon said, throwing his keys up and closing his fist around them as they landed back in his hand, 'I am minded to arrest him for being a—'

'Wizard,' he and Eleanor chorused together.

Clifford ordered more tea while Eleanor surveyed the empty plate in the centre of the table.

'Clifford, I'm so sorry! Hugh and I have pigged all the sandwiches while you were on your thoughtful car-fixing mission. We'll order some more with the tea.'

'Pigged, my lady?' He sniffed. 'Not a term I am familiar with. Perhaps—'

He was interrupted by the arrival of three tiered stands of cakes. Eleanor clapped her hands.

'I might not have pigged out on the sandwiches quite so much if I'd seen these in advance. Race you both to the last of the fruit cake. One slice per clue we've each discovered.'

Seldon let out a snort. 'Clifford, does the conversation ever take a logical tack?'

Clifford's face remained impassive. 'I really couldn't say, Chief Inspector. Not having experienced it myself.'

Seldon laughed at Eleanor's look of mock annoyance. Taking a piece of fruit cake after her, he took a bite and closed his eyes as he swallowed.

'Please excuse me if I've seemed a tad... brusque, Eleanor, but my superiors insist this case is cleared up not only quietly but also quickly, as you know.'

'But it was less than twenty-four hours ago that you arrived at St Mary's and confirmed Mrs Wadsworth was murdered. How can they possibly—?'

'True. And I've already started the usual checks for each of the suspects. Criminal record, bank account, any unusual or dubious personal connections followed up and so forth. I've held two extra men back in Oxford to take half the list each.'

'Bet you're not the most popular chap in your office today, then?'

He shrugged. 'I never am. I'm the boss.' He tapped his notebook. 'Miss Lonsdale also gave me access to the suspects' personnel records before I left. Obviously the war's made it decidedly tricky to trace people's movements, or to confirm them anyway, but then again, it never was easy. Actually, most of the staff have been at the school for a long time. The last appointment was the bursar almost a year ago. And before that, Miss Rice, the chaplain and Mrs Jupe, over two years ago, all of them. Miss Munn has been there twelve years, Matron and Miss Small for ten.'

'So, nothing's raised a red flag yet?'

'Its early days but the chaplain's academic background has raised some concerns. He's been through a raft of positions rather quickly for a chap of his age. A brief stint in a Derbyshire parish, a similarly short spell in a Warwickshire prison and then a slightly longer run at a Cumbrian asylum before coming here.'

Eleanor shrugged. 'Perhaps the poor chap's simply been trying to find a position that suits him.'

'Perhaps.' Seldon turned to Clifford. 'How are you getting on?'

'Well enough, Chief Inspector. I've learned quickly that the groundsmen all hold great respect for Mr Hepple.'

Seldon grunted. 'If the staff respect him that much, they may very well cover for him. I think you'll have to take anything you learn from Hepple's grounds team with a pinch of salt.'

'That noted, I did manage to check his alibi with two of his staff separately.'

Seldon leaned forward. 'And?'

'Both confirmed the timings Mr Hepple himself gave for his whereabouts during the set-up, preliminaries and start of the aborted Speech Day ceremony.'

'Mmm. Do you think Hepple's rumbled that he's being watched?'

'Possible, but unlikely. The majority of tasks he has drawn up for me mean that I will regularly be within sight of him. Indeed, my next assignment is to assist the gentleman himself in overhauling the woodworking machines. Despite his rationale that I am sufficiently skilled as I maintain the intricate engine on the Rolls, I was surprised he chose me over one of his more experienced staff.'

'Mightn't it be that he is, in fact, watching *you*, Clifford?' Eleanor said.

'Perceptive suggestion,' Seldon said. 'Or keeping you too busy to snoop around?'

Clifford nodded. 'Again, both are possible.'

Seldon rubbed his chin. 'And have you managed to glean any more about this mysterious intruder his young lad thought he saw and then didn't?'

Eleanor nodded eagerly. 'He has. I got Miss Small to give me a guided tour of the art room, where Hepple says young John saw the figure he thought was an intruder. Meanwhile, Clifford was watching from outside under the pretext of undoing the damage Gladstone had done to the flower beds below the window.'

Seldon snorted a laugh. 'A clever ruse. Digging up buried sausages was he, Clifford?'

'Leather slippers actually, Chief Inspector. Master Gladstone prizes his collection most highly.'

Seldon's brows met. 'And you brought them with you from Henley Hall?'

'Trust me, the path of least resistance with an overindulged bulldog in his advanced years is the only sensible course of action.'

'I can see that. Anyway, back to the case. I hope the artwork was still there?'

Eleanor nodded. 'Absolutely. The girls had made papier-mâché models of people as a mix of biology and art lessons.' She chuckled. 'Which had varying degrees of accuracy, I have to say. It was easy to spot those made by the little ones I'm temporarily in charge of. Big hands, huge noses and simply enormous heads.'

'Little ones?' Seldon muttered, scanning her face.

'What's strange about that?' she queried. 'They're only nine to eleven.'

His Adam's apple bobbed as he swallowed hard.

'Nothing. Nothing at all. So, what was your assessment?'

'Dubious.'

Clifford nodded. 'When her ladyship moved the model back and forth, from outside it simply looked like a stiff, lifeless form, not a burglar. However, it is worth remembering, Chief Inspector, that young John is only sixteen and, as Mr Hepple said, not the sharpest tool in the box. Also the sun was not as strong as on the day of Mrs Wadsworth's death and we were forced to conduct the experiment at a slightly different time, all of which will have affected the length of shadows thrown by the aforementioned model.'

'True. However, the other angle we may not have considered is Miss Small's connection to the models. After all, I assume it was her who had the pupils make them and her who positioned them in the art room?'

Eleanor thought for a moment. 'You know, I couldn't say, but it's most likely as she's head of art. And, of course, she did discover the body.'

Seldon grunted and made a note. 'I'd say Miss Small is rapidly shifting up our suspect list. Can I task you with exploring the whole false burglar alarm angle further?'

'Without question.' Eleanor eyed the remains of the fruit cake. 'And I'll crack on with winkling information out of the chaplain and the bursar. Load up the plates, Clifford.'

In the Rolls, Eleanor waved as Seldon drove away, then leaned back in her seat with a contented sigh. 'Thank you for everything you did today, Clifford.'

'My sincere pleasure, my lady.' He started the engine. 'Nothing hastens an investigation so well as a positive meeting of two perceptive and inquiring minds.'

'Three. You're absolutely as much a part of this as Seldon and myself. But you didn't do all you did this afternoon to further the investigation, I know. Uncle Byron was definitely right when he charged you with looking out for me, noting it would be an uphill endeavour.'

'Only in matters of the heart, my lady.' A mischievous look crossed his face. 'However, sitting cosied up in public, "pigging", I believe your term was, with a gentleman not even appropriately attired in a suit jacket is progress of sorts, I suppose.'

'Just get us back to St Mary's, you terror!'

CHAPTER 19

As they coasted down the high street of a tiny village just half a mile from St Mary's, Eleanor pointed out the window.

'Look, Clifford! That's the sweet shop I used to get all my sweets and cake from. I'd forgotten about that. I used to call it "Tuck Utopia".'

'My memory appears to be failing me, my lady. Sir Thomas More's reference to such a Utopia in his novel of the same name eludes me.'

'Very droll! You've no idea what a treat it was to actually be allowed to trot out to it so we could top up our tuck boxes. As long as we were accompanied, of course.'

'His lordship did endeavour to arrange for a personal delivery for you three times a term from that very shop, my lady, but the then headmistress forbade it.'

'He did?' She felt the beginnings of a lump form in her throat. 'I didn't realise Uncle Byron even knew the shop existed. He rarely made it to school.'

Clifford glanced sideways at her. 'Only because he was unfortunately engaged abroad when parents and guardians were invited to attend an event as I tried to regularly explain. There were very few each year, after all.'

'I know. It's fine, really. I hugely appreciate the wonderful job he made of taking me in, especially for a confirmed bachelor.' She smiled fondly. 'The wonderful job you both did, actually. I'm sure a troublesome nine-year-old was the last thing either of you expected or wanted to have thrust upon you. Better the troublesome thirty-year-old, perhaps?'

'I really couldn't say, my lady.' He winked. 'But neither came without the occasional redeeming merit.'

She laughed. 'But why did Uncle Byron think I would need a regular delivery from the village shop?'

The corners of Clifford's lips quirked. 'He was concerned your tuck box would otherwise never be replenished, given the remarkable consistency with which you acquired "sanctions" prohibiting you from visiting "Tuck Utopia".'

'Ah, very perceptive of him. One term I wasn't allowed to go at all. In fact, I was banned from leaving the grounds.'

He nodded. 'Autumn, 1903. His lordship mostly felt the need to supply you with regular deliveries, however, because you had usually consumed the larger part of your tuck box contents on our drive back to school before term had even started.'

She flapped a dismissive hand. 'You know how much I love a picnic. It was just the same then. But since we are stuck at St Mary's until we help Seldon solve this awful murder, I should like to take a few minutes skipping down memory lane. Especially as I am now too old for sanctions, thank you. So, please turn around so I can visit the shop and purchase an unladylike amount of goodies.'

'In the side compartment of your door, my lady,' Clifford said as he carefully reversed the car in the narrow high street.

She looked down at the stitched leather lining and the deep cylindrical fold in the corner that served as a pocket. She reached inside, her hands closing around a small soft object with a delicate metal clasp. 'Clifford! Oh my goodness, it's the little purse I had all the time I was at St Mary's.' She turned the grey silk pouch over and ran her finger down the few pretty coloured beads still clinging on by their frayed threads. 'Golly. Where on earth did you dig this out from?'

'His lordship was eager to preserve the few "treasured trifles" of your childhood, as he called them, that made it back to Henley Hall after you finished your final year at school.'

This time, the lump threatened to close her throat up completely.

'And you thought to bring this amongst everything else when you dashed home and packed up so hastily last night?' She turned the little silver bar at the top of the purse and opened it, smiling at the noise of coins jingling. 'And you've even filled it with pocket money!'

Clifford eased the car to a stop beside the wooden steps that ran up to the door of a tiny stone building. Hanging on two thin chains from its thatched roof, a fading home-made sign declared it The Village Emporium.

'Happy shopping, my lady.'

The ring of the shop's bell instantly transported Eleanor back to her childhood. Inside, every inch of space was lost to a sea of random foodstuffs and household items, all lined up with the methodicalness of a diligent shopkeeper with more time than customers. But it was the four low wooden shelves filled with glass jars of sweets in front of the counter that held her attention.

She chuckled at the memory of having once had a protracted discussion with the owner over his short-sightedness in wasting so much shelving on anything other than cakes, biscuits and sweets. She sniffed the air. Cough candies! Her eyes came to rest on an elderly man in a cable-knit cardigan leaning on the counter, beaming at her. Time, it seemed, really did stand still in here.

'Gracious! Good afternoon, Mr Brinkley.' Aside from the last strands of his once black hair having now turned white, he had hardly changed at all. Same shining chubby cheeks and jovial grin. Perhaps just a few more smile lines around his eyes, that was all.

'And the same to you, young lady.' He executed a courtly bow, as he had always done.

'You won't remember me, but I used to be at St Mary's, many years ago. And I couldn't pass by without coming in.'

He ambled from behind the counter, revealing that tartan slippers were still his preferred choice of footwear. Pulling four pink-and-white-striped paper bags from a bundle on a string, he tapped the jars.

'Butterscotch but only the big ones, aniseed twists but none of the broken ones, rhubarb and custards, and… pear drops' – his grin broadened – 'but only the red ones.'

Her mouth fell open. 'That's amazing! What an incredible memory you have.'

He began filling a bag with each of the named sweets with a small metal scoop.

'I shouldn't be too impressed, my dear. In my thirty-seven years here I've only met one incensed little girl with fiery-red curls who was determined she could run my business better than me. And only one amusing enough to nickname me Crinkley Brinkley, I believe.'

Eleanor's cheeks coloured. 'Oh gosh, I am so sorry. But, I'm not just here to shop for myself today. I'd love to take a selection of the biscuits and cakes the current girls favour. And a big bag of mint humbugs, please.' She pulled the little silk purse from her jacket pocket with a smile.

They chatted happily over how St Mary's traditions had hardly changed, whereas the village had dared to be so progressive as to install electricity in the big house and a telephone at the vicarage. Eleanor wished she had the time to stand there all day when the ding of the doorbell reminded her with a wince that poor Clifford was still waiting patiently outside. But as she turned and saw who had entered, she realised he would have to wait for a while longer.

CHAPTER 20

'Miss Rice. Good afternoon.'

'Lady Swift?' The school secretary paused in the doorway. 'I thought it was your Rolls that just passed me on its way to St Mary's.'

Eleanor nodded. 'I decided to take some time out since the Holly House girls are all busy with needlework club until five o'clock. I… I really fancied walking back to school.'

Miss Rice fidgeted with one blonde finger-wave that had escaped from its invisible pins and stared at the pile of sweet bags and boxes of cakes on the counter.

'In this heat and with so many packages?'

Mr Brinkley chortled. 'You should have come earlier, Miss Rice. The sweet treats are in short supply now until tomorrow's delivery.'

'Gracious,' Eleanor said, 'these aren't all for me. They're for sharing with my boarders back at school. But you're welcome to—'

Miss Rice held up a polite hand. 'No, thank you. I need to be strong.' She turned to the shopkeeper. 'Mr Brinkley and his wonderful selection here are half the reason I'm forever fighting to get into my dresses. But I'm a reformed character now, don't forget.' They both laughed at this obviously personal joke between them. She smiled at Eleanor and wandered to the back of the tiny shop.

Eleanor took her time packing all of her purchases into the two home-sewn shopping bags Mr Brinkley had insisted she borrow. In fact, she was waiting for Miss Rice to finish choosing which flavour of tinned soup she wanted.

'May I walk back to school with you?' Eleanor said as Miss Rice collected her purchase. 'I'd so enjoy the company.'

The young woman's big blue eyes widened. 'Really? Well, yes, of course, Lady Swift. Thank you. Can I carry your bags?'

'I'm fine, thanks. They're not heavy at all.'

With a cheery goodbye to Mr Brinkley, she steered Miss Rice out of the door and started down the steps, noting that Clifford had indeed driven off. *He must have seen Miss Rice enter the shop, Ellie, and magically read your mind, as ever.*

The short section of stone pavement ran out at the end of the village, leaving them to traipse along the road covered with the dusty grit of rurality. The chalky white soil was blinding in the searing sun and the air super-heated. Either side of them, native hedgerows of hawthorn, whitebeam and wild guelder roses flanked the long curving road. Eleanor wished she'd bought a drink back in the shop.

'Now, Miss Rice, do tell me all the best bits about working at St Mary's. It's such a treat to see it all from the other side after being a pupil.' She pulled a face. 'Albeit, that feels such a long time ago now!'

'Time passes and doesn't return,' Miss Rice said in an absent-minded way. At Eleanor's querying look, she gave a nervous giggle. 'Oh, silly me. Isn't that the right expression? I thought it meant we should use our time wisely. Which' – her flawless cheeks turned pinker – 'you have done so admirably, Lady Swift. I hope you don't mind my saying how in awe of you I am.' She started off at an energetic rate along the lane.

'Thank you, but I didn't realise you knew anything about me.' Despite the burden of her shopping, Eleanor easily kept pace because of her longer legs. 'Especially since you were spared sitting through my speech.'

'That was such a shame. I was so excited to hear what you were going to say.' Miss Rice demurely swished the many pleats of her sapphire-blue dress skirt with her free hand, clearly already feeling the stickiness of the outside afternoon air.

Something clicked in Eleanor's memory. *She was on stage, Ellie. That would never have happened in your day.* The secretary had been an elusive creature around school, seen only when one was summoned to the headmistress' study. She chose her next words carefully.

'It's clear Miss Lonsdale recognises how much your dedicated efforts help her keep the school running smoothly.'

'Oh, she is very kind. Not all headmistresses will take the time to say thank you or offer a compliment. She's quite the exception. I mean, I imagine that's so. I haven't worked in any other schools.'

'Well, what better sign of appreciation than to have included you in the staff line up on stage.'

Miss Rice's lively pace faltered as she stared down at her tin of soup. 'Actually, I wasn't there at Miss Lonsdale's invitation. It was just a rather unforeseen last-minute thing.'

'Oh dear, not a problem of yours, I hope?'

'Not me. The bursar. He, well, oh, Lady Swift, please don't think I'm being disrespectful but he is very concerned about his image you see.'

'Aren't most men? However discreetly they try to cover it up.' Eleanor gave her companion a conspiratorial nudge, prompting a quiet smile in return.

'Yes, I suppose so. But I'm not sure how many would have refused to be seen by a hall of spectators on account of temporarily needing a walking stick. It's only a twisted ankle.'

Hang on, Ellie!

'Do you mean the bursar insisted you took his place? And used the excuse that he wouldn't have to hobble on stage in front of everyone?'

'Of course he didn't say it quite like that.' Miss Rice frowned. 'Not like that at all, actually. But I've worked with him long enough'

– she gave a small shudder – 'and closely enough, to know his excuse of not wanting to inflame the swelling by walking any further than absolutely necessary was just a way to save embarrassment.'

'So was it a fair swap then?'

'I'm sorry? I don't follow you.'

'As you kindly took his place on stage, I hope he was a gentleman and reciprocated by covering whatever duty you normally perform in the event of a burglar alarm?'

'Oh, but none of us knew that it would ring, Lady Swift.'

'But still it did. And I've just remembered seeing you sprint off with several of the other staff. I can only guess you went because of the bursar being incapacitated. And, maybe, because he is not the kind of colleague to help out a less senior member of staff?'

'No, he certainly isn't. Which is why I skittered off to check the offices with everyone else when the alarm rang.' An angry look marred her pretty features. 'He's certainly better at taking than giving.'

Eleanor hesitated. 'Miss Rice, you can tell me in confidence. Does the bursar bother you… improperly, at all?'

'Oh goodness, no, Lady Swift.' She shook her head. 'It's quite sad, really. He just wants women to notice him, I think. In fact, he wants everyone to take an interest in him.' She shrugged. 'Just a fragile ego, I guess.' The secretary's face flushed a deep puce. 'Oh, I really shouldn't be talking about another member of staff like this. I think it's this heat. He works very hard, you know. I've seen him in his office ever so late, long after everyone has retired to their quarters.'

Has she indeed, Ellie!

'Am I right in thinking you live on site at school? And therefore you have some sort of boarding-house duty?'

'Halfway right. Shortly after Miss Lonsdale joined, my rooms in the village came to an unexpected end. She kindly offered me accommodation while I sorted out some other lodgings but, lucky for me, she quickly realised how useful it was if I was on hand. Not that she ever takes advantage, of course. So I have no evening duties, but if she needs something urgently, well, I'm just there, you see.'

'And that suits you?'

'Perfectly.'

Eleanor glanced at the woman's shapely curves. 'Isn't St Mary's a little… claustrophobic for an attractive young woman like yourself. No male visitors allowed after ten?'

Miss Rice dropped her soup with a gasp. 'Lady Swift! Whatever are you suggesting? I would never. It's… it's a sin.'

Eleanor retrieved the tin and held out what she realised was probably the woman's entire supper. Miss Rice grabbed it back.

'No, I mean a proper sin. I'm not married. But perhaps we should hurry along and get out of this heat. It appears we've both forgotten our hats, after all.'

Oops, Ellie! Somehow we didn't expect such a pretty young thing to be so traditional in her morals.

'Good suggestion.'

As they entered the welcome shade of the thick beech woods on either side of the road, Eleanor tried again.

'Did you know Mrs Wadsworth well?'

'She… she was very nice to me.' Miss Rice dabbed a finger under each eye. 'Sort of like an elderly aunt. She never passed the office without popping her head round to say hello. And she was always suggesting a book she thought I'd love. In fact, several times I found a new one on my desk just as I was nearing the end of the last one I'd borrowed from the library. Very thoughtful.'

'My condolences. She was popular with everyone I imagine.'

'Not… quite everyone. But I don't want to be the one to gossip any more than I already have, Lady Swift.'

'Goodness no. It's just that' – Eleanor leaned towards the young woman, bumping her with the bag over her shoulder – 'I confess I'm terrible at making the most awful faux pas in conversation. Too much time alone on my bicycle, probably.'

'You were so brave. I could never imagine doing anything like that.'

'Perhaps. Foolish, some say. Mostly men. But what I mean is, I'm rather socially challenged sometimes. And as I'm going to be at St Mary's until a replacement is found, I'm concerned I'll unwittingly go about stomping on all kinds of people's grief. It would be such a help to know who I can be less careful around. Just to save my blushes, you understand.'

'Oh, I see. Well, Miss Small for one. She repeatedly complained about Mrs Wadsworth letting the girls out of class late because it ate into their art time.'

The teacher who is the worst at timekeeping whining about another who was meticulous about it. Unlikely, Ellie? Although Mrs Coulson said Miss Munn had had the same complaint about Mrs Wadsworth.

Miss Rice stared straight ahead. 'But one person you really don't have to worry about is the deputy headmistress.'

Old news, Ellie. We know Mrs Coulson wasn't a fan.

'Really? Probably just the usual stresses and strains of professional relationships.'

Miss Rice shook her head. 'On, no. It went much further than that. The deputy headmistress insisted Mrs Wadsworth be sacked, but the headmistress refused. I was in the study at the time. Can you imagine?'

Now that is new news, Ellie!

CHAPTER 21

Eleanor left Miss Rice at the school gates and headed towards her room in Holly House. The boarders were all out on the hockey field, which was a shame because she fancied a diversion. A crowd of energetic young girls with a bent for mischief was exactly the tonic she sought as a break from the investigation.

In truth, she was too honest with herself not to admit there was more than just the case dominating her thoughts. The time with Seldon that afternoon had been so different from most occasions they'd met to discuss a murder investigation. For a start, they were now on the same side. Not that she had ever been on the murdering side, but it had proven a rare thing for her to be even on the same page as the police. Her parents' disappearance had been enough to instil a life-long distrust in her of all things to do with authority. She was sure that government powers, including the local Peruvian police, had somehow been involved in her loss.

Nevertheless, here she was now, working with Seldon. *No, Ellie, not with. Under. You're under Seldon's command, remember. That was the agreement.* Surprisingly, she wasn't finding that a problem. What was, was that he had seemed entirely focused on the case when they'd met, whereas no matter how much she tried…

A wave of guilt washed over her as she realised she was getting diverted from her desire to find justice for Mrs Wadsworth's murder. *This isn't the time, or place, Ellie to sort out your disastrous love life.*

'Botheration!'

'Problem, dear lady?' a male voice said from behind.

Too close behind, she found on spinning around and almost brushing her nose against a russet-and-mustard checked suit jacket. The man looked mid forties, and had pomaded brown hair and gleaming hazel eyes.

'Good afternoon. You must be the bursar.'

'Indeed, I am.' He wiggled his tweezered eyebrows as he hung the walking stick over his opposite wrist and held out his hand. 'And you are Lady Swift, of course.'

Eleanor groaned silently. She had promised herself she would keep an open mind on meeting him. But after only a moment in his company, she had to admit that the rather over-scented ointment in his hair was not the only oily thing about him.

She shook his hand firmly.

'Charmed.'

'As am I.' He gave another eyebrow wiggle. 'I came to sort out a minor paperwork matter with you. But perhaps there is something I can help you with first? Always happy to be the shining knight to a stricken damsel.'

She shook her head. 'St Mary's hasn't changed much since I was here. And I have an excellent memory and am horribly independent, so I shall be more than fine without any assistance. But thank you for your offer.'

He waggled a finger. 'No such thing as independent here, my dear. Not at St Mary's. We are all one happy family.'

Maybe. Maybe not, Ellie.

'So what's this paperwork you mentioned, Bursar?'

He tapped his nose with his left hand, displaying a gold signature ring on his little finger. 'I just need a few… private details of yours. For the records only, of course. Since you are technically a temporary member of staff. It's a necessary tedium, I'm afraid. The board of governors has insisted upon it.'

'Of course.' She gestured towards the gate and stepped back off the path. 'After you, Bursar.'

In the bursar's office, six oak roll-fronted filing cabinets filled one of the pale-blue walls, their tops home to a row of thick, red- and black-spined ledgers. A plain pine table with a hard wooden chair sat in the centre, like a lost island in an expanse of navy carpet. A mahogany desk with a green leather-tooled top and a heavily buttoned matching swivel chair occupied the far end, while a formidably solid waist-high metal safe dominated the furthest corner.

As she sat down, Eleanor mentally kicked herself for forgetting Miss Rice had said she would not be working, as she had Saturday afternoons off. That meant she was alone with this suited leech who was fooling himself her pointed rebuffs were merely her playing coy mouse to his cocksure cat.

'Such an enchanting address, Henley Hall,' he purred, before looking back down at the sheet of paper in front of him. 'Now date of birth, but only if the lady will forgive my asking?'

She frowned. 'What has that to do with me staying on to help at St Mary's?'

He held his hands up. 'Don't shoot the messenger. You are, of course, at liberty to take it up with the board of governors.'

Keen to move on the conversation, she decided not to argue. 'Twelfth of March, eighteen ninety-one.'

He rose and perched on the edge of the desk, leaning over to scoop up a sheaf of papers from the stitched leather tray to his left. 'Now, if you incur expenses while you are here, you will need to complete this set of forms to arrange reimbursement.'

'I shan't require reimbursement, whatever minor costs I might incur, thank you.'

'Generous to a fault, aren't you, dear lady? That will save me some more workload.'

'Don't you have an assistant for that? Apart from Miss Rice, I mean?'

That seemed to hit a sore spot. His brows knitted.

'Not as such. I did have an adjunct until a while ago. But she, well, between you and me, she really wasn't cut out for the role. Such a waste of time training and mentoring only to find the willingness not there, if you know what I mean.'

'I think I do.' She was careful to include no suggestion to her tone. In truth, she couldn't help wondering if the lack of 'willingness' to perform was more about 'duties' outside of the job's role. *But Miss Rice told you the bursar never tried anything improper with her, Ellie. She said he was all talk, and no trousers, or something like that.* She'd heard Mrs Trotman, her cook, use the expression, but she wasn't quite sure what it meant. Still, it seemed to fit.

'Gracious then, Bursar, you've been left to shoulder the whole burden alone.'

'Aside from Miss Rice sorting out my vast weekly influx of post and papers. And occasionally entering the figures for the very minor incidental accounts at the desk there. Oh, and acting as my secretary in making appointments, it all falls onto my shoulders.'

'No wonder then that I didn't notice you on stage at the Speech Day ceremony.'

'For the chance to hear you speak, I would most certainly have hung up my abacus for the duration.' He chortled and tapped his forehead. 'Just a little joke, no need for a calculation aid, of course. No, unfortunately I've had a spot of bother with the old pin here.' He indicated his right leg with the walking stick. 'An old war injury I foolishly angered sprinting up the stairs to my office yesterday morning.'

'I did wonder, but didn't like to ask.'

'It's nothing really, but Miss Rice made a great fuss about my needing to rest it.'

'So you took Miss Rice's advice? You let her go on stage and you stayed in your office, I mean?' *That's certainly not how she told it, Ellie!*

'What?' He shuffled some papers in his tray, not meeting her eye. 'Well, naturally, but only because it was an excellent opportunity to crack on with taming my burgeoning workload. I sat here with my head down until Mr Hepple's assistant phoned me with tales of a non-existent intruder.'

'But you managed to get some work done before you were interrupted?'

'Oh, yes.'

Out in the corridor, the school bell rang. The bursar checked his watch.

'Now, dear lady, it's teatime. And I have the sneaking suspicion that you might care to join me for a slice or two of well-deserved afternoon cake in the staffroom.' He slid off the desk and came round, offering her his elbow. 'Am I right?'

Dash it, Ellie! You haven't found anything useful out and you're not going to with other staff around.

'Actually,' she said as she skipped out of her chair, 'I have some business to attend to.'

He rolled his eyes. 'Not another female shrinking from the very idea of food to preserve her figure. How disappointing.'

'Mrs Wadsworth often remarked on my hearty appetite, actually. She was a wonderful housemistress. It's such a terrible business, wouldn't you say?'

His manicured brows shot up. 'Well, of course, I would. That dear woman. Such an unfortunate loss.'

'I imagine she made your life easier than some other staff?'

His left eye twitched. 'Not that I disagree, but in which regard do you mean?'

'In regard of her fastidiousness with things like lists and records. She must have kept beautifully ordered notes on how she spent her library and boarding house budgets?'

'Oh, I see. Yes, yes, she did. But then that is only the very basic beginning of the accounting process. It's really something of a science. Frightfully complicated.'

And frightfully dull, Ellie! Thank goodness Clifford is such an eager wizard with all that for Henley Hall. You'd be hopeless at it.

'Odd.'

He blinked. 'What exactly is odd, my dear?'

'It's probably just me, but someone mentioned that, in fact, Mrs Wadsworth often disagreed with you about how much of her budget she'd spent. Strange if she was so meticulous in her record keeping.'

He swallowed hard. 'Honestly, the truth is I... I did have the occasional disagreement with the lady about her budget. She did indeed keep meticulous records, as you say, but unfortunately, her... faculties had recently deteriorated.' He regarded her out of the corner of his eye. 'Perhaps you should consider a career in accountancy, my dear. Such a precise and enquiring mind.'

'Thank you.'

He coughed. 'Now, that's enough of that subject. If we don't hurry, there won't be any cake left.'

She smiled and headed for the door before he could reach it.

'Thank you, Bursar, but I'd hate to deprive you of the last of the cake. Enjoy.'

She made her escape, heading back to Holly House where she needed to finish setting up a surprise for her young charges.

CHAPTER 22

'It's hours 'til supper.'

'Who cares, it's Saturday!'

'That means the worst meal of the week!'

'On, no! You mean it's—'

'Shiver and run-run again!'

Eleanor smiled as she stepped out into the hallway. The gaggle of untidy-haired girls yanking off their brown outdoor shoes and ripping off their blazers stopped chattering and straggled into their customary three lines.

'Welcome home, girls, but, oh dear.' She pulled a face. 'Shiver and run-run tonight, is it? I always hated liver and onions when I was here too.'

This drew a collective gasp.

'You mean, miss,' Morton said, 'old girls called it that, all those years ago.' She yelped as Duffy dug her in the ribs.

Eleanor laughed. 'Yes, Morton, all those hundreds of years ago, we called it that too. And Woodster lived here back then as well, on the front door. And Oliver Windy McSpindy presided over the quadrangle on his weathervane roost. I always liked it when he faced west because it meant it would probably rain all afternoon and we'd escape having double hockey.'

The girls grinned at each other. Duffy stepped forward.

'Do you think, miss, while you are staying at Holly House you might be allowed to tell us a few stories about what St Mary's was like when you were here?'

'What back in the dark ages?' Eleanor held up a hand. 'It's alright, I'm not offended. And yes, I'd love to.'

The girls all jiggled excitedly and slapped each other's arms.

'Ah, but there is one major problem. I think we've all overlooked something, haven't we?'

'Pleeeease, miss,' half the voices called out.

She shook her head. 'That's not it.'

Duffy spun round and whispered to the others. They all put their hands together demurely and chorused, 'Good evening, miss.'

'Well done, but that's not it either.' She beckoned them under the arch and through the sitting room, then blocked their view of the long oval homework table. 'How can I tell you stories with my mouth full of...' – she stepped aside – 'CAKE!'

The screeches of delight made her clap her hands over her ears.

'Three cheers for Lady Swift!' Duffy shouted. 'Woohoo!'

'So, it doesn't seem very different now at all then, miss?' One of the three girls Eleanor struggled to tell apart said half an hour later as she reached for another Eccles cake, picking the escaping currants from the hole in the top of the crisp pastry. As if reading Eleanor's mind, she grinned. 'I'm Weston.' She wiggled her long blonde plaits.

'Thank you, Weston. And well, from what I've seen so far, St Mary's is still pretty much the same as when I was here.'

'See.' Morton slapped Duffy's hand as she went to bite into her chocolate slice. 'I told you this place is as dead as the hideous Latin we have to learn.' She gave an exaggerated yawn.

Eleanor laughed. 'We used to say that too.' She held her hands up as if directing an orchestra. 'Come on, girls. Latin is a language, as dead as dead can be—'

'First it killed the Romans, and now it's killing me!' the girls chanted before dissolving into fits of giggles.

Eleanor offered one of the plates to Elsbury, who she noted had eaten little despite Duffy's previous insistence she was their resident cake monster.

'Which would you rate the yummiest, Elsbury? Iced or Chelsea buns?' She turned the plate back and forth, making the others giggle again. A small smile brightened the quiet girl's face.

'Iced, miss.'

'Me too. But, then there's the larger dilemma, isn't there? Round or finger? Which is it?'

Elsbury shook her head. 'No, that's easy, miss. Always the round ones, because they're so much bigger.'

'Excellent choice. So good actually, I shall join you. There's one each.' She turned the plate again, smiling as the girl took one eagerly.

'Thank you, miss.'

'You are very welcome. Mr Brinkley helped me choose all the goodies.'

Harrison choked on her cake. 'You know Mr Slippers, miss? He was in the shop all that time ago… I mean when you were here too?'

She nodded, thinking the owner of the sweet shop was right. She had been more creative with the nickname she'd given him.

Morton let out a long whistle. 'He must be like a hundred and fifty!'

'Girls, how old exactly do you think I am?' She shook her head. 'You know what, please don't answer that.'

Elsbury put up her hand.

Eleanor smiled at her. 'You're at home when you're here, Elsbury, not in class. You can speak up without waiting for permission.'

'I was just wondering if you used to have the boarding house competition every year when you were here, miss?'

This received a resounding groan. Eleanor looked around at the glum faces.

'Yes, we did. But why are you all so gloomy about it?'

Morton pulled a face. 'Because it's a complete waste of time. Holly House never wins.'

Eleanor sat back and folded her arms. 'Hmm, now that's confusing, because I didn't see you girls as being so easily defeated. I had you down as being a plucky bunch.'

Duffy looked puzzled. 'What does that mean, miss?'

'Plucky? It means you're daring and up for an adventure.' She raised an eyebrow. 'And a lark and high jinks.'

'But we are!' Morton put down her iced ring and cringed as Duffy quickly shushed her. 'Although I probably shouldn't have said that, miss.'

This time, Eleanor led the round of giggles. 'Too late now, Morton, the cat's out of the bag! But come on, girls, tell me what is the problem about the competition? Why are you all so convinced you won't win?'

Duffy swallowed her mouthful. 'Because, miss, everyone thinks we're just babies. So whatever we do will just be thought of as a joke. It always has, every year, since forever.'

'It can't always have been.' Eleanor tried to think of something more encouraging to say. 'Holly House must have won once recently, surely?'

Elsbury shook her head. 'Holly House didn't win when you were here, did it, miss?'

'Not that I remember, but how could you possibly know that?'

'Because it's written in the b—'

'What Elsbury means, miss,' Duffy said, quickly interrupting and glowering at the other girl, 'is that we've found out that the last time Holly House won was 1871.'

'Hmm, so, is it still the girls who vote for the winning house?'

Morton nodded. 'Totally, miss. The teachers and parents watch, but they don't get involved at all. The head girl, Lydia Goldsworthy, runs the whole thing.'

Harrison groaned. 'And at the end, she'll march up on stage and delight in announcing that one of the other boarding houses has won. Again. What's the point of us wasting all our evenings working out an act and rehearsing it over and over just to lose?'

Morton leaped up, brandishing an iced finger. 'I say we mutiny. Like we learned Captain Bligh's crew did.'

Duffy looked doubtful. 'What, you mean storm the stage and steal the cup? Goldsworthy would likely whack you round the head with it before you could wrestle it off her. She's fearfully strong. You know she's been hockey captain three years in a row.'

Morton shook her head. 'No, silly! I mean, we refuse to take part. We can't lose if we aren't in the competition, can we?'

Weston, Harrison and Finsmore stared at each other. 'Are we allowed to refuse?' they chorused.

A clamour of insistent voices filled the room.

'We would be making history,' Duffy said loudly enough to silence the others. 'No boarding house has ever refused to take part. Well, not that's included in the you-know- what,' she ended in a loud whisper.

All eyes slid towards Eleanor. She put her fingers in her ears.

'La-la-la-la-la. Didn't hear a thing.'

Duffy grinned at her.

Elsbury half raised her hand and then snatched it back down at Eleanor's look.

'Two things, Duffy. First of all, as Holly House leader, you're actually going to lead us all into enormous trouble,' said the girl.

This brought a collective groan and shoves from the girls on either side of her.

Morton tutted. 'Don't be so wet, Elsbury. It'll be fine. Goldsworthy can't do anything to us… much.'

'What's your second grumble then?' Duffy said.

Elsbury swallowed hard. 'You'll be breaking your promise to us all.'

The room fell silent. Duffy flopped back down into her seat.
'I know.'

Eleanor glanced at Elsbury with a questioning look.

'On our first night here, miss, we all took a vote and voted Duffy to be leader. She said she would do everything to get us to win the competition. But we can't win if we don't take part.' She went round to stand next to Duffy. 'Can we?'

'I know,' Duffy repeated, leaning her head against Elsbury's arm. 'But when I promised I didn't realise it was impossible.'

Eleanor bit her lip, unsure if she should interfere. The girls stared gloomily at each other. Elsbury looked over at Eleanor.

'Are you allowed to help us, miss? The only rule is the girls are supposed to do it without their boarding mistresses' help, but you're not really our boarding mistress, are you? No offence, miss,' she added hurriedly.

'None taken, Elsbury. And if the Holly House council votes that I can help, then why not? I am, as you rightly say, not really your boarding mistress.'

Duffy squeezed Elsbury's arm.

'Council meeting!'

Eleanor busied herself tidying the plates while the girls dragged the chapel stools into a circle, whispering heatedly. She then wandered through to the small kitchen and set to washing up. As she finished, Duffy appeared in the doorway.

'Please may we ask you to come before the council, miss?'

'Of course, Duffy.'

In the sitting room, they were all standing respectfully in front of their stools, looking apprehensive. Eleanor perched on the spare one Duffy indicated, feeling like a giant as the girls each plopped down onto theirs. Something in the atmosphere transported her back to her school days. She felt that long-ago familiar air, the one charged with a mix of excitement and anxiety, and it made her heart skip. The stakes mattered to these girls. They mattered a lot. And, she realised with a jolt, that meant they mattered to her too. She mentally crossed her fingers, hoping she could think of something to help them.

Duffy stood up with her notebook. 'Lady Swift, as we have established you are not really our boarding mistress, would it be cheating if we asked you to be our secret weapon for the competition?'

Aware that all eyes were on her, Eleanor hesitated before answering. 'I don't think so.'

Duffy cleared her throat. 'Then, as the leader of Holly House, it is my duty and my honour' – she frowned as Morton giggled at this – 'to ask: will you be our secret weapon?'

'Pleeeeeeeeease,' the room chorused.

Duffy shuffled across the floor on her knees, stopping in front of Eleanor with her notebook held open.

'We took a vote and look.' She slapped the page. 'We all voted for you.'

Eleanor failed to stop her eyes from sliding over to Elsbury, who gave her a quiet smile and then stared at her hands.

'First of all then, thank you. I'm the one who is honoured to have been asked, but' – she held up a finger at the excited chatter that started – 'what is it that you think I can offer as your secret weapon?'

'Simple, miss,' Duffy said. 'You'll make sure we're pluckier than any Holly House girls have ever been.'

'Definitely,' Weston, Harrison and Finsmore cheered in unison.

Eleanor tilted her head and looked at Duffy.

'We heard you cycled across the world,' the girl said imploringly. 'There is nothing you couldn't do after that.'

Morton looked sideways at Eleanor. 'But more importantly, you let slip that you were naughty when you were here.'

'I'm sure I didn't,' Eleanor said with a smile.

'Oh yes you did, miss!' the girls chorused.

'Well, I can see I've been rumbled,' Eleanor said. 'Consider me your official secret weapon.'

At the cheer that erupted, she placed her hands over her ears again.

Still on her knees, Duffy shuffled over to Elsbury.

'Thanks, Piggy Piggerton. Maybe now I might get my name recorded as the leader who finally won the trophy after all those years!'

'I bet if she was still here, she'd jump up and down with excitement if... no *when* you do,' Elsbury said.

'Who's she?' Eleanor couldn't stop herself asking.

'The Holly House leader back in 1871 when our house last won the competition, miss.'

Duffy nodded. 'Until you arrived, Lady Swift, she was our heroine. Phylida Henley!'

Eleanor's throat closed up. *It couldn't be, Ellie? Why would no one have said before?* She stared at Morton.

'Are you sure that was her name?'

The girl nodded. 'Absolutely, miss. She led Holly House to victory in the competition and started some other, er, Holly House traditions too.'

'Are you alright, miss?' Duffy said.

'Fine, thank you. Duffy, please could you run and request Matron come and sit with you all for a short while? I need to go and ask someone a very important question.'

CHAPTER 23

'Why didn't you tell me?' Eleanor said before Clifford had even finished opening the door to his cottage.

'My lady?' He scanned her face, then took a deep breath. 'Ah. I see. I believe we need to walk and talk.'

'My mother was at school here, at St Mary's. And you never told me! I'm not the one who needs to talk!'

'I concur entirely. And I am deeply sorry, my lady. But please.' He gestured outside, whistling round the door for Gladstone to join them.

With the bulldog's lead looped around his neck, Clifford closed the garden gate. Eleanor set off at an exasperated pace, her hands shoved into her jacket pockets with Clifford a few steps behind and Gladstone bringing up the rear. The light was fading fast as they walked on in silence.

After taking a few moments to calm down, she shook her head.

'Clifford, I rarely question your reasons for anything, but why keep this a secret? And especially why not say when you knew I was coming back for Speech Day?'

He cleared his throat gently. 'My lady, there were a great many reasons not to tell you that your mother attended St Mary's.'

'When I was nine, maybe!' At the awkward silence beside her, she turned and stopped. 'Oh gracious, Clifford, I'm so sorry. I didn't mean to sound harsh. I know you only ever act with my best interests at heart. It's just that... well, I know it's irrational, but

I cherish any connection to her I can uncover. And not to know this!' She threw up her hands.

He shook his head. 'No, my lady, apologies need be reserved entirely for my side. Having wrestled with the conundrum for weeks before Speech Day arrived, I realise now that my prudent approach let me down. I thought if you knew before giving your speech, you would struggle all the more with your nerves and… your emotions.' He sighed. 'It is too late to undo the error, but there is a decanter of particularly fine brandy in the Rolls. Packed ready for the journey home when I had fully intended to tell you the whole story.'

She cocked her head. 'With a basket of walnuts and a generous wedge of especially mature Stilton?'

He gave her a relieved smile. 'Naturally. We aren't savages.'

Wishing it was acceptable to give him a hug, she settled instead for nudging his elbow with hers. 'Then you are entirely and irrevocably forgiven. As I sincerely hope I am too. Despite your protestations, I behaved badly just now.' She winced. 'Maybe it's the influence of being back at school. I was rather too much like the obnoxious child who joined St Mary's.'

His eyes twinkled. 'Perhaps "obstreperous" would be a more flattering description, my lady.'

They walked on in silence, with Gladstone lolloping in uneven zigzags across the lawn. Eleanor spoke first.

'I can see why you thought there was no chance I'd find out, Clifford. After all, I was only supposed to be here for an afternoon. I hope it hasn't been worrying you since we've stayed on?'

'It has occupied a great deal of my thoughts, my lady, if I am honest. Your unexpectedly staying on at St Mary's had already thrust you back to a period in your young life that must have seemed distressingly uncertain at the time. Regrettably, on top of that, there is the painful matter of you investigating Mrs Wadsworth's death…'

She smiled fondly at him. 'Thank you. You're always so thoughtful and protective. Neither of us ever imagined we would be looking for a murderer again, and certainly not here. But we are. And now I know my mother came here, please just tell me everything so I can settle in my thoughts.'

'With pleasure, my lady. But first, might I ask how the girls of Holly House learned of her having attended St Mary's? Assuming that is how you found out?'

'It is. But, hmm, that is a good question. Given that it was over forty years ago, I can't work out how they know. And certainly not how they discovered she was Holly House leader, among other things they hinted at.' She tapped her forehead. 'I'll definitely dig deeper into that later. They did say she had been their heroine until… until recently.'

'Until her daughter arrived,' he said softly. 'Even though I suspect they have no idea that is who you are.'

She shook her head. 'No, and neither shall they. Trust me, I'm not ready to face the onslaught of questions from a houseful of relentlessly enquiring nine- to eleven-year-olds.'

'Eminently wise, my lady.'

'Look, I know I shouldn't feel emotional about my mother after all these years, but sometimes it still catches me by surprise. And I'm not going to cut much of a figure as a strong, but caring boarding housemistress if I burst into tears every time they ask me something! And anyway, there's no reason for them to make the connection. Swift was my father's name, which mother took on marrying him, of course. When she was here, she was Henley, like Uncle Byron would have been at…?'

'Eton, my lady. His lordship was a proud Old Etonian to the very end.'

'Well, perhaps I may one day quietly champion St Mary's after coming round to the notion that it might not be quite the awful prison I always thought it was.' She held up a finger. 'But, don't you dare comment.'

He mimed buttoning his lip, which failed to hide the evident amusement her words had brought on.

'Oh, go on, Clifford. Whatever it is, let it out. You're itching to.'

She laughed as he pretended to unbutton his lip again.

'The question merely sprang to mind as to how you intend to champion St Mary's anonymously, my lady, since the establishment might not best benefit, or indeed ever recover, from being publicly championed by her most reprehensible pupil?'

He waited until she had settled sideways, leaning back against the bench's arm, sitting cross-legged, hands on her knees, and then cleared his throat.

'Where would you like me to start, my lady?'

'By joining me, please. Just for once.'

'As you wish.' From his trouser pocket, he produced a tennis ball and waved it at Gladstone before throwing it. From the other, he pulled out a bag of mint humbugs. 'These mysteriously appeared in the pocket of the coat I have been walking Master Gladstone in, my lady.' He sat at the furthest part of the bench. 'Most thoughtful. Thank you.'

She helped herself to a sweet. 'Well, I wish I had your talented, if rather questionable, sleight of hand. It took me ages to distract you sufficiently so I could slide them in without you noticing. Now, tell me everything, please.'

'Perhaps the logical start point is with your grandfather, Lord Grenville Henley, whom you sadly never met. He had two children, your mother, Lady Phylida Henley and your uncle, Lord Byron Henley. Lord Grenville Henley was quite the brilliant surgeon and physician, a highly respected and senior fellow of, what we now know as, the Royal College of Surgeons. He pioneered several new surgical procedures in his time. Tragically his wife, your grandmother, passed when your own mother was only six.'

Eleanor's hand flew to her mouth. 'She never told me that. Oh, Clifford, she grew up without a mother for most of her childhood, just as I did.'

'Most regrettably in both instances, yes, my lady.'

She shuddered. 'That reminds me of something Miss Small said about death.'

'My lady?'

She shook her head. 'It doesn't matter now.' She frowned. 'We really must talk to her again. Miss Small, that is. Miss Rice mentioned her in connection with Mrs Wadsworth and I'm in agreement with Seldon. She's definitely prime suspect material.'

Gladstone huffed up with the tennis ball and dropped it at Clifford's feet. They both jumped as he spun around and gave a deep woof that lifted his front legs off the ground.

A form appeared out of the evening gloom.

'Lady Swift, Mr Clifford! Thank heavens I've found you.'

'Miss Lonsdale.' Eleanor leaped up. One look at the headmistress' pale, drawn face told her all was not well. 'Goodness, are the Holly House girls alright? I was just on my way back to relieve Matron.'

'It's not the girls, but I have asked Matron to remain with them for now. I... I need your help. Your joint help.'

'Of course.' She glanced at Clifford, who nodded. 'Whatever has gone wrong, we can fix it, I'm sure.'

Miss Lonsdale shook her head. 'There is no fix for this, Lady Swift. It's Miss Small. She's... dead.'

CHAPTER 24

It was over three frustrating hours later that Eleanor heaved a sigh of relief at the sound of the familiar voice outside the headmistress' private sitting room. Clifford looked up from watching the model of the double-helix staircase as it slowly turned on what she assumed must be some sort of hidden mechanical turntable. The first time they'd been in the study it had obviously been switched off or broken. After a hesitant knock, Miss Rice's blonde waves bobbed around the door.

'Chief Inspector Seldon is here, Headmistress.'

Miss Lonsdale spun round, the relief evident in her careworn face.

Eleanor couldn't help noticing the tails of Seldon's long blue woollen overcoat swished out behind him, which added a certain grandeur to his tall presence. He waited until the secretary had left before addressing the headmistress.

'Miss Lonsdale. I apologise, but I need to get straight down to business.'

She eyed him coolly. 'Chief Inspector, good evening. Of course. After all, you are very busy and important.'

His fingers gripping his bowler hat tightened. He took a deep breath and looked across to Eleanor's side of the room. 'Lady Swift. Clifford. Thank you all for your patience. I apologise that it has taken me a considerable time to arrive here. Hence' – he held the headmistress' gaze – 'I need to get down to business because a single hour can make a difference in the appearance of a body.'

'Of course,' Miss Lonsdale muttered. 'My apologies. It has been a difficult few days. I am grateful that you have come out of hours. If you would all follow me.'

Eleanor threw him a sympathetic smile as she rose. The dark moons under his eyes and the shadow along his lean jawline, suggested it had been a long time since he'd seen his bed.

'Hello, Hugh,' she whispered as she passed him. 'Are you alright?'

'Strangely better now,' he muttered back. The hint of a smile threatened but dissipated as Miss Lonsdale turned to check he was following. 'Blast it. To business.'

The art room felt sombre and cold as Eleanor followed the headmistress and Seldon across the threshold. The long bank of windows gave onto an ocean of inky blackness. The pale-grey walls she'd noted reflecting the sun on her previous visit now seemed sterile, more the walls of a morgue than a classroom.

Seldon stopped, grunting as Eleanor bumped into him. Her breath caught as she looked down and saw Miss Small's body lying on the floor, half curled up on her side, her features twisted, her eyes wide and staring. Eleanor swallowed hard.

Seldon waved an arm toward three kneeling men in innocuous grey suits packing up a selection of items into leather bags and briefcases.

'They are with me. They also attended Mrs Wadsworth's death, but I don't think you met them.'

The shortest of them looked up, running his hand over his forehead.

'We're just about finished, sir. Got the few fingerprints there are, like you said. Just awaiting your say-so to move the deceased.'

Seldon nodded. 'Well done, all of you. You're sure you've covered everything, Morrison?'

An older, more world-weary version of the first policeman stood up stiffly, his knees cracking loud enough to reverberate around the room. Everyone winced.

''Fraid there's not much to get, sir.' He glanced at the two women.

Seldon motioned it was okay for him to elaborate.

'I mean, there's no sign of any struggle. No marks about the lady's person, aside from a few innocent-looking bruises, often more evident on fairer-skinned types. Pupils dilated and eye colour noticeably pale, veins prominent and dark. But again, in a lady of… minimal weight, and delicate constitution, not unusual at all. She has all the hallmarks of being no more a victim of anything than her heart having given up.'

Seldon nodded appreciatively. 'Miss Lonsdale, who found Miss Small?'

The headmistress tore her eyes away from the body. 'One of the cleaners.'

'At what time?'

'About eight forty-five.'

He turned back to Morrison. 'Time of death?'

The man thought for a moment. 'Let's see. It took us three hours to get here, so I'd say no more than an hour before she was found, given the state of the body when we examined it.'

Seldon jotted something in his notebook.

'Miss Lonsdale, does anything about the room or Miss Small's appearance strike you as unusual or out of place? Please look carefully.'

Miss Lonsdale stared around, taking her time to assess each of the long wooden benches with their untidy trays of paints and pots of brushes. Then she scrutinised the drying racks, the lines of tables and their adjustable-height stools, and finally the papier-mâché models against the far wall. With a quiet groan, she forced herself to examine the dead art teacher. She shook her head.

'No, Chief Inspector. If anything, the classroom looks a little tidier than usual. Miss Small was not known for her organisation, bless her. And she… she seems much as she did when I spoke to her at afternoon tea. Except, of course…' She indicated the body.

'Of course. Has she the same clothes? No change to the way her hair was left untied?'

'Honestly, I didn't notice what she was wearing.'

'Thank you.' He caught Eleanor's eye, making her frown as she struggled to interpret the message behind his look. 'Morrison, you can remove the body and fill out the medical report in the vehicle.'

'Sir.'

The three of them snapped the clasps of their bags closed. The one who hadn't spoken produced a grey-white sheet from beside him and laid it over Miss Small. Eleanor shuddered. It reminded her too much of her time as a nurse during the war again. The third man retrieved a slim stretcher she hadn't noticed leaning against the wall.

Clifford cleared his throat. 'Miss Lonsdale, perhaps you would prefer me to show the chief inspector's men the most discreet way out to their vehicle?' His voice was gentle.

The headmistress shook her head. 'A very kind offer, Mr Clifford, but it is my duty. Miss Small was a valued member of St Mary's. It is the least I can do to escort her from the school. Miss Rice has already ensured the staff and girls are all elsewhere. Where are you parked?'

Morrison pointed out the window. 'The wagon is—' He bobbed an apologetic head to Seldon. 'Sorry, the, erm, vehicle for the deceased is parked by the kitchens, madam.'

'Make sure you go extra carefully,' Seldon said. 'Allow Miss Lonsdale a moment with the deceased before you leave. We are not pressed for time now.'

'Got you, sir.' Morrison discreetly tapped his nose.

With just Seldon and Clifford left in the room, Eleanor tilted her head.

'Hugh, why did you want Miss Lonsdale out of the way?'

'Because I can tell she is already convinced this is a case of death by natural causes.'

'How can you possibly know that? You haven't spoken to her without us.'

He spread his hands. 'Too many years on the police force. The point is, I shall have to rely on you and Clifford to be impartial observers in her place, as it were. Now—' He waved around the room.

Eleanor started over by the long benches. Clifford didn't move.

'I'm afraid, Chief Inspector, that I have only seen this room from outside, while pretending to dissuade Master Gladstone from decimating the flower beds.'

Seldon grunted. 'Then it's down to you, Eleanor. Can you spot anything different since you were last here? Anything at all?'

'Nice there's no pressure then,' she muttered. After examining the benches, she shook her head.

'Nothing here. I'll… oh, hang on! The vermillion paint is missing. Miss Small showed it to me when she was explaining why the room smells as it does.'

'What the deuce is vermillion?' Seldon marched over to her side, notebook in hand.

She rolled her eyes. 'Red paint, you art philistine.'

'I had no idea you were such an expert.'

'Hmm, well, I used to take art classes in this very room. But actually, Clifford would probably say *I'm* the world's biggest art philistine.'

'Most assuredly, my lady,' Clifford's measured tone called across the room. 'But vermillion, that is surprising.'

'Why?' Seldon beckoned him over to the paint benches.

'Vermillion, Chief Inspector, has in the last two years commonly been replaced by cadmium red due to its less toxic properties.'

'Toxic?' Eleanor and Seldon chorused.

'Mercury sulphide. Formed by pounding mercury and melted sulphur together. When heated in a chemical container or furnace, the vapour from the original black mercury sulphide condenses into a vivid red crystalline version. It then undergoes a complicated washing and further physical reduction process to produce the final pigment used by artists since pre-Roman times. Vermillion has also been used to colour royal seals made from sealing wax since medieval times.'

'Remarkable,' Seldon said, making hasty notes.

'Indeed, a most ingenious, if hazardous, method.'

Eleanor laughed. 'I think Hugh meant more that you know such obscure things. He hasn't experienced your impression of a walking encyclopaedia first-hand like I have. I'm not sure it has anything to do with Miss Small's death, though.'

'Nevertheless, excellent information following on from an excellent observation,' Seldon said. 'Well done, both of you. Miss Lonsdale will be back soon though, I should think. Anything else?'

'There's nothing else in here except the models.' She pointed as she walked over to the line of papier-mâché figures leaning against the wall. 'Oh, but of course. Hugh, maybe you don't realise this is the room in which young John reported seeing the figure he thought was a burglar on Speech Day?'

He looked up from his notes with a frown. 'No, because no one has said until now! But then again, I omitted to ask. Blast it, I need some sleep to think clearly.' He brushed an unruly lock of chestnut curls from his eyes. 'And to magic up ten minutes for a haircut.'

'I think it suits you long.' Her cheeks coloured as he jerked up to stare at her. She tried to hide her blushes. 'So, erm, it appears to have been one of these models that Hepple's young lad saw. You see how they all have wooden boards on their feet? That's to support them so they can be displayed standing up. Only one of them' – she looked along the line – 'where are you Patrick Papier?'

'Patrick what?' Seldon's deep voice tickled her ear.

'Papier. Forget it. I noted when I was in here with Miss Small that one had lost his clay base… here he is! Oh!' She picked up the figure. 'It's been fixed.'

'Lady Swift, gentlemen?' Miss Lonsdale called from the doorway, discreetly wiping her eyes. She was clearly making every effort to make her voice cheerful as she said, 'I believe now is the time for that much needed round of tea.'

Eleanor nodded and whispered to Seldon, 'There's nothing else here I can see.'

'Then,' Seldon shut his notebook, 'lead on.'

CHAPTER 25

The clock struck midnight. Eleanor rubbed her eyes.

'A long night, my lady,' Clifford said from his uncomfortable perch on the opposite settee back in Miss Lonsdale's private sitting room.

Seldon grunted. 'I imagine it will run into a long morning soon enough.'

The headmistress returned with the secretary, who set down a large tray of tea things with a plate of biscuits. 'Thank you, Miss Rice. I should think we'll be self-sufficient from herein.'

The secretary scanned the other woman's drawn features in concern.

'It's no bother to stay, Headmistress.'

'Really, dear, you've done enough. I'm sorry to have called upon so much of your Saturday evening.' She smiled gratefully at Clifford, who had set about distributing cups and side plates.

Seldon waited until the four of them were alone before getting straight down to the matter at hand.

'Miss Lonsdale, you don't want to hear this, I know. But despite my men finding nothing immediately suspicious about Miss Small's death, the fact remains that she died soon after Mrs Wadsworth was murdered. And it was she who found the victim's body in the library.'

'I understand.' She accepted the tea Clifford held out to her. She hesitated, and then sighed. 'But your medical man, whatever his name is—'

'Morrison.'

'Yes, him. He was correct in his assumptions that Miss Small was not blessed with robust health. She has had several turns, you might call them. Feeling dizzy, saying her heart suddenly felt fluttery.'

Eleanor's ears pricked up. 'Matron must know about that. I could ask her.'

Miss Lonsdale frowned. 'Her spells will have been recorded in the medical records, naturally. There is no need to speak to Matron unnecessarily.'

Seldon swallowed a large glug of tea with the sigh of a man running on empty.

'Nothing is unnecessary in the case of suspected murder. I'm sorry, but Lady Swift will need to do as she has suggested. It might jog Matron's memory about something she didn't think important enough to record. The difficulty we'll have is that I imagine school was in normal operation again after Speech Day and all the staff would have been scattered around doing myriad things?'

Miss Lonsdale nodded. 'Of course. Life has to continue to timetable for the girls. Would I be correct to assume that, if Miss Small's death turns out *not* to be of natural causes' – she shuddered – 'you anticipate the murderer being one and the same for both ladies, Chief Inspector?'

'From experience, absolutely. From facts, I can't say. But I propose to start with the same suspects.' He pulled out his notebook again. Eleanor smiled as Clifford produced hers from his pocket and held it out to her.

Miss Lonsdale had put her hands together, whether in prayer for Miss Small or to think better, Eleanor wasn't sure. After a moment, the headmistress spoke.

'Well, Chief Inspector, your man Morrison calculated Miss Small's time of death at no more than one hour before the cleaner found her. That means, I take it, you want to know where your remaining suspects were between seven and nine?'

He nodded. 'It would be a great help.'

She frowned. 'Let's see. We can probably easily rule out Miss Munn and Mrs Jupe. They would have been with their girls seeing as they're both boarding housemistresses.'

'That should be easy to verify reliably then. Miss Lonsdale, could you ask one of your staff not on our suspect list to discreetly enquire if either of them left their boarding houses between the same times, seven and nine?'

'Of course, Chief Inspector.'

As Miss Lonsdale left, Seldon leaned back in his chair and grunted. 'I didn't want to say anything insensitive with Miss Lonsdale in the room, but Miss Small was in my mind a leading contender for Mrs Wadsworth's murder. And now…' He threw his hands up and shrugged.

A thought struck Eleanor. 'Hugh, your fingerprints man said he'd found some prints, yes?'

He nodded. 'Jones. What of it?'

'Well, I think you've got a hideous problem in front of you, same as you have with Mrs Wadsworth. How on earth are you going to discreetly fingerprint the entire staff when technically there is no murder again, and no one is allowed to know about any of this?'

'Thank you, Eleanor. Honestly, I don't know. We haven't been able to come up with anything to check for the fingerprints found at the scene of Mrs Wadsworth's death. Even if this wasn't all hush-hush, I still wouldn't have the authority to demand all staff, teaching and nonteaching, have their fingerprints taken. Officially, Mrs Wadsworth's death isn't even murder. I mean, there's no direct evidence as yet.' He shook his head wearily. 'I had intended to wrestle with that problem tomorrow, but' – he glanced at his watch – 'I suppose it *is* tomorrow.'

Clifford topped up the teacups. 'Fingerprinting is still quite a fledgling science, I believe, Chief Inspector? One that few members of the general public actually associate with the police? Am I right?'

'True. I don't know what percentage really even know we use them.'

'Of course!' Eleanor nodded to Clifford. 'Most people who know about fingerprints see it more as a matter of science rather than criminology.'

'Bravo, my lady.' Clifford offered her and Seldon the biscuit plate.

Seldon took a Garibaldi and a custard cream and looked from one to the other.

'Oh blast it, you two, I'm supposed to be the detective, but I'm mystified. How does any of this help us?'

Eleanor waved her digestive at him. 'And a brilliant detective you are, as you well know. But my brain is full of school life since I not only went to St Mary's, but I'm also stuck back here at the moment.'

Seldon frowned. 'And what exactly, please note the word, *exactly*, has this to do with matching the fingerprints found on the ladder in the library, and now, in the art room?'

Eleanor leaned forward. 'We get the girls to do a science project.'

Seldon's brow creased even further. 'How…?'

Clifford coughed. 'The whole point of fingerprints, Chief Inspector, is that each one is unique, like snowflakes. Not meaning to teach you to suck eggs, of course.'

Seldon's frown vanished, replaced with a look of comprehension. 'You can teach me to suck eggs if you come up with a ruse like that. Good man!'

Eleanor nodded eagerly. 'Exactly, you've caught on. The girls do a science project to show that everyone's fingerprint is unique. And the only way that can be proven is if ALL the school have their fingerprints taken.'

'Staff and pupils!' Seldon said.

'Including grounds staff.'

'Brilliant!'

He slapped the coffee table as Miss Lonsdale came back into the room. She looked as if she was going to remark on it, but then seemed to change her mind.

'Chief Inspector, I've been able to verify that both Miss Munn and Mrs Jupe were with their boarders at the time of Miss Small's death.'

'And Mrs Coulson?'

'Unfortunately, or fortunately, depending on how you view it, she was engaged in a variety of tasks that took her all over school.'

It was Eleanor's turn to groan quietly. 'One for me to interrogate tomorrow, then.'

Seldon peered sideways at her when Miss Lonsdale's back was turned. She pointed to the scowling face he had drawn in her notebook on her doodle of the horseradish jar representing Mrs Coulson. For the first time that evening, his lips rose into a quick smile.

Eleanor quickly whipped to another page as the headmistress turned around.

'Miss Lonsdale. The inspector has come up with a great idea for getting the staff's fingerprints.'

'Really? I'm listening, Chief Inspector.'

Having the good grace to blush, Seldon outlined Eleanor's proposal. Miss Lonsdale nodded approvingly.

'Surprisingly impressive. It's almost as if you had attended St Mary's yourself.' She looked pointedly at Eleanor. 'And I will make a great show of allowing the girls to take my fingerprints first. Right now, however, I think we need to call a halt to this meeting. Despite the horribly late hour, I still have a raft of things to do. And, Chief Inspector, the longer and later you are here, the more suspicious the staff will become.' She shrugged. 'We do not even really know if there was anything suspicious about Miss Small's death, do we?'

Seldon looked as if he was going to argue, but then changed his mind.

'Yes. You're right. And it's a long drive back to my office, so I might be lucky to actually arrive in time to start work again in the morning.'

'My sympathies. And my gratitude. Good night all.' She gestured towards the door.

Out in the corridor, Eleanor poked Seldon in the ribs. A lot harder than she intended, it turned out as he yelped. 'Oops! Sorry. I know you're tired, but we haven't finished discussing everything we need to, have we?'

'Not by a long way. But Miss Lonsdale is right, I need to not be seen here any longer. That was a rule of my involvement in the case.'

'Pah! Then let's make it that you aren't seen.' Eleanor strode ahead, calling over her shoulder. 'What are rules at St Mary's made for, Clifford?'

'Breaking to the point of no return, I believe, was always your modus operandi, my lady.'

CHAPTER 26

The wind snatched the heavy oak door from Seldon's hand and banged it back against the outside wall.

'Blast it.' He pulled his hat further down over his head.

Clifford stepped round him and peered out into the lashing rain. They all ducked backwards as a large branch whipped past only inches from their faces. A fork of lightning split the sky, making them shield their eyes.

'Oh, well,' Eleanor said. 'No one ever died from getting wet.'

'Actually, my lady—'

'Just run!'

They arrived at the door to Clifford's cottage panting, eyes stinging and drenched through to their underclothes. Eleanor and Seldon helped each other peel their soaked jackets from their shoulders in the tiny entrance space. By the time they'd gone into the sitting room, Clifford had somehow lit the fire and the sound of a kettle boiling on the stove filtered out to them. He darted up the narrow ladder-style staircase and disappeared through the elongated hatch in the ceiling.

Gladstone lumbered sleepily out from the kitchen, trailing a patchwork blanket on his back like a cape. On seeing Seldon, he broke into a lopsided canter and jumped up at the inspector, knocking him into one of the armchairs.

'Oof! Good evening, Gladstone. Or is it morning now? Ugh! Seriously, Eleanor, can't you teach him to say hello without using his tongue?'

She chuckled through her shivering. 'You try teaching an overindulged bulldog anything. Especially at his age.'

Clifford slid back down the ladder, one arm draped in swathes of fabric.

'My lady, Chief Inspector. The fire will soon catch and warm refreshments will be ready in a trice. Please avail yourselves.' Laying the pile on the tiny dining table, he strode through into the kitchen.

Eleanor tucked a towel around her shoulders and pointed to a thick, navy dressing gown.

'Perfect for you, Hugh.' She gratefully wrapped herself in the other, which swamped her. Tugging the soft velvety shawl collar up round her chin, she fumbled behind her for the waist sash. 'Dash it, my fingers are too cold to work properly.' Noting that Seldon seemed hesitant, she picked up the navy dressing gown and waggled it at him. 'You'll only regret arguing. You know what Clifford's like. He'll take an hour to explain the vagaries and intricacies of pneumonia or some such. That will just eat up more minutes you could have been on your way home. Oh, where is the sash for this robe?'

Seldon snorted. 'Hopeless!'

Her breath caught as he spun her by the shoulders and reached through her arms with the sash before tying it gently against her hip.

'Thank you,' she said, her cheeks burning and her heart skipping.

Clifford meanwhile had stoked the fire and arranged the arm-chairs in front of it. He disappeared again before stepping back in to join them.

'Oh, Clifford!' She pointed at the dressing gown he was now wearing. 'And I didn't even have to beg you.'

He adjusted the perfectly aligned fold of his gown's shawl collar. 'Purely in the name of saving time, my lady.' His eyes twinkled. 'Entreaties can be very long-winded, in the case of certain parties, I have learned.'

'Fibber.' She smiled fondly. 'Honestly, one could think you have engineered the whole thing.'

'Even wizards cannot actually command the weather, my lady.'

'Perhaps not, but they can arrange an impromptu midnight feast and dressing gown party. It's perfect. Thank you.'

In front of the fire, Seldon stopped trying to separate the pages of his sodden notebook and gruffed. 'We've no time for faffing about with food.'

'Quite so, Chief Inspector.' Clifford turned and disappeared back into the kitchen.

She sighed again. *Has the man no romance, Ellie?* Mind you, she'd seen first-hand on her birthday that he had.

Seldon tucked his collar tighter around his neck. 'What kind of man packs three dressing gowns for an anticipated stay of only a few days?'

She laughed. 'The world's best butler, silly.' She settled in the patterned armchair by the fire and forced herself to focus. Gladstone settled against her legs. 'Right, to business then. As we're assuming Miss Small was murdered, and by the same killer as Mrs Wadsworth, are we happy with Miss Lonsdale's report? That Miss Munn and Mrs Jupe didn't leave their respective boarding houses?'

'For the moment, yes.' Seldon dropped into the armchair beside her. 'You can verify that tomorrow. For now, they are off our suspect list. Ah, just a small one, Clifford,' he said with evident sorrow as a decanter of warmed brandy and three glasses appeared on the card table Clifford set down in front of them.

They discussed the case for a few minutes longer until Clifford reappeared with two long wooden boards filled with a variety of cheeses, ham slices, wedges of soft seeded bread, a large pat of creamy butter and a host of relishes and pickles. But the undisputed centrepiece of the mouth-watering spread was a large oval plate bearing a pyramid of golden-brown Stilton and walnut scones, hot from the oven. Seldon inhaled the rich buttery aroma, his stomach grumbling loudly. Gladstone instantly came to and let out an expectant round of woofs.

'Dive in,' Eleanor said. 'Not you, Gladstone! Thank you, Clifford. I don't know how you've conjured up this incredible past-midnight feast, but it's perfect.'

He bowed, then poured three large brandies, drew up one of the classroom chairs and perched on the edge.

'If I might mention a point that has sprung to mind. Miss Munn told you, my lady, she had passed Miss Small "dashing", I believe was her word, down Long Passage during the commotion caused by the burglar alarm being rung.'

'That's right. But we can't check that with Miss Small now. Sadly.'

Seldon grunted. 'And she was lining up nicely as a chief suspect.' He shrugged. 'Sorry, a little unfeeling, but now, as I said before, the field's wide open.'

'True, Chief Inspector,' Clifford said. 'However, my point is that it seems unlikely that Miss Munn would fabricate an alibi so easy to disprove.' As the others nodded through their mouthfuls, he continued. 'Ergo, it would not be imprudent to conjecture Miss Small might have witnessed something, hence her panic. Something which resulted in the murderer feeling she needed to be eliminated, perhaps?'

Seldon took a long swig of his brandy, clearly savouring the fiery warmth trickle down his throat. 'But why wait until today to silence her then? If Miss Small was going to tell someone, she would probably have done it by now.' He frowned. 'You also told me Miss Munn said she'd heard someone on the main stairs? Without realising it, she might have heard something useful.'

'Indeed, Chief Inspector, she could be a valuable witness.'

Seldon eyed him over the rim of his glass. 'Or the murderer.'

'Excellent point,' Eleanor said, imitating Seldon's tone. She peeked at him as she scribbled in her notebook, but he was oblivious, having taken another bite of his scone.

Gladstone shuffled over and licked the crumbs from his dressing gown.

'This is so criminally good, it really should be illegal.'

Eleanor rolled her eyes. 'Maybe you and the scone should get a room?'

He grunted. 'I'm too exhausted to think about finding any sort of hotel with any sort of a bed for the night, thank you.'

She put down her drink and turned to Clifford.

'Since he's finally admitted he's all in, you can stop pretending now.'

'Good news, my lady.'

Seldon's brows met. 'Blast it! Stop pretending what?'

Eleanor pointed to his washed-out face. 'That we had any intention of letting you drive home in this storm. Especially after what is clearly at least two nights of no sleep and probably a week without a decent meal.'

He drained his glass. 'Well, I appreciate the thought, but that's precisely what I'm going to do.'

'Warming brandy, isn't it?'

'Too warming to stop at one but I have managed to do so—'

Clifford cleared his throat. 'My error, sir, I appear to have forgotten you intended to leave tonight.' Ignoring Seldon's confused look, he refilled his glass. 'This is, in fact, your third double measure.'

'Clifford! No wonder my brain is like a fog.'

Eleanor laughed. 'And your cheeks are all rosy. Although that might be because you're snuggled up in Clifford's dressing gown.'

Clifford indicated the hatch in the ceiling. 'Chief Inspector, there is a newly laundered set of nightwear beside the freshly made and, I must say, surprisingly comfortable bed. Your wet clothes will dry by the fire tonight. In the morning, I shall show you a very discreet way back to your car. Would breakfast of eggs, bacon, toast, pancakes and sausages at twenty to six suit?'

For a moment, Eleanor thought Seldon was furious. Then he let out a deep rich laugh and she saw it had just been the dark circles under his eyes and the washed-out hue of his face.

'Agreed.' He ruffled the bulldog's ears and slipped him a piece of ham. 'So long as I don't have to fight Gladstone for the sausages in the morning. I'll arrest you both later for conspiring to intoxicate a police officer while on duty.'

Eleanor slapped his arm. 'That's the trouble, Hugh, you're never *off* duty.'

He smiled at her. 'Well, tonight I am. And I'm very grateful. And horrified at how easily you tricked me.'

'Oh, don't be. One thing investigating murders is quickly teaching me is the art of deception. Clifford though' – she jerked her thumb at her butler – 'he's just a born scallywag.'

He bowed. 'Most kind, my lady.'

Eleanor sighed with relief as Seldon settled back in his chair, swirling the brandy in his glass with one hand and loading up another scone with the other. The knot in her stomach from worrying he might not have arrived home safely slowly unravelled.

He seemingly savoured another bite of the scone, swallowed and sat up a little straighter.

'Now, before I actually fall asleep in this chair and waste Clifford's kind offer of a bed, we'd better get a step closer to solving a murder.'

CHAPTER 27

Clifford, having made sure there were ample liquid and solid provisions remaining, and that Gladstone had a bone so he might leave them to eat in peace, perched himself back on the edge of his chair. Seldon unstuck two more pages of his notebook and shook his head at the smudged writing.

'Well, at the risk of repeating myself, Miss Small's death has left this case wide open. We'll have to concentrate on the remaining suspects and hope something comes up. Right, Eleanor, you were going to check with Matron over the bursar's supposedly gammy leg?'

She gave an involuntary shudder. 'Everything about that man is a tad gammy to my mind.' She flapped a hand at her butler's disapproving sniff. 'Honestly, Clifford, if you were female you'd recoil from his reptilian charms too. Anyway, I did check and Matron said that he had been to her to ask for painkillers and a walking stick.'

'Mmm.' Seldon ran his hand along his jaw, the gentle rub of it passing over his five o'clock shadow sending a tantalising quiver down Eleanor's back. 'Miss Rice told you that the bursar insisted she go on stage in his place. And the bursar said Miss Rice made such a fuss about his leg, he let her go on his behalf to keep her quiet. Correct?'

Eleanor nodded.

'But which one's telling the truth?' He wrapped a thick slice of cheese in breaded ham.

'If the bursar's the one lying, he could have made up his leg injury so he could kill poor Mrs Wadsworth. But then again, he would have needed to get her off the stage first, wouldn't he?'

'Hence the burglar alarm. He was, after all, the one who rang the bell.'

Clifford held up a finger. 'Indeed, Chief Inspector. But only on receiving word from Mr Hepple's lad that there was an intruder.'

Seldon frowned. 'Then they could be in it together. Perhaps the bursar paid Hepple to tell the lad to say he'd seen an intruder. After all, you and Clifford both think the story's flimsy and you've said Hepple's men are loyal to him.'

She nodded. 'We do, and they are. I'll confront him about it tomorrow.'

'No, you will not.'

'Says who?'

Clifford silently aligned the relishes and pickle dishes back into perfect order.

Seldon held Eleanor's gaze. 'Me. It's too dangerous. And besides, if he is the killer, it will alert him that we're on to him. Can you instead come up with a devious ruse to verify irrefutably if the bursar's injury is real or not?'

Mollified, Eleanor rubbed her hands. 'Can we ever!'

'Good. Then I'll dig further into his background. Hopefully, that won't prove too hard. He only joined St Mary's fairly recently.' Seldon glanced up. 'Eleanor, I can't repeat enough how careful you need to be now. Miss Small's death, if it is murder, shows just how wrong I was when I told Miss Lonsdale none of her other staff were, in my opinion, in danger.'

She tutted. 'Don't worry, I'm not really staff, the girls of Holly House will vouch for that. Anyway, I have my secret weapon. I've got my bodyguard and private wizard here, remember.'

Clifford's lips twitched. 'Ah, I have been meaning to ask which costume you would prefer me to wear, my lady?'

Seldon shook his head with a quiet smile as he watched Eleanor layer paprika relish to the top of another Stilton scone and then did the same. 'Back to business. What can you add about Hepple, Clifford? Anything?'

'Something indeed, Chief Inspector. Or it may be nothing at all. I investigated the nearest outbuilding to this cottage, which is the furthest one from the main school building. Her ladyship and I noticed Mr Hepple acting suspiciously on entering it early this morning. Amongst an exceptionally fine set of wood chisels, I found this carefully wrapped in tissue paper.' He unfurled his hand to reveal a small blue woollen bobble.

Eleanor gasped. Her voice trembled. 'Clifford! Oh gracious, I know exactly what that is.'

Seldon scanned her face. 'Take it easy a moment.'

'I'm alright, it's just that this' – she took the bobble from Clifford's palm – 'is from Mrs Wadsworth's cardigan.'

Seldon looked up sharply. 'Well, that puts a different spin on things. Hepple wasn't on stage with the other staff and he basically raised the alarm, which neither of you believe was a genuine call. But, Eleanor, how can you be sure that's where the wool thing is from?'

'Because Mrs Wadsworth taught me every day for half my childhood and it was her favourite piece of clothing. And it is still hanging on the back of her chair in the staffroom.'

Seldon started to speak, but she held up a hand.

'Yes, I'll go and confirm if her cardigan is missing any bobbles tomorrow as soon as I can.'

'Thank you, Eleanor. I do appreciate this is not easy for you.'

'Investigating murder never is. And yet you do it every day.'

He stared at his hands. 'Someone has to.'

She peered at Clifford. 'Why didn't you tell me you found this?'

'Purely because we became involved in a rather pertinent, and long overdue conversation, my lady.'

'About my mother. Of course.' A flicker of something she couldn't quite distinguish crossed Seldon's face. 'But hang on, what about the row Miss Rice told me about? Between Mrs Coulson and Miss Lonsdale when Mrs Coulson tried to get Mrs Wadsworth sacked?'

'Over what?' Seldon said, pen at the ready.

'She didn't say. And I couldn't press the matter at that point.'

Clifford arched a brow. 'Too weighed down by boxes of cakes and sacks of sweets, my lady?'

'Something like that.' She winked. 'Clifford and I will winkle it out of Miss Lonsdale tomorrow.'

Clifford cleared his throat. 'My lady, perhaps it might be better if you were to meet with Miss Lonsdale alone? I fear the lady is more upset over a second death at the school than she is showing.'

'Nonsense, Clifford! She thinks the sun itself shines out of your pockets.'

'I was merely thinking that in the lady's present state of distress the matter might be a delicate one to discuss.'

Seldon let out a deep, rich chuckle as he glanced at Eleanor. 'Then you absolutely have to be there, Clifford. Never send a bull into a china shop unfettered!'

With the men clearly enjoying the joke between them, Eleanor finished her brandy with a roll of her eyes and waved her notebook. 'You'll probably want to add Matron to your fiendish digging, Hugh. Clifford and I wangled a way to check if you can hear the alarm in the sanatorium. That's where she said she was when the alarm went off and she insisted she couldn't hear it.'

Seldon picked up his pen. 'And?'

'An outright lie. Clifford had a brilliant idea on learning that Mr Hepple tests the alarm every Saturday morning when the girls are always outside doing sport or whatnot. So earlier today' – she rubbed her eyes – 'gracious, earlier yesterday, I happened up to Matron's flat on the pretext of wanting to meet Tripod.'

Seldon winced. 'I can't believe I'm asking, but I'm too intrigued. What tripod?'

'Not what, *who*. Tripod, her three-legged cat, obviously.'

'Obviously,' he muttered. 'And you could clearly hear the alarm?'

'Even above all the exaggerated cooing noises I was making over the scraggy old puss. Actually, he's quite sweet but don't tell Gladstone. So, you use all your official channels to see what you can unearth about her as well as the bursar. Clifford and I, in the meantime, will find out what she was really doing.'

'Excellent.' Seldon nodded, then frowned. 'I have to say, this red pickle stuff is amazing.' He spread another spoonful on a slice of thickly buttered bread. 'What is it?'

Eleanor gave a mock tut while Clifford served them both another slice of cheese and ham. 'There's no time for faffing about with food, remember?'

'That was before. It's now almost' – he squinted at his watch – 'two in the morning and I'm losing the ability to make sense of anything, thanks to you two.'

Clifford rose. 'A few hours of sleep, perhaps?'

'Amen!' Eleanor and Seldon chorused, wolfing down their last mouthful.

As Clifford tidied up in the kitchen, Seldon helped Eleanor clear the table. His hand brushed hers as they both reached for the last plate.

'Eleanor?'

She stopped, something in his tone making her throat catch.

'Yes, Hugh?'

'Thank you again.'

'No trouble,' she said, more casually than intended. 'You know how I seem to struggle to not get caught up in these ridiculous investigations.'

'I actually meant for this.' He pointed to his brandy glass. 'But thank goodness my men can't see me. Their detective chief inspector swathed in a borrowed dressing gown, hiding out in a girl's school in the early hours. A little squiffy and' – he rubbed his hands over his cheeks – 'probably blushing now just to make a complete fool of myself, blast it!'

She looked up at him impishly. 'You look better with colour in your cheeks. Someone needs to look after you if you aren't going to.'

For a moment neither of them spoke.

Then Seldon cleared his throat. 'Yes, well. It's been stupidly busy these past weeks. But on this case, I couldn't do any of this without you… without you both. I'm eternally grateful.' She waited as he seemed to fight to find a few more words. 'And more tired than I have ever been, I admit.' Her breath caught as he reached out absent-mindedly and gently tightened the sash on her dressing gown. 'I'm truly glad you stopped me leaving tonight, albeit by highly questionable methods.'

She tried but failed to flap a nonchalant hand since her arms were trembling, wishing he would scoop her into his and hold her for one long delicious moment.

'Whatever it takes to keep someone safe, Hugh. That's what friends are for.'

His lips moved, but nothing came out. He stared at the floor and then at her hands.

'Is that what we are, Eleanor? Just friends?'

She swallowed hard. 'Honestly, Hugh, I'm… I'm not sure.'

'Me neither. But I like the sound of it.' His gaze met hers. 'For starters.'

For starters, Ellie! She bit her lip, not trusting herself to speak.

At the head of the path to the boarding house, Clifford struggled in the strong wind and lashing rain to open the gate for Eleanor.

She peered out from under the enormous hood of the waxed coat he had insisted she wear. She hesitated.

'Yes, my lady?' he shouted above the storm.

'He's a good man,' she shouted back. 'Hugh, I mean. Despite all his gruff exterior. And his irritating stubbornness over policy and protocol. And his dashedly awkward way with women. At least with me. All that aside, he's a good man, wouldn't you say?'

Clifford shook his head. 'I shall cancel my order for a loud hailer first thing in the morning.'

'What?'

'My lady, despite my best efforts, you have not heard what I have been saying for the last sixteen months. The chief inspector is indubitably a very good man. It's heartening you've finally drawn the same conclusion without having heard a single word.'

She laughed. 'It's official then, Hugh is indeed a decent chap. You, on the other hand, are the most devious monster I have ever encountered!'

He winked. 'Too kind.'

As she stood on the doorstep of Holly House, she waved to him. He nodded, then vanished into the darkness. She half turned and jumped. *What was that, Ellie?* A weak crack of lightning did a poor job of illuminating the grounds. She waited, heart racing, for the next flash. This time she saw it clearly. Someone was hiding on the other side of the hedge at the edge of the path, watching her. For a moment she contemplated striding over there, but the image of Miss Small lying on the art room floor flashed into her head. Deftly, she slid the key in the lock, hopped over the threshold and locked the door behind her.

Peering through the glass, she scanned the hedge. But whoever it was had gone.

CHAPTER 28

The last of the chapel bells calling the girls to Sunday matins filtered in through the half-open door of Miss Lonsdale's office. The storm had exhausted itself in the night and fingers of sun teased an extra genial glow from the yellow ochre walls and cushions. Even the portrait of the old headmistress seemed less austere. Yet the recent events had left a sombre pall over the room and its occupants.

Eleanor rubbed her eyes, still tired from the long night before. She was halfway through formulating her words to grill Clifford about what he and Seldon had talked about once she'd left – *I'm sure it wasn't about you, Ellie, was it?* – when the headmistress cut into her thoughts from the doorway.

'I am sorry to have kept you waiting, Lady Swift. Ah, Mr Clifford too.'

Eleanor scanned the headmistress' face. She looked as tired as Eleanor felt. She was obviously struggling with the recent turn of events more than she was letting on, as Clifford had suggested.

Miss Lonsdale seemed oblivious to Eleanor's gaze.

'On the table, please, Miss Rice.'

The secretary's pretty face and curvy frame appeared behind her, arms balancing a coffee tray. 'Would you like any notes taken, Headmistress?'

'No, thank you. We will merely be chatting.'

'The coffee isn't quite ready, though. I'll just wait to pour.' Before Clifford could reach the table, Miss Rice quickly set about arranging cups on saucers.

Eleanor peeped sideways at her with quiet interest while addressing her hostess.

'So, Miss Lonsdale, I sincerely appreciate the chance to reminisce further over my days here.'

'And I to hear more of your adventures,' the headmistress said. 'I can take care of our guests now, Miss Rice. Thank you.'

The secretary's shoulders sagged. She pulled the door closed behind her, the latch clicking but not quite catching. Clifford caught Eleanor's eye and tapped his ear. She nodded.

Miss Lonsdale looked between them before dropping her voice.

'Miss Rice is a very dedicated employee, Lady Swift. Where else would you find a young woman of her age and, forgive me, her looks, who would willingly volunteer to work at the weekend?'

'We're not questioning that. Rather more, why she seemed so eager to stay and even more reluctant to leave.'

'Lady Swift, you continue to surprise. Modesty is a most becoming trait, as St Mary's girls so quickly tire of being told.'

Eleanor looked blankly at Clifford.

'My lady, I believe Miss Lonsdale is suggesting Miss Rice was hoping to hear of your adventurous exploits first-hand.'

Miss Lonsdale nodded. 'She has spoken of little else since she brought me your letter confirming you would come for Speech Day.'

Something tugged at Eleanor's befuddled thoughts, but Clifford got there first.

'Would Miss Rice normally have been part of the staff on stage at Speech Day?'

'No. But bless her, she certainly gave enough hints that she wanted to be. I'm afraid I needed her to be by the telephone in case of an emergency.' Her composed look faltered. 'I have had words with the bursar for asking her to take his place at the last minute without my permission.'

So maybe Miss Rice isn't lying, Ellie? Has the bursar fooled Miss Lonsdale as well?

Clifford rose silently and pushed the door fully shut. Once they were seated, Eleanor took the notebook he offered her.

'Something has been puzzling me, Miss Lonsdale. On Speech Day, Miss Munn said she'd heard someone on the main stairs on her way back to the hall after checking her area for intruders. But I've gone through the movements of the other staff who responded to the alarm with Clifford, and I can't work out who it could be.'

'Nor I.' Miss Lonsdale took her coffee from Clifford with a grateful nod. 'But it is possible there was no one there at all.'

'Gracious, is Miss Munn the sort to make things up?'

'Not to my knowledge. She is, in fact, refreshingly transparent. St Mary's itself, however, is another matter. Architectural features such as lofty ceilings, arches and grandiose stairwells do their job of impressing the parents and reflecting the elegance we hope our girls will eventually attain. They also, as a side effect, tend to mask the precise location of a sound's origin which, incidentally, the wilier errant girls use to their advantage.' She looked at Eleanor. 'Like our current Holly House. But certain alumni might understand that better than others.'

Eleanor laughed. 'You're so diplomatic. Now you've reminded me, I do indeed remember. There are lots of nooks and discreet spaces around school where one might be engaged in something extracurricular, shall we say, without being discovered. Even if it involved making quite a noise.'

'Flanking paths,' Clifford said.

Miss Lonsdale nodded. 'Why, yes, Mr Clifford. So knowledge-able.'

He turned to Eleanor. 'Certain surfaces other than floors and walls within the fabric of a building can facilitate the transmission of sound along what are known as "flanking paths". These paths fool the ear as to the source of the original sound. For instance, it may appear someone is walking up a certain flight of stairs, when in fact they are descending another.'

She eyed him ruefully. 'Like that makes it any clearer. But, thank you. So we're saying Miss Munn could have heard someone in any number of places adjacent to where she thought they were?'

'We are,' Miss Lonsdale said.

'Then I suppose it was just another teacher checking their area. Well, we'd better move on to the… other matter.'

Miss Lonsdale accepted a coffee top-up. 'The "other" matter? Oh my!' The headmistress stared at the blue woollen bobble Eleanor placed in her hand. 'This… this is from Mrs Wadsworth's cardigan' – she looked up – 'as I am sure you have already deduced.'

Eleanor nodded. 'It's so distinctive, I couldn't mistake it for anything else. I checked on the way here and there are several missing, not surprisingly given its age, but that's definitely one of the missing ones and it had been snipped off.'

Miss Lonsdale closed her hand over the bobble and let out a long breath. 'But Mrs Wadsworth wasn't wearing her cardigan when she was killed. That is something of a comfort.'

Eleanor glanced at Clifford, who indicated he was as lost as she was. 'I'm going to have to ask you to elaborate,' said Eleanor.

'Of course.' Miss Lonsdale looked towards the door and rose. 'But not here. Lady Swift, Mr Clifford, do bring your coffee. This way, please.' She led them to her private sitting room. With the door shut and the three of them seated, she sighed heavily. 'I had sincerely hoped this would not need to come to light.'

Clifford picked up her coffee and held it out to her. 'No secrets will go beyond her ladyship, myself and the chief inspector unless it is strictly necessary, madam.'

'I don't doubt that for a moment. It's just that this involves a confession on my part. I broke St Mary's number one rule.' Miss

Lonsdale stared again at the wool bobble. 'You found this in the furthest outbuilding?'

'Yes, among Mr Hepple's carpentry tools.'

'That poor man.' The headmistress sighed. 'He's lost two women he loved dearly now.'

Eleanor's eyes widened. 'You mean—'

'Yes. They were having an affair, if you can call it that, as it was more for company than anything else. I found out by accident soon after I joined St Mary's. Both were widowed and obviously very lonely and had been loyal employees for many years, so I wrestled with my conscience over my duties as headmistress. To my shame, I turned a blind eye, despite it being strictly against the rules for staff of opposite genders to fraternise.'

'There is no shame in compassion,' Eleanor said.

Clifford nodded. 'But perhaps another member of your staff was not so compassionate? Mrs Coulson maybe?'

Miss Lonsdale nodded. 'Nothing escapes you two, does it? But yes. She discovered their relationship as well. She felt forcefully that they did not uphold the school's moral code and insisted I removed them both from the school immediately as they were corrupt influences on the children. It promoted the most fearful row. I had to forcibly stop Mr Hepple packing his bags. The only way I could placate Mrs Coulson to some extent was to ban Mr Hepple coming into the main building and to remove most of Mrs Wadsworth's teaching duties.'

So that's the real reason why Mrs Wadsworth didn't teach any more, Ellie!

Miss Lonsdale shook her head sadly. 'It affected Mrs Wadsworth very badly too. Because they could no longer meet, she retreated into herself and became very distracted. The other staff knew nothing of the real reason. That is one thing to Mrs Coulson's credit, she didn't go round tattling about it. However, everyone else saw Mrs

Wadsworth's change in mood and behaviour as being a degeneration of her faculties. It was very sad to watch.'

So that's what the bursar was talking about, Ellie. Maybe he was telling the truth about her getting her budget wrong?

'You did everything you could, madam, and beyond,' Clifford said. 'Some connections are just not meant to be, experience has shown time and again.'

Eleanor couldn't miss the tinge of sadness behind his usually measured tone.

'So it seems unlikely Mr Hepple would have harmed Mrs Wadsworth?'

Miss Lonsdale shook her head vigorously. 'Unless, Lady Swift, something drastic happened between them. But even so, I could not believe he would ever harm that woman. Unlike… unlike, and it pains me greatly to say this as I do not want to cast aspersions, unlike Mrs Coulson.'

Eleanor leaned forward. 'What do you mean exactly?'

'Loyalty forbids me to say, but I feel, given the circumstances, I must.' She sighed. 'My last confession. Mrs Coulson said that if I wouldn't get rid of Mrs Wadsworth, she would. And by whatever means necessary!'

CHAPTER 29

By late afternoon the following day, Eleanor was in desperate need of a diversion. Clifford had disappeared off on an errand and she'd shouted herself to a standstill encouraging the Holly House girls on the hockey pitch. Furthermore, when she let herself into Clifford's cottage, Gladstone was too busy chasing dream rabbits in his quilted bed in the kitchen to be dragged out on a walk.

She returned to the sitting room and stared wistfully at the chessboard that sat waiting for her promised rematch with Clifford. She'd lose again, for sure. Mentally rolling up her sleeves, she looked over at the main building of St Mary's.

'Right, Matron. It looks like the perfect time for you and I to have that chat then.'

At the door of the sanatorium, the sound of a hushed voice made Eleanor pause. She took in the unexpected sight of Matron on all fours in front of the end storage cupboard, its double doors wide open.

'You'll get me into such trouble!' Matron hissed.

Eleanor scanned the rest of the room but couldn't see anyone else. *What on earth, Ellie?*

Matron's anxious voice came again. 'And what am I supposed to say if we get caught? Tell me that.'

Her front half disappeared inside the cupboard, causing the skirt of her blue-and-white uniform to ride up her calves. Eleanor crept a few tentative steps into the room and took advantage of the partition curtain to hide behind. From this view, she could see the five inner shelves of the cupboard. All were stocked with different-sized packets and boxes and a variety of glass bottles, mostly brown with a short row of smaller blue ones on the top shelf. But whatever Matron was doing was obscured by her bent over form. *There has to be someone hiding by the side of the cupboard, Ellie, but why?* She craned her neck further.

Suddenly Matron cried out and shot backwards onto her heels, clutching her hand. Several of her thick brown curls tumbled out of their restraining pins under her starched white cap.

'Right, that does it!' She shuffled stiffly onto her feet and grabbed one of the blue bottles. Sliding it into her pocket, she arranged a handkerchief on top, taking care to tuck the edges down firmly.

Eleanor decided this was her best moment to find out what was going on. She crept back to the door and poked her head round as if she'd just entered.

'Is everything alright, Matron?'

The woman's hand flew to her chest. 'Oh, Lady Swift. You gave me such a fright!'

'So sorry, but I was passing and thought I heard you shout.' Eleanor walked briskly over to her. Trying not to make it obvious, she glanced down the side of the cupboard, but there was no one there. She scratched her head. 'Do you need help, Matron?'

'Honestly, yes.' She hurried over to the door, looked up and down the corridor, before closing it quietly. 'We mustn't get caught. I wish there was another way but I haven't found it yet.'

'Another way to what?'

'Deal with him.' She pointed to the bottom of the cupboard.

Eleanor dropped to her haunches and laughed.

'Tripod! What are you doing in there?' Two bright-green eyes in a fluffy black-and-white face blinked at her. About to reach forward, she paused as Matron tapped her shoulder.

'I shouldn't, Lady Swift. You'll end up with one of these.' Matron showed her a long welted and decidedly angry scratch across the back of her hand.

Eleanor tutted at the cat. 'You ungrateful puss!'

He looked haughtily at her, unmoved. Suddenly, his tiny pink nose twitched.

'Aha!' Eleanor reached into her pocket and pulled out a handful of Gladstone's liver treats. Tripod gave a plaintive mew. Eleanor shook her head. 'Only if you play nice.' She placed a line of treats from the cupboard out onto the floor.

'Well, I never did,' Matron said as the cat hopped out and devoured them. Eleanor pointed to the scratch on Matron's hand. 'Shouldn't you put something on that? My butler, Clifford, always seems to have some fearfully spiteful concoction about his person, which he insists on dousing me liberally with whenever I end up with the tiniest scrape.'

Matron looked at her quizzically.

'I anticipated finding a little of the unorthodox in you, Lady Swift, but, well, forgive me for saying, you're actually nothing at all like I expected.'

Eleanor laughed. 'I get that a lot. Now.' She turned to the still-open cupboard. 'Which of these magic potions is what you need?' She ran her finger along the line of brown bottles while surreptitiously reading the labels on the blue ones on the shelf above.

'Oh no, no! No need for anything in there.' Matron bustled her to one side before locking the cupboard. 'I've plenty of iodine to hand. You'd think the girls here were boys, the amount of unladylike cuts and scrapes they turn up in here with.'

'Ah, that's where I get it from then. So I would have been less accident prone if I hadn't attended St Mary's?'

Matron laughed. 'Very possibly.'

'Well, can I help with the iodine?'

'No, thank you.' Matron washed her hands in the sink, watching Eleanor in the reflection of the mirror above. 'Thank you for your help with Tripod, though. Now, you run along and have some minutes to yourself before the Holly House litter straggle home looking like they've fought their way out of a tied sack thrown in the river.'

'I'm growing horribly fond of them.'

'Naughty is as naughty does.' Matron splashed some purple iodine on a clean cloth and dabbed at the scratch. Turning around, she went to put her hands in her pockets but seemed to falter as if remembering the bottle there. 'I've a small duty to see to, Lady Swift. Will you excuse me?'

'Of course. Two very quick things, though. Who is it that dislikes Tripod so much?'

'Pardon?'

'You were worried when you realised I'd seen you talking to someone. More so, when you also realised the sanatorium door was open, and he was in the cupboard. Just so I know and don't let slip by mistake.'

Matron's lips pursed. 'Just between us, it's Mrs Coulson. She made such a fuss when Tripod arrived and immediately came up with stipulations about where he could and couldn't go. Quite ridiculous! He's a cat. You can't make rules like that with them, they'll find a way to come and go as they please.'

'Even with only three legs.'

Matron scowled. 'Honestly, I think she would have had Mr Hepple drown him in a bucket if she could.'

'And this is one of the places he's not allowed?'

'Absolutely! If she'd spotted him, she'd have got straight down to her old trick of making trouble. Trust me, she's good at that.' Her cheeks coloured. 'But listen to me, saying all sorts of things I shouldn't be. Please don't mention this conversation, will you?'

'Of course not.' Eleanor leaned in and whispered, 'She was more terrifying than the headmistress when I was here and she had four canes in her office, all with my name on.'

Matron nodded, looking thoughtful. 'To be fair, Mrs Coulson has had a point on occasion. I mean, if the staff openly break the rules and get found out, what do they expect? Of course, she was going to go hell for leather to make trouble for them. But if people can't be properly discreet... well, there we are.'

Mmm? Perhaps Mrs Coulson hadn't kept the affair between Mrs Wadsworth and Mr Hepple quiet after all, Ellie?

Matron grabbed a black book from the counter as she bustled over to the door. Pulling it open, she beckoned to Eleanor. 'I'll need to lock this behind us.'

'Of course. Now, what was that other thing I wanted to ask you? Oh yes, why didn't you hear the burglar alarm in your flat on Speech Day? I heard it very clearly when I came to meet Tripod for the first time. It's far too loud to sleep through if one were to have dozed off.'

Matron's face had already fallen before Eleanor finished speaking. She pushed the door closed again and leaned against it. 'Curious as a cat, aren't you?'

'Do you know that is a long-running bone of contention between Clifford and me? He insists a ferret is a far nosier creature.'

Matron stared at her. 'Please don't tell anyone. The truth is... if you're staff, life never stops. Especially if you're the matron. I always have a place to be and a job to do. And on the afternoon of Speech Day, I was exhausted. I just needed a few minutes to... to relax.'

Eleanor patted the other woman's arm. 'Then why didn't you say?'

Matron hesitated. 'Because, Lady Swift, trouble follows trouble.'

As she disappeared around the corner of the corridor, Ellie nodded.

She's right, Ellie. Trouble does follow trouble. So let's see what sort of trouble we're following, shall we?

Keeping close to the wall, she set off after her prey.

CHAPTER 30

Stealth, Ellie, stealth! Good thing you're excellent at that. Bull in a china shop indeed! This tailing the suspect lark is… blast!

At the corner of the school's main entrance, disaster struck. Matron spotted Miss Rice emerging with a parcel and spun around.

'So, herein lies your solution, my lady.' Clifford's measured voice cut into Eleanor's panic as she too spun on her heel. She stared at him and then down at the magazine he held.

'What solution?' she whispered. 'And what are you doing here?'

'Endeavouring,' he whispered back, 'to provide you with a plausible cover.' Holding the magazine up, he pointed to a page as Matron hurried past. 'As you can see, my lady, the hedging at the front of the school is similar to the one shown here, perfect for the Italian garden at Henley Hall.'

Eleanor eyed her prey escaping. 'There *is* no Italian garden at Henley Hall, Clifford! And I can't let Matron out of my sight.'

'Then I suggest we head the lady off.'

She rolled her eyes. 'Of course. Only to head her off, I'd need to know where she's going. And if I knew where she was going… I wouldn't be following her!' Her voice had risen to a shrill whisper at the end.

'Don't you, my lady?'

'Infuriatingly I don't. But clearly, you do. Lead on, dash it!'

Gesturing for them to take the path heading in the opposite direction to the one Matron had taken, Clifford led the way. Finally he ceded to Eleanor's insistence that he put her out of her misery of 'feeling the total dullard'.

His eyes twinkled. 'I can but try, my lady. It struck me as quite the contradiction that Matron is clutching a Bible after the colourfully irreverent language she used earlier this afternoon in the rose garden which I "accidentally" overheard.'

Eleanor wrinkled her nose. 'I didn't notice it was a Bible she was carrying. But is it really so surprising she might have let loose something inappropriate? If she thought no one was so shameless as to be earwigging, of course. Everyone needs the outlet of a discreet profanity once in a blue moon.'

He straightened his perfectly aligned tie as he cleared his throat. 'Not everyone, my lady. If you will forgive my contrary opinion.'

'Everyone except you, I mean, obviously. Ah! I see. You think she's scurrying off to the chapel?'

'That is precisely my conjecture. She is taking the indirect route for discretion, and the Bible is merely an aid for whatever deception she is perpetrating.'

Eleanor tugged on the elbow of his suit jacket, ignoring the quiet tut this received. 'Listen. In that case, we need to cut through Long Passage. We'll end up at the perfect vantage point and it's the quickest route out to the quadrangle from here.'

'Perhaps, but it could arouse suspicion if we were spotted.'

'Pah! Don't worry. I think I know how to sneak down Long Passage unobserved!'

She followed his gaze to the very visible scar on her wrist. 'Okay, last time I did get caught, but that was just unlucky.' She ducked under an archway and beckoned for Clifford to follow. 'By the way, what was Matron's oh-so shocking impiety over?'

'I believe the lady fell foul of the rugosa roses, my lady. Their thorns are notoriously vicious if one is not prudent. She seemed to be collecting a small posy of the few rare blue blooms.'

'Pilfering all of Hepple's prize roses, tsk tsk. He won't be happy about that, I'm sure.'

'Mr Hepple is not happy with anything at the moment. But perhaps we should focus. We are almost at Long Passage, are we not?'

'We are. Through this door here, a short sprint up those steps midway along the corridor, then whip through the narrow door over there on the right.'

'Sprint, my lady? Rather conspicuous, to say nothing of unorthodox, for a lady of the manor.'

'For heaven's sake, you sound like Seldon. There's no one here to see us.' She jumped as someone bumped backs with her.

'Goodness, sorry. Are you alright, Lady Swift?'

Eleanor turned to find Miss Rice bent over, collecting the papers she'd obviously been carrying.

She joined the secretary and Clifford in picking them up. 'Yes, I'm fine, Miss Rice. So sorry.'

'No problem, really. Can I help you? Not lost or anything?'

'No, no, thank you. We are just getting inspiration for some renovations I'm thinking of having done back at home.'

'Oh, in that case, I'd best get on with delivering these budget reports for the bursar. Do say if I can provide you with the name of any contractors. I love St Mary's, she has so many very pretty features, doesn't she?' She walked off, her blue skirt swinging with the sway of her shapely hips.

Eleanor watched her disappear before looking up at Clifford, who was still staring after the secretary.

She chuckled. 'As does she, wouldn't you say?'

He gave her a withering look. 'I was, in fact, wondering exactly where Miss Rice had appeared from since neither of us heard her coming.'

'Flanking paths,' they chorused.

'Indeed. But Matron first perhaps, my lady?'

'Matron? I almost forgot about her.'

In the small quadrangle, at the diagonal corner to where the chapel stood, Clifford pulled out his pocket watch and flipped open the case. He nodded.

'A matron on a covert mission, for sure.'

Eleanor bent forward.

'What? The inside of your watch case is mirrored? How have you been my butler for sixteen months and I've never noticed that?'

'A good question, my lady. The mirrored section is a removable addition of his lordship's invention to better enable discreet observation in instances such as this.'

They both watched as Matron, after a brief glimpse in their direction, slipped into the chapel. Eleanor shadowed her at what she hoped was a discreet distance, Clifford bringing up the rear.

Inside, the familiar heady mix of candles, polish and a whiff of damp hit Eleanor's nostrils. She looked around at the high stone gothic arches that felt every bit as imposing as she remembered. The hard wooden pews looked just as austere and uncomfortable as she recalled as well. The weak light penetrating the enormous stained-glass window behind the altar was poorly augmented by just a few of the candle-lit candelabras hanging on long chains from the elaborate rib-vaulted ceiling.

'Why do chapels and churches all smell the same?' she whispered, shivering at the same time. 'And why are they always so cold?' She held up a hand to stop Clifford from regaling her with the precise reasons.

Hearing a noise, she quickly ducked behind a latticed screen.

'Whoa!' She lost her balance and nearly fell.

Clifford put his finger to his lips.

'I know,' she whispered. 'But I almost broke my neck!' She looked at the floor where she'd slipped. 'Candle wax!'

Clifford pointed to the right side of the chapel, his eyes twitching from side to side as he listened intently. Motioning upwards, she followed the direction of his finger to the tiny gallery behind the pipes of the ornate gothic organ. Turning her head, her sharp ears caught the whisper of voices. She peered cautiously further round the edge of the screen but the shadows obscured any sign of who it might be from both of them.

She crooked her finger and mouthed, 'Follow me.' She tiptoed along the left-hand wall using the solid wooden Bible rests of the side-facing pews for cover. Three quarters of the way along, she dropped to her haunches. Clifford lifted the tails of his jacket and followed suit.

Your favourite old hidey-hole. Let's hope it's still here, Ellie!

It was. Beside her, a hip-height rectangular section of the wood panelling of the wall was outlined by a faint dark line. She pushed cautiously on the bottom of the panel. It swung upwards quieter than any proverbial chapel mouse. Through the gap, the bottom of a sturdy set of wooden steps was visible. Clifford nodded appreciatively then ducked nimbly through after her.

She climbed as fast as she dared without making any noise. On the final rung, she turned and beckoned Clifford up. From their cramped position, the brass grillwork of the air vent was inches from their faces. She rose slowly and pressed her eye to the cold metal. Directly across, only fifteen feet or so away, two shadowy forms were still whispering heatedly in the small stone gallery.

'You need to do something,' a female voice hissed.

Matron, Ellie.

'You said you wanted to help,' said a taut male voice she almost recognised.

'I did. Really, I do. But not like this. Not any more. It's gone too far.'

'But you know I can't carry on otherwise!'

'I… I know, but you have to face up to your actions. You must do what is right!'

That's it, Ellie. She turned her head to Clifford and mouthed 'Chaplain'. He nodded.

'Please.' The chaplain's voice cracked. 'I feel terrible about it but I beg you, say you'll keep covering for me?'

'No. This is positively the last time. You are a chaplain. You must… confess. Do what is right or I will have to speak up. I mean it.'

The thud of unsteady feet on stone steps echoed through the chapel. A moment later the chaplain's feet stumbled past them below. The scuff of his heels died away, leaving an eerie silence. A few minutes later Matron's feet appeared at the bottom of the steps and disappeared in the opposite direction to the chaplain.

Eleanor turned to Clifford. 'What was all that about?' she whispered.

He shook his head. 'I don't know, my lady, but unless there is another explanation, it doesn't look good for the chaplain.'

CHAPTER 31

The end of supper and the rambunctious return of the girls to Holly House couldn't come soon enough for Eleanor. As the front door slammed against the hallway wall, she bounded out through the sitting room's arch with a cheery, 'Welcome home, girls.'

'Thank you, miss!' they chorused, hanging their blazers in a messy line on the hooks and hurling their muddy shoes underneath.

Duffy stepped forward, pulling awkwardly on her jam-smeared jumper.

'We… we wanted to say another thank you, miss.'

'How lovely. And beautifully well-mannered, of course. But what for?'

Duffy hesitated until Morton poked her in the back.

'For yelling so loudly for us on the hockey pitches earlier.'

She laughed. 'Good job no one else noticed though. It wasn't very ladylike, was it?'

Duffy giggled. 'Miss Munn noticed and the games mistress from the other school.'

'Well, then I'm probably in trouble.'

'Not at all!' Morton pushed her way to the front. 'Miss, we've never won two matches in a row before.'

The others all shook their heads.

'We're usually rubbish at hockey,' one of the blonde pigtailed trio piped up.

Eleanor laughed. 'So was I. I think I only really liked the running and shouting. Not that bit with the ball.' She wrinkled her nose, earning another collective round of giggling. 'But I'm sure it's good for something.'

Duffy waved her hand. 'Competitive spirit, cooperation and confidence. Or that's what Miss Munn says.'

'Probably. But not so for knees and shins, huh?' Eleanor pointed along the row of scraped and dirt-flecked legs. 'Just as well it's bath night.'

Morton groaned. 'Oh, but that takes hours! There's never any time left for doing something fun before lights out.'

'Hmm. But perhaps not, if you have an incentive to be quicker.'

The group stared at each other until Morton's face broke into a grin. 'Have you… have you got another surprise for us, miss?'

Duffy elbowed her in the ribs. 'If it isn't rude to ask, miss?'

'No, it isn't.' A doubt flittered through Eleanor's mind. She dismissed it. 'Well, not to my thinking anyway. But don't quote me on that. However, the surprise is ready. It's just awaiting a gaggle of sparklingly clean girls in their pyjamas. And in swapped dressing gowns, of course.'

'Woo-hoo!' Morton yelled as she thundered up the stairs, followed by the others. All that was, except Elsbury, who straggled up last. Something in the girl's demeanour reminded Eleanor of her younger troubled self. She stepped to the bannisters and leaned over.

'Everything alright, Elsbury?'

'Yes. Thank you, miss. Everything… everything is always alright.'

Oh gracious, Ellie! That's what you used to tell yourself every day you were here.

Twenty minutes later, a thunder of footsteps back down the stairs showed bath time was over.

'May we come in, miss?' an eager voice called through.

The gaggle of faces were now scrubbed to a shine, and the hands held out for her inspection looked remarkably clean. She nodded.

'You'll do. Right, into one long crocodile, please. Hands on the shoulders of the person in front of you. Eyes shut tight. No peeping. Under the arch we go. Left. Right. Left.' She led the giggling line through into the sitting room.

'Okay, you can look.'

'Jigsaw puzzles! Hooray!'

The collective shout made Eleanor wince a little.

Duffy looked from the puzzles to Eleanor. 'For us? Really?'

'Yes, all for you. Now, shall we start puzzling?'

'Thank you, miss,' voices called as they scampered between the boxes, dividing up into twos and threes.

'Ooh, this is a zoo picture. Morton, it's got a monkey that looks just like you.'

'Must be the prettiest monkey ever then.' Morton made chimpanzee noises as she plumped down onto her knees.

'I want to do the seaside one!'

'And me! Shuffle up.'

'I want to do the historic London landmarks!'

Elsbury hovered on the edge of the group, peering over the hunched forms of her housemates.

'Come on, Piggy Piggerton,' Duffy called, 'you can join us.'

Eleanor held up another box. 'Or you might fancy a map of the British Empire?' She frowned. 'I'd prefer a map of the world, but I suppose this has got most countries on it. Elsbury? I could do with some help if you do.'

The young girl smiled shyly. 'I'd love to, miss.'

Duffy looked up from her puzzle. 'Of course you would. You're a total geography swot!'

'Well, I hadn't guessed that,' Eleanor fibbed and dropped into a cross-legged position on one of the few spaces left on the rug. 'Which is it first, Elsbury? Corners and edges, or like colours in piles?'

'Corners and edges. Definitely, miss.'

'A puzzler after my own heart!'

Time passed in happy chatter. The puzzles took shape. Dressing-gown sleeves were repeatedly shaken to reveal a host of missing pieces, resulting in more giggles. Eleanor paused to hand out the quarter-pint milk bottles chilling on the kitchen floor. The girls lined up and took one each. She glanced at the clock she'd wound back an hour before they'd come in.

'An hour left, so, let's make the most of it before it's time for lights out.'

Duffy looked at the clock and then at her but said nothing.

Retaking her place beside Elsbury, Eleanor held out the box of pieces.

'Please can you tell us a few of your travel stories while we puzzle, miss?' the young girl asked more boldly than Eleanor had heard her speak before.

'Absolutely. But first, how's the fingerprinting project going?' She'd been dying to find out from the moment the girls had returned but she desperately wanted to avoid the feeling that she was using them to investigate.

The girls all stopped puzzling and crowded around, eager to share their part in the project. As Elsbury had volunteered to organise it, she filled in Eleanor on their progress.

'We've fingerprinted all the girls so far, miss. We're allowed to go into the other classes and ask for them.'

Eleanor nodded. 'And what ink are you using?'

Duffy giggled. 'Just our pen ink. It's great fun, miss. I've got loads of prints of my fingers!'

'And what about the teachers?'

'We've asked most of them as well, miss,' Morton said. 'And the other staff.'

Duffy scowled. 'Old Hepple and his garden cronies didn't want to have their fingerprints taken, but the headmistress told them they had to. She had hers taken first.'

Eleanor frowned. 'So, has anyone refused outright?'

Elsbury, who had left the room for a moment but had returned, shook her head. 'Even Mr Hepple gave us his in the end, miss.' She held up a large piece of card on which smaller pieces of paper had been stuck, each one with a set of fingerprints on and a name underneath. 'There're more in the classroom.'

Eleanor clapped. 'Well done, all of you!'

Elsbury put the card on the table, her face animated. 'It was jolly interesting, miss. We learned that fingerprints were first used in England in 1855, I think it was, but they used fingerprints to seal contracts back in ancient Babylon.'

'Seal contracts? Really?' Something tugged at Eleanor's mind. She frowned and looked around at the... expectant faces. 'Oh, sorry! Yes, I promised to tell you some of my travel tales while you puzzled. Now, where would you like to know about most? Africa? India? Turkey? China, or Persia perhaps?'

A rabble of voices answered with different replies.

Eleanor held up a hand. 'I vote Elsbury chooses since it was her idea. Fair?'

'Fair,' the room agreed in unison.

This seemed to delight and daunt Elsbury in equal measure.

'China, please,' she mumbled, eyes bright with excitement.

'That's so amazing,' Duffy said close to an hour later as the last of the puzzles were finished and Eleanor's final tale ended. 'You must be the bravest, most adventurous woman in the world. I want to be like you when I grow up!'

'And me!' another voice called.

Maybe, but I'm not quite so sure their parents would approve, Ellie!

'Thank you. But other ladies have done similar things. I certainly wasn't the first. Now, it's time for bed.'

Duffy jumped up. 'But we forgot. We were supposed to be sorting out our entry for the house competition this evening, miss!'

Dash it, Ellie, so did you.

'No matter, we've got ten minutes while the last of you finish your milk. Now, give me a clue. What sort of thing would you like to do?'

Duffy stood up. 'Holly girls. House meeting!'

CHAPTER 32

Twenty minutes later they were still thinking of what to do.

Duffy groaned. 'It's really hard when you know the entire school is just going to laugh at you.'

'That's the problem,' one of the pigtailed trio chimed in. 'We don't stand a chance.'

Eleanor clapped her hands. 'Now, I'm sure you wouldn't be the butt of everyone's joke but I know what it's like if something feels like that.'

Morton gasped. 'You do? I thought old people never felt that way.'

Duffy shoved her off her stool with a glare.

'It's supposed to be educational,' the blondest of the trio said.

'Like a song,' added the second.

'Or a poem,' the third said. 'Yuk! That would be so hard to do. All that rhyming and everything.'

'We should tell a story,' Elsbury blurted out. Her cheeks coloured as all eyes turned to her. 'Like Mrs Wadsworth used to tell us.'

Eleanor nodded. 'An excellent idea. What sort of story do you think, though?'

'An adventure story. Like the ones you've told us.'

'We could tell one of yours, miss!' another voice cried.

'It's a lovely sentiment, but that wouldn't fit the criteria of it being something of your own, would it? However, you could make up a story between you.'

'Yes!' Duffy leaped up. 'But rather than read it out, we could act it out!'

Figuring trying to dispatch them off to bed now would be hopeless, Eleanor went over to the basket of notebooks and pens and returned to the circle.

'And you could dress up,' she said as she handed them around.

Duffy jumped up and slapped her hand over her heart. The other girls copied her. Eleanor wondered what on earth this was, but then her own heart faltered as Duffy spoke.

'As leader of Holly House, I promise this will be the best entry ever since Henley was leader!'

Mother. Oh, Ellie!

In the dormitory, Eleanor gave them a few minutes to say their prayers and braid each other's hair. Elsbury was the only one who'd made it into bed, so she set off to the furthest end of the two rows to start her goodnights.

'You had a great idea, Elsbury. The girls are really grateful.'

The girl shrugged her shoulders, her arms just bumps under the covers. 'I... I don't normally say things in the group like that.'

'But when you do, you say very wonderful things that help your friends.'

'I do?'

'Yes. The girls are very lucky to have you as a friend.'

'I suppose.' She shrugged again and bit her bottom lip. 'Friends are better than family, aren't they, miss?'

Eleanor held back the sad frown that threatened. For the first time, she realised the young girl was fiddling with something under the blankets.

'Have you got a special doll or teddy bear under there?'

'No, miss. Something else.'

'May I see? If it isn't too private, of course. You don't have to show me.'

Elsbury peered over her shoulder at the covert pillow fights that had started up around the dorm. Pulling out her arms, she held up a music box covered in mother-of-pearl. With an awkward smile, she thrust it towards Eleanor.

Eleanor took the box gently. 'Who gave you this? It's beautiful.'

'The headmistress. Father sent it by post.'

'With a note, perhaps?' Regretting the question at the single tear this drew, Eleanor reached for a handkerchief and offered it to the girl.

'Yes, miss. But… but I threw it away. Was that a terrible thing to do?'

'I don't think so. But I'm sure your father cares very much about you. He sent you this present after all.'

'Do you think so, miss? The note said he couldn't come to the end-of-school competition day. Just like he couldn't come to Speech Day.' She stopped and closed her eyes. 'I just wish he would come to something. Just once.'

Eleanor swallowed the lump in her throat. 'I know what it feels like to wish someone was around more. But I have learned that it doesn't mean they don't love you. Or miss you even more than you miss them.'

The young girl balled her hands into fists. 'But, he can't miss me, can he, miss? Or he'd be here. Instead, he's always so busy. Always travelling abroad.'

Eleanor patted the girl's hand awkwardly, unsure if anything she said might bring on more tears. In both of them. She looked at the music box.

'Have you opened it, Elsbury?'

The young girl shook her head. 'No, miss.'

'Can we do it together?'

Elsbury nodded. As they both slowly opened the lid, a doll-like ballerina rose, turning as the pas de deux from *Swan Lake* tinkled in the background. Elsbury gasped for behind the ballerina was a hand-painted portrait of her. And, small though it was, the doll's features were a perfect miniature replica of the young girl.

'That's… that's me!'

Eleanor nodded. 'Maybe that answered your question, Elsbury. Your father must have had it specially made. How much time do you think he spent scouring jewellery shops to find one which could create a musical box with his beloved daughter as the ballerina?'

Elsbury stared at the doll as it turned. She shook her head. 'I… I don't know, miss. Ages?'

'Ages and ages. And plenty more ages after that. Sleep well, Elsbury.'

'Thank you, miss.' The young girl closed the music box and slid it under her pillow. 'I will now.'

After all the girls had settled in bed and she'd turned off the lights, she crept downstairs to where Miss Rice was waiting.

'Are they all asleep?'

Eleanor shook her head. 'No, but I don't think they'll give you any trouble. They're exhausted. It's so kind of you to look after them at such short notice. It's only for half an hour at most.'

Miss Rice shrugged. 'It's no problem. I can read my book here as well as in my room. I'm just curious as to why you didn't ask Matron.'

'Oh, I've asked her so often in the last few days, I thought I ought to give her a break. See you in half an hour.'

She hurried out the door before Miss Rice could ask her any more awkward questions.

*

In the chapel, the woman froze on seeing Eleanor sitting at the organ.

'What... what are you doing here?'

Eleanor turned to her.

'You know, Matron, I simply cannot understand how all these pull-out stop things work.'

Matron swallowed hard and darted a glance in the direction Eleanor had seen the chaplain stumble off in earlier. 'How... how long have you been here?'

'Long enough.' Eleanor scanned the woman's face. 'You missed hearing the burglar alarm on the day Mrs Wadsworth died, not because you were in your room, but because you were here with the chaplain, weren't you? You meet him in this spot quite often, don't you?'

Matron's eyes filled with tears. 'He's such a troubled soul. With... with no one else to turn to.'

Eleanor patted the pocket of Matron's uniform where the small blue bottle had lain earlier that afternoon.

'Morphine will do that, I believe. If it becomes an addiction, that is.'

Matron's face crumpled. 'He's a good man. He's barely twenty-six.'

'A war injury?' Eleanor asked gently.

Matron nodded. 'Like so many. Too many. The chaplain was shot in the stomach in Ypres.'

Eleanor blanched, remembering her time as a nurse in military hospitals during the war.

Matron wiped her eyes with the back of her hand. 'The field surgeons did their best, and he's lucky to be with us but... the pain.' She turned to Eleanor. 'Even though it's subsided, he's haunted by it. And... and he reaches out.'

'To you, to supply his addiction?'

'I'm not proud of what I've been doing, Lady Swift.'

'Perhaps not, but errors of judgement founded on noble intentions can never be completely condemned. And earlier on, you did him the best service.'

Matron shook her head and yanked a handkerchief from her sleeve. 'No. No, I didn't. I gave him another bottle.'

'I saw. But you also gave him another ultimatum. But this time you'll stick by it.'

'But… but I'm so worried about what he'll do.'

'Don't worry about that. I know someone who will make sure we help him. Please trust me.'

Matron stared at her wide-eyed. 'But addictions can't be tolerated at St Mary's. Nor what I did for him. I—'

Eleanor grasped the matron's shoulders. 'Listen. Don't mention this to anyone, including Miss Lonsdale, until I ask you to. Okay?'

Matron nodded, then bowed her head and hurried away after the chaplain.

Eleanor shook her head slowly as she watched her go.

Oh, Ellie, how many more sad secrets do you have to uncover before you can catch a killer?

CHAPTER 33

'Another dead end, I'm afraid.'

Seldon's words of greeting as he hurried down the steps into Dunningswade's historic Queen Bess Coaching Inn made Eleanor's heart sink.

Straight to business it seems, Ellie.

He hung his bowler hat on the coat rack, dropped into a seat at the table and pulled out his notebook.

She tried her sweetest smile. 'Hello, Hugh. How have you been these last few days?'

'Busy.' He looked up. 'Sorry. Force of habit, too many years on the job. I'm fine, if rushed. And you?'

'Very well, thank you. Now, I'm happy to get down to the matter in hand, but only while you eat something.'

He hoicked his pocket watch out from his waistcoat and stared at it in disbelief.

'Drat! I'll try, but I should be leaving for London in half an hour.'

'Aha! Then you're in luck.' She waved an arm around the black-beamed walls and ceiling and the displays of medieval weaponry hanging either side of the inglenook fireplace. 'Dunningswade is still quaintly but hopelessly lost in the sixteenth century, so you actually have four hundred years to reach London in time for your appointment.'

Seldon shook his head in amusement, then glanced around at the sound of a reprimanding cough. Having materialised at

Eleanor's side, Clifford nodded discreetly at the offended-looking middle-aged couple taking their seats at the next table.

'Perhaps, my lady, noting that Dunningswade is, in fact, "modernity immersed in tradition" might be a more pleasing description. If you will forgive the correction, of course.'

She resisted the urge to poke out her tongue at him. Instead she asked, 'What delectable delights have you ordered for us, Clifford?'

'Three Ye Olde Peahen and Mead Pies with Trowte Uppon Soppes as an accompaniment. That being the entire menu on offer.'

Modernity, my eye, Ellie!

'Right, let's get started,' Seldon said once Clifford had taken up his usual perched seating position. 'The bursar and the matron. All the leads I set my men to follow have come to nothing.'

'Nothing at all?'

'Well, nothing out of the ordinary, Eleanor.' He shook his head. 'Not being allowed into St Mary's to investigate myself is thoroughly frustrating.' He looked up from his notebook. 'Not that you aren't doing an incredible job. You both are. I hope I've made that clear.'

'You have, thank you.' She fanned her neck with her napkin. With the low ceiling, the June heat was oppressive.

'Anyway, there is some other news. That fingerprint scheme of yours turned up trumps. Well, in one way. We found two sets of prints on Mrs Wadsworth's ladder, as I'm sure you remember.' He paused as a buxom waitress resplendent in white frills and a matching bonnet set a pewter goblet beside his hand with a cheeky grin. Eleanor felt a frisson of jealousy as she watched the woman sashay away, still batting her lashes at him over her shoulder. 'Tasty.'

'Hugh!' Eleanor gawped at him.

He took another swig of his drink. 'Whatever this stuff is, it's more than passable.'

She bit back a relieved smile. *Bless him, Ellie, he really has no clue how dashingly attractive he is. Thank goodness!*

'Well, I'm not a fan, it tastes vile. What is it, Clifford?'

'Revolting, my lady. But authentically so, I'm sure.' He turned to Seldon. 'The two sets of prints, Chief Inspector?'

'Ah, yes.' He referred again to his notebook. 'They were Mrs Wadsworth's and—'

Eleanor leaned forward. 'Yes?'

'Miss Munn's.'

'Oh!' She turned several pages of her notebook back and forth. 'Why am I so disorganised? Don't answer that. Aha! Here it is. Miss Munn said something about the library steps.' She held it out sheepishly to Clifford. 'Any idea what my hieroglyphics say?'

He peered at it through his pince-nez. '"Rabidly?" "Racily?" Ah! "Rarely took her up on her otter."'

'Offer! With two F's. As well you know, you terror! But even if Mrs Wadsworth had only rarely taken her up on her offer, her fingerprints would still be on the ladder. And she'd know that. So maybe she saw no point in using gloves if she's the killer, or had no time to put them on?'

Seldon shook his head. 'Most people have no idea fingerprinting is possible as we've said, so the fact that her prints were on the ladder gets us nowhere, really. Plus, we have determined absolutely no motive for her to kill Mrs Wadsworth. Admittedly, we're actually pretty thin on motives all round. But I'm sticking with my hunch that we are dealing with just one murderer for now, and Miss Munn also has a perfect alibi for Miss Small's death.'

'Dash it! So I suppose even though you found her prints, she's still off our suspect list?'

Seldon and Clifford nodded.

'Okay. What about Miss Small's art room?'

'Plenty of fingerprints around the classroom, obviously. The trouble is, even with the fingerprints of the entire school to hand, thanks to your excellent ruse, it's not an exact science matching them up. Not yet, anyway. Give it a few more years.'

Eleanor frowned. 'What do you mean?'

'Well, we managed to match most of the prints we could read to pupils and staff, but there were a couple that didn't quite fit, but that's not uncommon.'

'Perhaps an outside workman was in the classroom recently?' Clifford said.

Seldon nodded. 'That often happens. Someone comes in who isn't normally there to fix something or make a delivery or whatever and leaves their prints all over the place and, of course, we don't have a match. I'll check with Miss Lonsdale if anyone's been in lately.' He sat back. 'Miss Lonsdale hasn't passed on any more alibis for our other suspects relating to Miss Small's death to me. Have you uncovered any?'

'Sadly not,' Clifford said. 'But we do have a few schemes in mind, do we not, my lady?'

She nodded. 'Fiendish ones too.'

Seldon stared at her. 'Then perhaps you should tell me what you've got planned?'

Eleanor shook her head. 'Perhaps we shouldn't.'

Clifford cleared his throat. 'Plausible deniability can be a useful tool when facing interrogation from further up the chain of command perhaps, Chief Inspector?'

'Ah, food.' Seldon's stomach rumbled loudly at the sight of the waitress bearing three golden-brown pies with rich gravy bubbling from thick crusts.

'Thank ye, fair maiden,' Clifford said matter-of-factly as he turned the plate inspecting his meal.

'Welcumen, sire.' She giggled. With another coquettish wiggle at Seldon, she disappeared with her tray.

'Don't encourage her, Clifford,' Eleanor grumbled quietly.

The corners of her butler's lips imperceptibly quirking didn't miss her.

Seldon attacked his pie with gusto. 'While you're terrorising the staff about where they were at the time of Miss Small's death, I'll chivvy her autopsy along. The department can be notoriously slow at the best of times, but they've suffered the same level of budget cuts we have so they're horrendously behind. They haven't even done the Wadsworth woman.' He gave Eleanor an apologetic wince. 'I mean, Mrs Wadsworth, yet.'

'Can't you pull rank, Hugh? Get them to yank your dead bodies to the front of the queue.' She wrinkled her nose. 'That didn't come out right.'

Clifford cleared his throat. 'I imagine, my lady, the deceased need to be examined close to the order in which they died otherwise vital clues can be missed as the body changes state.'

'Yes. And, anyway, pulling rank wouldn't help as Mrs Wadsworth and Miss Small aren't the only bodies I've sent in this week.'

They all stared at their pies.

'Oh, Hugh,' Eleanor said. 'I really don't know how you do what you do every day. You deserve a medal. Genuinely.'

He smiled. 'For what? Being the grumpiest policeman in England?'

She laughed. 'Okay, two medals. Now, we'll tell you what *we* found out about Hepple and Mrs Wadsworth.'

Clifford rose. 'Perhaps you would excuse me a moment, my lady, Chief Inspector?'

He strode away towards the long oak bar, leaving her frowning after him. She turned back to Seldon.

'Anyway, Miss Lonsdale confessed something to us.' She looked around and lowered her voice. 'When we showed her the woollen bobble Clifford found, she told us that Hepple and Mrs Wadsworth had been having an affair. Incredible, isn't it?'

Seldon's brows rose, but he shrugged. 'Human nature will always find a way to achieve a burning desire.'

'Like an all-consuming passion? Like… true love?' she said more breathlessly than intended, running her hand over her notebook as her cheeks coloured.

'More like taking a life.'

She sighed to herself. *There goes another lost romantic moment, Ellie.*

Seldon continued oblivious. 'How long had Mr Hepple and Mrs Wadsworth been engaged in their liaison?'

'A fair while. Before Miss Lonsdale joined, she was certain of that.'

'Hmm, a lover's tiff turned sour?' His pen darted across his notebook with his customary short, efficient strokes.

'Miss Lonsdale didn't think so.'

He grunted. 'So, do the entire staff know?'

'No, the only other person who knows is Mrs Coulson.'

'How is the notorious jar of horseradish treating you, by the way?'

'Like an unwelcome idiot cousin.'

That drew a deep, rich chuckle. He stared up at the sagging ceiling for a full minute before looking down and shaking his head. 'I don't think it's Hepple. Apart from anything else, he wasn't the one to report seeing the intruder. And it would have been most unlikely no one would have noticed his absence on the rear door. Or that another teacher wouldn't have spotted him in the school.'

'I agree.' Eleanor drew a line through Hepple's name on her list. 'Speaking of Horseradish Coulson.'

Clifford, having returned with a tray of tea things, sniffed. 'I believe the deputy headmistress' first name is, in fact, Isobel, my lady.'

'Yes, but that isn't funny, Clifford!'

Seldon laughed again. 'What about her?'

'Well, just wait until you hear what Miss Lonsdale told me she'd said.'

She relayed the whole scenario of Mrs Coulson's attempts to have Mrs Wadsworth sacked and her threat to get rid of her by any means.

Seldon frowned. 'Incriminating, for sure. But why not go after Hepple too?'

Eleanor struggled to put it charitably. Clifford beat her to it.

'I believe her ladyship wishes to say Mrs Coulson has minimal regard for the staff engaged in manual, rather than educational, employment. To the point that they almost do not feature in her view of the school at all.'

'Yes, that. Delicately put, Clifford.'

Seldon nodded. 'I know the type. And how recently was this affair between Hepple and Mrs Wadsworth exposed, Eleanor?'

'Quite recently. Miss Lonsdale found out shortly after she'd started. '

'Recent enough for Mrs Coulson to still be enraged that she had been overruled by the headmistress?'

'Are you thinking, Chief Inspector,' said Clifford, 'that Mrs Coulson might have shaken Mrs Wadsworth from the library steps in a fit of rage?'

'It certainly sounds like she had the motive to. Plus, she might have considered it her last resort to preserve the precious reputation of St Mary's.'

'So,' Eleanor said, 'she takes over as number-one suspect then?'

'Steady on.' Seldon held onto the end of her pen, stopping her from circling the name. 'We've still got several other candidates, including Matron, the chaplain and—'

'Actually, we can cross Matron and the chaplain off. I think.'

'Really?'

Seldon tucked into the remains of his pie as she explained. Once she'd finished, he picked up his pen again.

'Eleanor, do you believe Matron really was in the chapel supplying the chaplain with morphine when the burglar alarm rang and Mrs Wadsworth was murdered?'

'I do.' She watched in amazement as he crossed both names off his list of suspects. 'Just like that?' she asked.

A flush spread up his neck. 'You've proved to be right before, Eleanor. I'm learning.'

Without a word, she too crossed out Matron and the chaplain's names in her notebook, trying and failing to hold in a smile.

'So we are planning to grapple with the bursar next.' She gave an involuntary shudder at the image this brought to mind. 'It was one of your tasks for us to follow up. But we haven't had a chance yet to check out the legitimacy of his "old war injury". However, I do remember another snippet of information that may, or may not, prove useful. Miss Rice mentioned he often works late, which doesn't fit my impression of him at all.'

'Why not?'

She glanced at Clifford. 'At the risk of being reprimanded for publicly assassinating a man's character with unfounded observations, to my mind the bursar's interests lie purely in the wrong kind of figures.' At Seldon's blank look, she added. 'Not the sort that you enter into accounting ledgers.' She imitated the waitress' coquettish wiggle, which made Seldon blush.

Clifford cleared his throat as he topped up their teacups. 'Why then might the gentleman be working late, do we presume?'

'Because he needs to catch up on all the work he never does during the day because he's too busy leching after the female staff.'

'Or perhaps because he wants to make irregular adjustments to his ledgers unseen, my lady?'

'Okay, it could also be that.'

'Right,' Seldon said. 'I'll try to lay my hands on a set of the school's accounts from last year. Not that I'll understand them.'

'Show them to Clifford,' Eleanor said. 'He's the most ferocious bloodhound when it comes to financial rectitude. Certainly when it comes to Henley Hall's myriad household accounts.'

Clifford raised an eyebrow. 'I'm sure you have appropriately trained men available to you, Chief Inspector.'

Seldon shook his head. 'The fraud team is as down on personnel as we are. I might indeed have to call on you.'

Clifford bowed. 'Then it will be a pleasure to be a "ferocious bloodhound" in the pursuit of justice.'

Eleanor laughed and turned her notebook towards Seldon so they could check their amended list of suspects tallied.

Staff eliminated (for now)
Miss Small – dead!
Mrs Jupe – alibi for Miss Small's death
Miss Munn – fingerprints on ladder but alibi for Miss Small's death
Mr Hepple – had bobble from Mrs Wadsworth's cardigan, but loved her!
Matron – taking morphine to Chaplain at time of Mrs Wadsworth's death – believe her
Chaplain – in chapel with Matron

Staff not eliminated
Mrs Coulson – left stage so opportunity – wanted Mrs Wadsworth dismissed as believed she was a bad moral influence so motive (No alibi for Miss Small's death)
Bursar – off stage so opportunity – faked injury (?) Maybe fiddling accounts (?) and Mrs Wadsworth found out (?) so motive (No alibi for Miss Small's death)

Miss Rice – left stage so opportunity. Said Bursar asked her to swap and be on stage, but maybe lying? Why would she want Mrs Wadsworth dead? No motive (No alibi for Miss Small's death)

Eleanor tapped her pen against the doodle of the bloated toad she'd drawn to represent the bursar.

'Clifford and I will start with him the minute we get back to school.'

'Let us not forget Miss Rice.' Clifford waved at the waitress for the bill. 'There is still the conundrum over whose story is correct about why she was on stage at Speech Day.'

Seldon grunted. 'Hopefully your cunning ruse this afternoon will encourage the bursar to reveal more about that?'

Eleanor felt faintly sick. *Let's hope Miss Rice was right, Ellie, and that's all he reveals!*

CHAPTER 34

'Are you sure this is the best time to catch him, Clifford?'

'I have it on good authority, my lady. The method you have suggested I feel, however, is still' – he cleared his throat – 'highly questionable.'

'Too late. Now, it was Hepple's men who told you of the bursar's habits?'

'Indeed. Mrs Jupe and another female member of staff regularly find an hour to play tennis before supper twice a week.'

She grimaced. 'That man has nothing but slime coursing through his veins. No wonder she was so scathing about him.'

She peered around the corner of the kitchen and refectory dining room.

'Here come the ladies now. Mind you… Gracious!'

'My lady?' He went to crane his neck forward.

'Mrs Jupe's tennis skirt is a tad on the short side, wouldn't you say?'

He jumped back hastily. 'I shall take your word for that.'

'Hmm, if she really thinks he's such an oily tick and he regularly happens by when they're playing, why would she risk showing an extra inch of leg?'

'I have noted that the lady is unusually tall. Perhaps finding suitably lengthened tennis attire has proven difficult?'

'You're right, of course. Well, if it was me, I'd have sewn a bed sheet to the bottom so that my skirt flapped around my ankles rather than have him ogling anything he shouldn't.'

'Admirably decorous, my lady.'

'Not really, I'd just like to spoil his lecherous fun.'

'Equally laudable. The grounds staff informed me he walks the less conspicuous way round, via the pool, netball courts and then the short run of woods at the top end of the field.'

'Perfect. My old haunt. I know just the spot.'

On reaching the small copse of red-berried rowan and black-fruited elderflower trees, it looked to Eleanor much as it had done when she was there as a child. One of the few areas left to its own devices, the jumble of branches had woven themselves into a thick, low canopy over a tall carpet of meadow foxtail and cocksfoot grasses, punctuated by the odd militant fern.

'Gracious, I used to love it in here. I made a den in the middle of the trees. I was forever hiding out and swinging from the branches.'

'And frustrating Mr Hepple beyond all measure, we've since learned.'

'I know. It's incredible that he's still here, isn't it?'

'Not really, my lady. A guaranteed job is likely to attract longevity of service, whatever the employment.'

'True. But what I meant was that, unbeknown to me at the time, he was a part of my life then and for this short period, he is again.'

'The roots of our past run deep, my lady.'

She looked over at the trees again. 'I'm glad we've discounted him for the moment. I'd hate to send Hepple to the noose. It would be like chopping off and digging out one of my own roots. Let's hope our murderer is the slimy reptilian bursar then.'

'Actually, that is a common misconception. Reptiles are generally not slimy—'

'Not now, Clifford!'

'As you wish.' He produced an extendable monocular from somewhere she couldn't fathom and trained it on the half-visible figure moving with a pronounced limp in the distance. 'I believe the aforementioned reptile is slithering his way towards your trap as we speak. Good luck, my lady.'

He took a step backwards and vanished into the box hedging behind him. Eleanor sprinted across the path, threw two hands onto the top of the waist-high wooden fence marking the forbidden zone of the copse and swung herself nimbly over it. Undaunted by the sound of ripping skirt fabric, she looked about.

'Hello, old friend,' she whispered, patting the twisted trunk of one of the ancient elderflower trees, before hauling herself into it.

From her hidden vantage point ten feet up among the foliage, she could see the bursar making his way along the path, still leaning heavily on his borrowed walking stick.

Perhaps he isn't acting, Ellie? That's quite the performance, given that there's no one around.

She crawled out as far as she dared on the thickest branch and waited. When the bursar was only a few feet away, her plan went awry as she made the acquaintance of a particularly grouchy wasp that took umbrage at her intrusion and stung her forehead with a searing barb.

'OW!' She lost her grip and landed in an awkward heap on the scrubby grass below, her left ankle stuck out an angle.

'Oh goodness, dear lady, are you alright?' The bursar ran a hand across his over-pomaded hair as he reached the fence. 'Not feeling quite so "horribly independent" as you described yourself when we first met now, perhaps?'

'Not quite,' she called back, gritting her teeth at his syrupy tone. 'Stupidly, I've got myself into the most ridiculous situation trying to relive a childhood memory. I used to love this little copse, you see.'

'Aha! The stricken damsel does need a shining knight, after all. Just a moment, dear lady.' He cleared the fence with inches to spare without, she noted, the use of his stick. Despite the pain in her leg, she watched him carefully, nodding to herself as he landed on both feet without so much as a wince. Dropping beside her, he pointed to her forehead. 'Didn't St Mary's teach you insects are dangerous?'

Biting back a retort that it was reptiles in human form one needed to avoid, she forced a laugh instead.

'Really, you think I'd be old enough to know better than going head to head with nature at my age.'

'Youthfulness never learns. It's a very becoming feature.'

She frowned, the angry welt on her forehead stinging even harder.

'Perhaps you might be kind enough to find something I could use to help me limp back over the fence, Bursar?' She went to stand but cried out as her ankle gave her an even sharper stab than the wasp's barb. 'Dash it! I've really twisted it.'

'Of course, my dear. I'll be but a trice!'

As the bursar disappeared nimbly back over the fence on his mercy mission, Clifford stepped out from behind another tree and placed one of the milk crates from Holly House in front of the fence.

'My lady, your ankle. I must—'

'We don't have time, Clifford. He'll be back in a moment.'

It was only three or four minutes later that the bursar returned, a little breathless, with a small pair of steps. He pulled up short as he took in the sight of Eleanor leaning on *his* side of the fence.

'Dear lady, how did you manage to climb back over the fence with your injured ankle? I'm perplexed.'

'Oh, Bursar, my sincere apologies, I got back over as best I could. You see, the minute you left, I pictured scrambling over and, even with your kind and gallant assistance, my mind couldn't conjure up anyway to do so while maintaining even an inch of ladylike modesty.'

'I had hoped to see,' he said distractedly.

'To see what?'

'Goodness, no, no, not to see anything.' He feigned horror. 'Never. I meant, erm, I had hoped to help you maintain your modesty and ensure you didn't further your awful injury at the same time.'

'You're so kind. Would you mind terribly if I borrowed your walking stick? I'll limp straight to Matron and get it sorted out.'

'With sincere pleasure, dear lady. Allow me.' He pressed the stick into her hand. 'I don't suppose you would take my arm and let me accompany you?'

'I don't suppose I would! I might be an "old girl", but I refuse to feel like one.'

A very painful few minutes later, she was grateful to be sitting with her foot up on an armchair in Clifford's cottage while he fussed about her, proffering all manner of ointments, pain-relieving powders and a seemingly endless supply of ice.

'How on earth did you happen to have all this to hand, Clifford?'

'Somehow it seemed judicious when you insisted the only way to snare the bursar was to take some sort of fall, my lady. I was immediately transported back to your first summer at Henley Hall as his lordship's ward.'

'The one where you and I fought like cat and dog, perchance?'

'That would be it. Also, the one where, despite being only nine years old, you refused to yield to reason, stricture or pleading and fell from the tallest tree in his lordship's orchard.'

'I remember. That hurt too. Anyway, at least we've definitely proved that the bursar's so-called injury is a total fiction.'

'Unlike yours, my lady.'

'Whatever. The point is, we've got him!'

'But have we?'

'Yes!' She took in his arched brow and groaned. 'Oh, go on, break it to me gently. I'm an invalid, remember.'

'We might have uncovered the deception of his leg injury—'

'Exactly! Why on earth fake something like that? Obviously so he could swap with Miss Rice and be in the school office when the bell rang. He'd have had time to dash to the library unseen and hide before Mrs Wadsworth got there. Then, all he had to do was make sure he wasn't spotted on his way back to the office.'

'Indeed, and if he were to be fiddling the school's accounts, Mrs Wadsworth is exactly the sort of precise-minded individual to have discovered his wrongdoing.'

'So, it's him then, surely?' She scanned his face, then slowly shook her head. 'Isn't it?'

CHAPTER 35

The mantelpiece clock in Miss Lonsdale's study chimed nine times that evening. Eleanor groaned, wishing her ankle would stop throbbing.

'Come on, Hugh. Where are you?'

Clifford snapped the case of his pocket watch closed for the umpteenth time. 'Punctuality cannot be easy to maintain in the chief inspector's line of work.'

'Miss Lonsdale didn't seem to think so. She's severely annoyed Seldon hasn't rung.'

'The lady carries enormous responsibility in heading up such a prestigious school. I—'

'Alright, Mr Even-Handed. Either way, she waited over an hour for Hugh to call and now she's had to leave to go to High Table with the sixth form.'

'Perhaps we should take advantage of the chief inspector's lateness to reconsider our conclusion concerning the guilt, or otherwise, of the bursar?'

'Okay, what was your deduction again?'

He cleared his throat. 'Unfortunately, I feel your ruse, although faultlessly carried out—'

'Clifford! Get to the point, please.'

'The result might easily have been achieved without personal injury had reason and prudence prevailed.'

'The weightier point!'

'As you wish, my lady. That point is, all we have proved is that the bursar's injury is false, or exaggerated. We are assuming that he faked it in order to kill Mrs Wadsworth because of the timing. Suppose, however, he faked it at that specific time for a different reason? The man has a large, if fragile, ego. And what better time to display an old war wound than when the school will be full of military men and their very sympathetic wives.'

'Speech Day!'

'Exactly. Assuming this as a possible alternative scenario, it begs the question why, if that is the case, would such a man then negate his chance of such sympathetic adulation by insisting that Miss Rice took his place on the stage?'

They spun around as Miss Rice's blonde finger-waves bobbed around the door.

'So sorry to interrupt, Lady Swift, but it's Detective Chief Inspector Seldon on the telephone.'

Was she listening at the keyhole, Ellie?

'Thank you. Put him through. Miss Lonsdale will be back shortly.'

Even though she was expecting it, the jangle of the telephone made Eleanor jump.

'Hugh? Oh, Miss Rice, it's still you. Yes, thank you. Please put the inspector through now.'

She tapped the arm of her chair impatiently until the crackling stopped. A sharp click was followed by silence.

'Hello?'

'Eleanor?' Seldon's deep voice came down the line. 'Is that you?'

'Hugh! What's going on? You're an hour late.'

'That's the least of our problems, I'm afraid.' He sounded tired again. And… *depressed, Ellie?*

She forced a laugh. 'You know you really need to work on your greetings.'

'Seriously, Eleanor, you need to listen. Not protest. Not question. Not argue. And definitely not make life any more difficult than it became an hour ago, blast it!'

She turned to frown at Clifford but realised he had disappeared in his usual silent fashion.

She pulled a face at the handset. 'Listening.'

'Thank you. There are a few things you need to hear and you aren't going to like any of them. But first, why have you answered the telephone? I was expecting to be put through to Miss Lonsdale.'

'You're so late, she's had to go. She won't be back for at least another twenty minutes or so.'

'No bad thing. I'll call back and tell her after I've told you then.'

'Told me what?'

'Miss Small's autopsy came in.'

'And?'

'Natural causes.'

'Nonsense! I'd bet Gladstone that she was murdered.' There was silence at the other end. 'Alright, I'm listening.'

'Finally. Thank you. Now, you did everything you could. I understand how immensely frustrating it is, trust me. Clifford's vermillion paint theory was a good one, but that was quickly dismissed by the boys downstairs. Apparently, Miss Small would have needed to have ingested a large dose for that to be the cause and—'

'Let me guess. There was none in her stomach. Just as there was none around her mouth or on her clothing. But we only half thought it might be that, anyway.'

'Precisely. And… Mrs Wadsworth's autopsy is back too.'

'And that's the same, isn't it?' She held her breath. 'Hugh?'

'Yes. Natural causes of injury.' Again, papers were shuffled. 'Blow to the side of the head caused fatal internal bleeding due to the force of the fall sustained.'

'Due to the force with which she was *thrown off the ladder!*'

'Eleanor, you promised.'

'I didn't, actually, but I am trying really hard. It's just that, oh dash it!'

'I know. This matters enormously to you. Which means it does to me. But my hands are totally tied. Hopefully, you'll see that when I get the chance to finish.'

Clifford came through the door and she beckoned him over hurriedly.

'Hugh, wait a moment.'

Clifford strode over and placed a tall glass of something that looked like cold tea beside her.

'Err, thank you.'

'I needed a ruse to check Miss Rice wasn't listening in, my lady.'

'Ah!'

'Eleanor?' Seldon's voice called. 'Who's with you?'

'It's Clifford. He was checking Miss Rice wasn't eavesdropping.' Seldon's tone was urgent. 'And was she?'

Clifford leaned into the handset. 'No, Chief Inspector.'

'Good. Now, are you in the loop, Clifford?'

'Both autopsies back. Both natural causes,' Eleanor said.

Clifford nodded. 'Yes, Chief Inspector, I am up to date with developments.'

'Actually you're not,' Seldon's weary voice said. 'Neither of you are yet. Mrs Wadsworth's case – and Miss Small's – have both been closed. Both death by natural causes, both accidental. And' – he hastened on at Eleanor's gasp – 'no I cannot pull rank. This has come from the top.'

Eleanor was stunned. 'You're telling me your superior has closed the case even though you don't agree, Hugh?'

Seldon sighed. 'No, not my superior. My superior's superior!'

'The chief of police?'

'No, Whitehall. It seems someone at St Mary's informed Sir Oswald Goldsworthy, Private Secretary to His Majesty, that the police were carrying out unwarranted murder investigations at his daughter's school.'

'Oh no!' *Sir Oswald Goldsworthy, Ellie! That's the head girl's father.*

Seldon laughed mirthlessly. 'It gets better. My superior informed me that he was also informed by Sir Oswald that he'd been told the police were using unauthorised, and untrained, assistants to spy on the girls. One, of course, being his daughter!'

'But, Hugh, that's not true! Well, the spying on his daughter part. Have you any idea who it was who told Sir Oswald?'

'No idea. I take it as you've asked me, you've no idea either?'

'No… not that I've got any evidence for.'

Mrs Coulson, Ellie, it must be! She never wanted an investigation in the first place. Unless it's the killer and they're scared we're getting too close? Maybe they're one and the same!

'I hope you're not in trouble, Hugh.'

'Let's just say I've acquired more black marks to my record than you ever did in your entire history as a pupil there. If, of course, that's possible.'

'Dash it, I so wish you were here. I probably still wouldn't say the right thing, but I'd love it all the same.'

'Absolutely, you wouldn't. But I'd still jump at the chance.'

'Look, don't worry, Clifford and I will come up with a plan.'

'No, Eleanor! No! All the free rein I should never have given you up to now ended an hour ago. Just as mine did. You both need to pack up investigating immediately. That's an order. With apologies for having to be so direct. If it gets out that you're still there investigating on my behalf for even a day longer—'

'Oh, alright. Instructions received and understood.'

'Thank you. I knew deep down you would. My superior's dispatched me on a case miles up north with the hope that Sir Oswald will huff and puff for a day or two and then let it drop. Without, hopefully, insisting on any sackings. I'll be gone for several days. You won't be able to contact me, I'm afraid.'

The door opened and Miss Lonsdale entered. She stopped short and looked from one to the other.

'Has the chief inspector finally graced us with a call?'

Eleanor nodded mutely and handed over the receiver. A few minutes later the headmistress placed the receiver on the cradle and leaned back in her chair.

'Lady Swift, what a relief.'

Eleanor nodded briefly, not trusting herself to speak.

'You and the chief inspector did a remarkable job, given the restraints you were under. And Mr Clifford, of course. And I do understand exactly why you felt Mrs Wadsworth's death – and Miss Small's to a lesser extent – was suspicious. But even you must be heartened by the news that both deaths were simply tragic accidents.' She spread her hands. 'Lady Swift, I'm also eternally grateful for all your time and efforts with the Holly House girls. And, Mr Clifford, you too, in helping Mr Hepple and his team.'

He gave a brief bow from the shoulders. 'It has been a pleasure, Headmistress. And my sincere gratitude for the use of the spare cottage. It has served myself and Master Gladstone most admirably.'

'Excellent! Well, I'm sure you've both got some packing to do, so I'll let you go. Thank you once again for all your splendid efforts on St Mary's behalf.'

CHAPTER 36

In her temporary bedroom in Holly House, Eleanor stared glumly at the disorganised chaos. She hadn't even got around to unpacking properly, and here she was forced to leave. And now, after Seldon's news and the chance to get justice for her favourite teacher gone, she felt too bereft to even tackle packing up the small amount she had pulled haphazardly from her cases.

Despite the mixed feelings being back at her old school had evoked, she realised she was going to miss it. And the girls. Especially the girls. They were all in lessons so she wouldn't even have a chance to say a proper goodbye.

She dropped onto the edge of the bed. Maybe a part of her didn't want to leave because she'd discovered a connection with her mother that she'd never had. She'd stayed in this very boarding house. No doubt charging noisily up the stairs and drawing silly faces in the steam of the bathroom mirrors, giggling over apple pie beds and swapped dressing gowns just as she herself had without ever knowing. And before she'd taken that all in, and possibly discovered more, she had to go.

'Come on, Ellie. Buck up,' she said aloud.

'Actually, my lady,' Clifford's measured tone came through from the landing outside. 'Instead, might I suggest we make short work of packing.' His suited arms appeared in the doorway holding two cases, the rest of him remaining out of sight. 'Together?'

'Clifford!' She ran to the door, noting that – inevitably – he was respectfully facing away so he couldn't see into her room. 'Much as

I heartily wish you could be, you can't be in Holly House. What about St Mary's protocol?'

'I told Miss Lonsdale that you were in no state to pack your own things. And as the girls are in lessons for several hours yet, there is no fear of them catching me. The lady did not argue. Too much.'

'Thank you, but—' She grabbed the pristine handkerchief he held out and tried to stem the salty streams coursing down her cheeks. 'Oh, Clifford, I can't believe I'm going to let Mrs Wadsworth down. I feel so terrible. She was so kind to me when I really needed someone. I don't believe a word of the natural-causes verdict. Nor for Miss Small. She was so young and so passionate. And she's gone too. And whoever did it is going to walk scot-free. It's so wrong. I've failed them both.'

Clifford cleared his throat. 'I can only offer the consolation, small I know, that it is not you who has failed either lady.'

'You blame Hugh?'

He shook his head. 'No, my lady. He is, as we both noted, a good man, just one caught in an impossible situation. If he had refused to stop the investigation, he would simply have been removed, and a replacement appointed who would have done so.'

She sighed. 'I know. In truth, we were only able to investigate Mrs Wadsworth's death – and Miss Small's – because he bent the rules. Which was as hard for him to countenance as it ever is for you. And he made it clear he may already have lost his job over this. And that if we carry on investigating, there will be no "if" about it.'

'My lady, with your permission, I should very much like to take you home with immediate expediency. The brandy, walnuts and Stilton still await in the Rolls, although we might choose a less emotive topic than we had planned for our return journey. I promise, however, to tell you everything I can about your mother tomorrow if that would suit?'

'Deal. Thank you.' She dried her eyes. 'But how do you intend to help me pack without entering my bedroom?'

'That is easy, my lady. I have learned an important lesson from you on this venture. Sometimes rules are meant not to be bent, but broken.' At her gasp, he opened the first suitcase, holding it across his arms with the lid obscuring his view. 'However, I was recently introduced to a new style of packing which previously, and surprisingly, had never occurred to me.'

She laughed. 'Tell me, how does that new style go exactly?'

'It's ingenious. I believe one simply pulls every item of clothing out of wherever it may have been hurled and rams it in the nearest case until it is full. And then, and this is the really ingenious part, one simply moves on to the next one.' The suitcase shuddered slightly.

'You mean like this?' She hurled the first muddle of clothes into the waiting case.

A groan came from the other side. 'Y-e-s, my lady. Regretfully, just like that.'

In the Rolls she buried her face in Gladstone's soft wrinkles. As they drove away from Holly House, she looked out the rear window and shook her head.

'You know, Clifford, I just couldn't bring myself to write the girls a goodbye note since the ink would have run all over the page with more tears, dash it.'

'Perhaps a letter, which I shall take to the post office as soon as it opens in the morning? They would delight in receiving a missive from you. Which, I hope you will tell them, was penned in your house pyjamas, fighting a wilful bulldog for space on the chaise longue?'

She smiled. 'Followed by supper in the kitchen with the staff I have missed so much. And finished off with an unladylike amount of Uncle Byron's favourite port and Stilton crackers through into the small hours over a chess rematch I will inevitably lose?'

'Absolutely, my lady.'

She sat back and closed her eyes as the Rolls rounded the last bend in the driveway before the school's gates. But rather than drive through them, she felt Clifford bring the Rolls to a stop.

Oh, not now, Ellie! Whatever it is, we just want to get out of here as quickly as possible and lick our wounds. She opened her eyes. 'Clifford, why have you stopped? In fact, I don't care. Just drive on, will you?'

'Would that I could do as you bid, my lady. But… we have a problem.' He pointed through the windscreen.

She followed the direction of his finger.

'Oh, my!'

A line of Holly House girls, arms linked, stared back at her. She could see now why he'd stopped. They were completely blocking the driveway between the two small stone gatehouses.

'Oh gracious, Clifford, what are they doing? I can't really have managed to teach them to be extra naughty in just a few days, can I? I tried so hard to be strict and stick to St Mary's rules.'

'It would appear you failed, my lady. You have bred a veritable band of insurgents, it appears, which' – he turned to her, his eyes twinkling – 'I am highly delighted to see. But—' He pointed in the rear-view mirror as Miss Lonsdale appeared behind the car, her black gown billowing out behind her.

She marched up to Eleanor's window and rapped on the glass. 'Lady Swift.'

Eleanor groaned and wound down her window. 'Miss Lonsdale, I'm so sorry. I had nothing to do with this. They are a delightful group of girls, really.' She looked back at them. 'And… and it is such a wrench to leave them so suddenly.'

The headmistress glanced at the girls, her lips pursed.

'It seems they feel exactly the same about you. To the point that the entire Holly House contingent left their classes without permission and set up this impromptu roadblock the minute they found out. Although how they did, I don't know.'

'Sorry, found out what?'

'That you were leaving right now, of course. Appearing unbidden into my study the ringleaders, Duffy, Morton and Elsbury, were most insistent, if hearteningly articulate, in detailing just how much the end of term was inconceivable without you. Normally, I wouldn't brook such behaviour. But' – she seemed to wrestle with herself – 'apart from the inconvenience of arranging for yet another temporary housemistress, I would rather avoid any further disruption for the children. At least until the end of this term. Which as you know is only a few days away.'

'Oh gracious!' Eleanor muttered again, accepting another pristine handkerchief from Clifford. She waved at the girls' anxious faces, noting Elsbury was in the middle of the line with Morton and Duffy on either side. 'That's so very kind of you, Miss Lonsdale. But… you were rather insistent only a short while ago that I left.'

Miss Lonsdale hesitated for a moment. 'Nonsense. That was when you were here, well,' – she glanced at the girls, and lowered her voice – 'investigating Mrs Wadsworth's and Miss Small's deaths. Now that those are all cleared up, I'm inviting you to stay until the end of term purely in your capacity as temporary housemistress of Holly House.'

Oh, Ellie? What about Seldon? She wrestled with her conscience. *He didn't actually say you had to leave the premises, Ellie. He just said stop investigating. If you stay, at least you won't be letting these children down the way you've let Mrs Wadsworth down.* She stared at the Holly House girls again, who were collectively holding their breath. Despite herself, she found herself nodding.

'Good.' Miss Lonsdale straightened up and addressed the girls. 'Lady Swift has agreed to stay on. Now—'

A shrill cheer drowned out her next words. Eleanor followed Clifford in slapping her hands over her ears. Miss Lonsdale waited until the noise had died down and continued.

'Now, girls, get back to your classes immediately. And remember, this sort of behaviour will not be tolerated on another occasion. Be very clear about that.'

She waited as the children filed past Eleanor's window muttering, 'Thank you, miss,' none of them daring to linger or say more. Miss Lonsdale turned and followed the last of the girls into the main school, leaving Clifford to restart the Rolls and turn the car around.

Eleanor leaned back in her seat and closed her eyes again.

'Perhaps, if it's all the same to you, Clifford, before we unpack we might just first go—'

But for the second time, she was interrupted by the Rolls stopping. She opened her eyes and smiled.

Inside his cottage, Clifford went straight through to the kitchen and put the kettle on. She collapsed into one of the armchairs, Gladstone laying his heavy head and paws in her lap. Clifford reappeared in his flowery apron.

'Thank you for once again reading my mind, Clifford. I don't think I can face going back to the boarding house just yet. It's been rather a rollercoaster the last few hours. And I'm stunned at the action of the girls.'

'I am not, my lady. Not at all.'

'But what do I know about children? About nine- to eleven-year-old girls especially? Although I suppose I was one once. But when I agreed to stay on for the investigation...' She frowned. 'But let's not talk about that. Anyway, I thought the girls would view me as some sort of creature from another planet.'

'Tentacles and head-to-toe silvery scales tend to bring that impression out in children, my lady.'

She laughed. 'I didn't realise you'd noticed, you terror! But seriously, I'm so touched that they asked if I could stay.'

'I feel "insisted" might be a more accurate description.'

She sighed. 'You know, Clifford, I have no idea what the next few days will bring, but it can't be anything like the last few!'

CHAPTER 37

'Miss, this is so much fun!' Morton spun excitedly round the Holly House sitting room, arms out like an aeroplane. She ended up in a tangle with the curtains, sweeping a row of books off the windowsill. 'Oops!'

'I'm delighted to hear it, Morton,' Eleanor said over the other girls' giggles. 'But if you're that enthusiastic you'll actually fall off the stage. And your entry needs to be taken seriously, remember?'

'Yes, miss.' Morton bundled the books vaguely back in place. 'We're going to show the rest of the school we aren't babies!'

Duffy stood and tapped her notebook with her pencil like a bandmaster assembling her musicians. 'Right! Girls who are playing a character in the performance? Do you all know who you are supposed to be and what you're supposed to do?'

Half the girls nodded vigorously.

'And prop girls? You've practised your poses for each set change?'

The other half leaped up and demonstrated they had.

'Excellent,' Eleanor said. 'You've all worked very hard. Well done. I can't wait.' Out of the corner of her eye she noticed Elsbury sitting slightly out of the group, looking as though she was attempting to appear as happy as the others.

'Oh no!' Duffy, only having sat down a second ago, leaped up. 'We've forgotten we're one person short. For the non-speaking part.'

This drew a collective groan of panic.

'But that person needs to be on stage most of the time,' one of the impossibly similar trio called across.

Duffy tutted. 'I know that, silly, but it's not my fault. We'll have to go through the whole list of characters again and see who we can do without.' Duffy's eyes fell on Eleanor. 'Miss, you remember you said you would be our secret weapon?'

'Yes, I did, Duffy. And?'

'Could you be—?'

Eleanor shook her head. 'I can't actually be in your wonderful play, can I? It was all of you who told me I'm not allowed to be.'

'What would Henley have done?' Elsbury said shyly.

Even after the emotional turmoil of the day, Eleanor smiled at the quiet girl's words. That evening, after lights out, she planned to sit on the very chapel stool she was perched on and absorb any connection she could with her mother. A delicious chance to lose herself in imagining the nine-year-old version of the unflappable, protective, ever-loving person who had been taken from her so early in life.

'That's right, Elsbury,' she managed. 'What would she have done, I wonder?'

'I don't know, miss,' Morton said. 'We're still one short either way, aren't we?' She flopped into the centre of the circle. 'Please help us think of something.'

'Mmm, a non-speaking part? Perhaps I do have an idea…'

The girls leaned forward, several toppling off their stools. 'Yes, miss?'

'Well, as long as no one hides any sausages in their pockets, we should be fine.'

Duffy frowned. 'Sausages, miss? Are you sure?'

'Very! Now how about another run through from the top?'

An hour later, the girls were wrung out from going over their lines and poses.

Eleanor rose from her stool. 'Milk and a break, girls?' She walked through to the kitchen and loaded the quarter pint bottles onto a tray.

'Do you need some help, miss?'

Eleanor spun round.

'What a kind offer, Elsbury.' She reached into a cupboard for plates. 'How about you set out the biscuits?'

'Biscuits? After supper, miss? Really?'

'Really. You've all earned an extra treat. And it's nearly the end of term. I think a special night is in order.' She smiled and bent back down to be at the young girl's height. 'I'd like to let you all know how much it means to me that you asked Miss Lonsdale to let me stay on.'

'It was quite plucky, wasn't it?'

Eleanor held out the biscuit tin. 'It was beyond plucky.'

Elsbury stared at the floor. 'Please can I say something that might sound silly, miss?'

'Go ahead.' Eleanor pulled two of the milk crates over for them to perch on, wincing at her ankle pain. 'I'm all ears.'

Elsbury giggled. 'That's a funny saying. Imagine if you really were.' She slid her hand into her dressing gown pocket and pulled out the music box she'd shown Eleanor. She held it like a talisman, as if it would give her courage. 'What I wanted to say is that since you've been here...'

'Yes?'

'Well... it's that, we've talked more and more about Henley. All of us have.'

'That's probably because we've been talking about the competition a lot. And Holly House hasn't won since she was here.'

'I don't think it is that, miss. You remember you said that you used to have the bed I'm in now?' As Eleanor nodded, the girl continued. 'Well, that used to be hers too. Somehow, it feels as though she's... she's here. Not really here,' she hurried on, 'but here, you know... in spirit.'

'Oh, Elsbury! I think it absolutely does!'

'So do I. And you don't think that sounds... silly?'

'Of course not.' Eleanor tilted her head. 'But how do you know she used to sleep in your bed?'

Elsbury clapped her hand over her mouth. 'I can't say.'

'Quite right. Secrets are to be kept.'

'Yes, miss.'

'Your music box really is beautiful, by the way.'

Elsbury turned the tiny brass key at the back and opened the lid. 'I don't know what the music is, but I love the ballerina. She looks very happy.'

'She really does.' They watched the ballerina slowly pirouette. Eleanor sighed. 'I was never any good at ballet. Too clumsy, not elegant like her.' She stood up and picked up the biscuit tin again. 'It's lovely talking with you, Elsbury.'

'Thank you, miss.'

'Now, how about you go tell the girls lights out is officially forty minutes later tonight and you can choose collectively what you'd like to do with your extra time.'

As Eleanor returned to the sitting room, she was pulled up short by the sight of the girls sitting in neat lines across the three settees.

'Hello? What mischief are you all up to now?'

'Mischief, miss?' Duffy frowned at the burst of laughter from Morton beside her.

Eleanor set down the tray. 'It looks like you're doing something I probably should pretend I haven't seen or heard. I'll be in the kitchen if you need me.'

'See!' Elsbury whispered as Eleanor turned her back. 'Go on, ask, Duffy. You're house leader.'

'Miss?'

Eleanor turned back around.

Duffy stood demurely, pulling on her sleeves. 'Would you play a game with us, please?'

'Is that all? Of course, I'd love to.' She wriggled onto the end of one settee and looked around the horseshoe of excited faces. 'What are we playing?'

'Truth or dare!' the whole group cried in unison.

Oh, help, Ellie. What have you agreed to!

'Is that really the truth?' Duffy said fifteen minutes later.

Morton pouted. 'Cross my heart. And promise on Woodster.'

'Go on then.'

Eleanor watched as Morton scampered from the room. The sound of the door slamming back against the hallway wall was followed by three sharp taps of the iron doorknocker's woodpecker beak on his dented circular plaque.

'Right, next it's…' Duffy pulled another scrunched piece of paper from the battered wicker basket in front of her. She opened it and clapped her hands. 'It's Lady Swift!'

Eleanor dutifully stood and went into the middle of the circle, mentally crossing her fingers, hoping they wouldn't ask anything she couldn't reply to.

A council of whispers followed until Duffy finally broke the group up with, 'No, we can't ask that.'

Elsbury stood up. 'Then I will. Someone needs to if we're ever going to find out.' A hush fell around the room. 'Miss, when you lived at Holly House…' She paused, clearly feeling the nerves that had caused the others to bottle out. 'Did you… did you used to sneak out after lights out?'

All eyes swivelled to Eleanor.

'I did, girls, yes. Although I definitely shouldn't be admitting that.'

'But you promised to tell the truth. And you have, haven't you?' Duffy shuffled forward on her knees. 'Really, you did?'

Eleanor nodded. 'I'll go and make my promise on Woodster. One moment.'

When she returned from tapping the door knocker, she paused under the archway. 'I probably should tell you though that I also got an awful lot of sanctions over going out after hours. I don't encourage you to do the same.'

Duffy giggled. 'You just needed to be better at it, miss.'

One of the blonde trio leaned forward. 'Is that what you were doing the other night, miss?'

'What? When?'

'In the storm. You came back ever so late, and ever so soggy. With a man shining a torch for you.'

'That was my butler, Mr Clifford. You've all seen him around by now. But perhaps you didn't recognise him in his big co— One minute! How could you have seen me arriving back with him?' She gasped. 'It was you? Hiding in the hedge, watching as I came in the front door!' This received a series of nods in reply. 'More than one of you? Whatever were you doing out in the rain? You must have been so cold and wet.'

'Who cares, we had food!' Duffy said.

'Lots of food!' the blonde trio chorused.

Eleanor frowned. 'But the door was locked.' She groaned. 'Tell me you didn't use the trellis?'

'Too slow,' Duffy said. 'We used the one by the bathroom window.'

'Oh dear. So it was a midnight-feast run. I'm just glad none of you caught a cold from it.'

Duffy looked confused. 'Why would we have? It's only a second across to the sanatorium and then it's all indoors.'

Eleanor ran through her mental map of St Mary's. 'But how did you get to the kitchens?'

Morton threw out her arms. 'Through the passage.'

'Which passage?'

'The secret passage underneath the staffroom corridor. You know, from the book.'

'Girls, I'm confused. Which book?'

'The Holly House Book of Secrets,' the room chorused.

'Henley started it,' Elsbury said.

Duffy looked confused. 'It must have been here when you were, miss. It's been here forever.'

Morton dug her in the ribs. 'But it was lost for ages, remember? It says so at the front.'

Again all eyes swivelled to her. Desperate to see something her mother had apparently started, if not written, she chose her words carefully.

'Are adults allowed to read it? If they're old girls who didn't get the chance when they were here? And they promise not to tell another adult as long as they live?'

Another hastily convened council erupted. Duffy turned to her.

'We've voted. And we all agree, but only if it's you.'

'Thank you, girls. That means so much.'

A few minutes later, the hairs on Eleanor's neck stood up as she ran her finger over the pages of her mother's writing. It wasn't quite what she remembered, but there was no mistaking those scrolling Y's and the way it was all at a slight angle.

Duffy leaned over Morton's shoulder. 'So you've never read this before, miss?'

She shook her head slowly. 'No, never. I must have left before it was found again.' She caught Morton's eye. 'Yes, I left in the nineteenth century which sounds positively medieval now we're in the twentieth.'

Morton giggled. 'More like BC, miss.'

Duffy nodded and then caught Eleanor's eye and blushed. 'Sorry, miss. But look. If you turn the page there's another map that shows the passageway that leads from the hall to the library.'

Eleanor's eyes shot up from the page, her mouth falling open. *Ellie, that's it!*

They looked at her and then one another in confusion. Duffy shrugged to the others.

'Are you alright, miss?'

No, Ellie, you're not!

CHAPTER 38

The packed hall was stifling, the June heatwave still searing on, although ominous clouds were gathering. *We're in for a storm, Ellie.*

She felt lightheaded. Even though she would never admit it to Clifford, her ankle was seriously swollen. She tried to swallow her anxiety, but her mouth was painfully dry. From her vantage point, Eleanor watched the staff in the wings assembling in a line ready to file onto the stage and then down to the front-row seats. The boarding houses would need the stage for their productions.

She had finally stopped the girls rehearsing an hour after official lights out, but neither she nor they had slept a wink. First, she'd asked Matron to stand in for her while she limped over to Clifford's cottage. And then on her return, she'd lain awake, pretending she couldn't hear the whispers and giggles coming from the dormitory. But at the same time, she'd imagined it was her mother planning her house's winning entry all those years ago when she'd been a border there.

And then until the early hours she mulled over what she and Clifford had talked about. And planned.

She shook her head and tried to focus on what was going on around her. Mrs Coulson was solemnly leading the procession across the stage, the staff in their swishing black teacher gowns looking as if they were in mourning for their dead colleagues. All except the bursar, who'd chosen a loud navy-and-pink houndstooth suit as if in denial. He was still making a great show of leaning on his borrowed walking stick. She looked round the hall. *Well, he finally has his audience, Ellie.*

She and Miss Lonsdale had both agreed it would be better if she wasn't with the staff, an easy decision for both of them. Especially Eleanor. She had an appointment to keep.

As the last of the teachers stood beside their chairs, Miss Lonsdale strode in from the wings and up to the lectern.

'Ladies, gentlemen, girls, it is such a pleasure to have us all here together again. This time for St Mary's Annual House Competition. This year it will be followed by a shortened version of Speech Day. Unfortunately, as many of you know, Speech Day was canc—'

Three short, sharp rings of the school bell rang through the hall. There was an immediate uproar. Shouts of 'Not again!' echoed around the room.

Eleanor waited until Miss Rice appeared and hurried up to the headmistress. Then she quietly left her seat.

The library felt eerily quiet after the turmoil in the hall. Eleanor took a couple of deep breaths. Silence could hold a malevolence all of its own, she thought. She shifted uncomfortably as she stood at the top of the tall A-frame ladder that had been the scene of Mrs Wadsworth's final fatal moments.

Something brushed her shoulder. She didn't need to turn to know what it was.

'Hello, Henley, I mean *Mother*,' she whispered. 'I'm trying to be brave, no, *pluckier* than I've ever been before.'

A door creaked and stopped as if the person opening it had expected it to be silent. And it would have been if Clifford hadn't adjusted the hinges out of line to make sure it creaked. The presence at her shoulder faded into the background, but she knew it was still there. She picked out the book that had lain beside Mrs Wadsworth's body from the top shelf and flicked it open.

'What's the game, then?'

Eleanor put the book down on the top step and turned towards the voice, her heart beating wildly.

'Game? I don't follow.'

Hepple looked up at her, scowling. He held an old sack in one hand, the sort she'd seen the grounds team using when clearing up.

'You knows what I means. You're responsible for that blasted burglar bell ringing again, ain't you?'

Keep calm, Ellie.

She forced a smile. 'Actually, no, Mr Hepple. Clifford rang the bell from the school office as I asked him to.'

'Asked him to?' He started at her for a moment, then shook his head. 'I've had enough of this nonsense.' He half turned as if leaving.

Eleanor hung further off the ladder. 'Oh, but don't go yet, Mr Hepple. I was about to explain exactly *how* you murdered Mrs Wadsworth and Miss Small. And why.'

Hepple paused and then turned back slowly.

'I see. Go on then, *Lady Swift*.'

The menace he put into pronouncing her name made her shiver.

'Well, where to start? Why not with the burglar alarm? When it rang tonight, you were confused, weren't you? Because even though young John has just come running to you with tales of another intruder in the art room, you knew it wasn't true. Which is why you haven't reported it. And why you were so confused when the bell rang anyway.' She paused for breath.

'And it made you wonder, didn't it? Because you knew there was no intruder this time. Or the last time. Anyway, just now you made sure all your staff were rushing off to check their respective areas and then you sprinted to the art room to find out what exactly was going on, didn't you?'

Hepple's mouth set in a thin line, but his eyes blazed. 'I was just doing my duty in checking out what one of my team told me they'd seen.'

'If that were the truth, Mr Hepple, then why did the note I pinned to Patrick Papier have you running here?'

'Patrick what?' Hepple shook his head. 'You're talking in riddles!'

'Let me explain. Patrick Papier was the papier-mâché model you saw just now in the art room. You remember? The model turning on the same mechanical turntable you disconnected in Miss Lonsdale's room so she would think it was broken and hand it over to you, the handyman who can fix anything, as she described you to me. You see the *first* time I went into Miss Lonsdale's study her model staircase wasn't turning. But the *last* time I went in it was because you'd finished using it and returned it to her, with the pretence of having fixed it.'

'And what's me fixing Miss Lonsdale's turntable got to do with you getting your flunkey to ring that bell and upsetting everyone?'

'Everything. You see, one of the girls I'm temporarily housemistress to was given a beautiful music box. When you open it, an elegant ballerina rises up and turns slowly. Just, I realised last night, like Miss Lonsdale's double-helix staircase. And just like the papier-mâché model that you set up on Miss Lonsdale's turntable to throw shadows on the wall of the art room as if it were an intruder on Speech Day. Why? So you could send your assistant John on a perimeter walk, having already put the idea in the young lad's mind that there might be intruders around.'

'What a load of rubbish,' he blustered.

'And so you could get young John to report the intruder on the porter's phone while you nipped into the art room, put the model back in its place and hid the turntable. I reckon that it was you Miss Munn heard while she was looking for intruders. Flanking paths, you know. But I digress. Why such an elaborate plan? I'll answer my own question, shall I? So that if Mrs Wadsworth's death was seen as suspicious, you weren't the one to have claimed there was an intruder, that's why. And also, so you had an alibi, as apparently you were guarding the rear door all the time.'

Hepple put one hand in the bag he was holding. 'So, Lady Swift, all this nonsense is so as you can accuse me of murdering Mrs Wadsworth?'

Eleanor shook her head. 'Oh no. Not just Mrs Wadsworth, Miss Small too, remember. But I'm getting ahead of myself. Let's rewind. When you reached the art room, a few moments ago you saw the note pinned to the model, the note that is I imagine' – she pointed to his jacket – 'now somewhere on your person.'

His hand flinched towards his pocket. 'What blasted note? You're talking in riddles again!'

'No, Mr Hepple, I'm not. As well you know. The note in Miss Lonsdale's handwriting telling you to hurry to the library urgently.' She laughed. 'I know, but it was Clifford's idea. We needed something that you couldn't ignore. Clifford wrote it. Honestly, between you and me, he has the most dubious extra skills for a butler. Including, I've recently found out, forging another's handwriting.' She shrugged at Hepple who stared back at her, rage in his eyes. *If looks could kill, Ellie, you'd already be dead.*

'Alright, Lady Swift,' he said through gritted teeth. 'Seeing as you thinks you're so clever. What else do you think you know?'

Eleanor pretended to think, her heart racing. 'Where to begin? I know Mrs Wadsworth was never having an affair with you, Mr Hepple. She wasn't having an affair with anyone, poor woman.' At his look she hurried on. 'In fact, it was Miss Lonsdale who was having an affair with you, wasn't it? And still is.'

Hepple snorted. 'Do you really think the headmistress of one of the most fancy girls' schools in the country is going to have an affair with the head of her maintenance team? Do you really think—'

'That it's very lonely at the top? That feelings and physical attraction transcend social boundaries? Yes, I do. I'm sure you were surprised to find yourself drawn to her as well, but if any of us had control over our hearts, life would be much less messy. And who would ever have suspected the two of you? The very idea! The reality, however, is vastly different. Murderously different, in your case.'

Hepple's eyes narrowed and his spare hand strayed back to the bag.

Eleanor tapped her chin thoughtfully. 'Only Mrs Wadsworth found out about your affair and went to Mrs Coulson as the second most senior member of staff, since she obviously couldn't go to Miss Lonsdale. Mrs Coulson probably never even let her finish her first sentence. I can picture it. A flustered Mrs Wadsworth gets as far as the words "Mr Hepple" and "affair" and Mrs Coulson sweeps from the room like a hungry wolf. *Wrongly* she thinks she has just heard a confession from a member of staff, rather than a report on the misconduct of her headmistress. She rejoices that she can finally get rid of the bumbling English teacher she has despised for lowering St Mary's standards for years.' Eleanor wrinkled her nose. 'Ironic then, that Mrs Coulson went to Miss Lonsdale and insisted Mrs Wadsworth and you, Mr Hepple, be sacked instantly. You and she were, in fact, the very ones dragging St Mary's standards through the gutter.'

Hepple's eyes never left Eleanor's. 'If what you says is true, then when Mrs Coulson came to Miss Lonsdale demanding Mrs Wadsworth be sacked, why didn't she do it? She could have got rid of the only person who knew of our supposed affair.'

'Simple. Because if she'd sacked Mrs Wadsworth she would have needed to also sack you, Mr Hepple. Mrs Coulson would have been suspicious to say the least if she hadn't. And she couldn't bear the idea of sacking you, could she? Back to a life of loneliness. No more secret liaisons. But you began to panic that Mrs Wadsworth would tell someone else. Someone else who would actually listen without jumping to conclusions. The board of governors, perhaps? So you decided to kill her on the day when you would have the perfect alibi – Speech Day. Even if Mrs Wadsworth's death was treated as suspicious, you would have a watertight alibi. But congratulations on your ruse of cutting a bobble from Mrs Wadsworth's cardigan and wrapping it like a special memento. After all, it was she you were accused of having an affair with. That almost fooled us completely.'

Without a word Hepple strode to the door and closed it as silently as he could. Producing a bunch of keys from his pocket, he locked it. When he turned around, his face was deadly. He put his hand in the bag and slowly withdrew a shotgun.

Eleanor gripped the ladder and swallowed hard.

You need that pluck now, Ellie.

CHAPTER 39

Eleanor tried to ignore the throbbing pain in her ankle. And the shotgun pointed at her. *You just have to keep him talking, Ellie…*

She cleared her throat. 'You know what really puzzled me for some time, Mr Hepple? *How* you killed Mrs Wadsworth. Nipping into the art room next door and hiding Miss Lonsdale's turntable took a matter of a few minutes with little chance of being spotted. But making it all the way to the library, killing Mrs Wadsworth, and making it back without any of the other teachers seeing you? Or your own grounds team missing you? Well, that was another matter. Unless, of course, there was a secret passageway, but I think we can discount that possibility.'

Because you know there isn't, Ellie. You checked the maps in the Holly House book. There's no secret passageway from the art room to the library.

Hepple scowled. 'Then why don't you tell me how I did it, as you seems to have all the answers, Lady Swift?'

She tapped her chin. 'I will, although as I said it did have me puzzled for some time. Because my butler very, very rarely makes mistakes. But when Clifford first saw Mrs Wadsworth's body and the steps, he jumped to a natural conclusion. We both did because we recalled the accident my uncle had had on the same make of steps when he was overreaching for a book. Only Mrs Wadsworth wasn't overreaching, was she? Because she died before she could. You made sure you had no need to even be in the library when it happened.'

Hepple stepped towards her. 'You really does have an overactive imagination, don't you? All them fanciful stories Mrs Wadsworth filled your mind with in them daft classes, I reckons.'

Keep him talking just a little longer, Ellie.

She smiled sweetly. 'Well, indulge my overactive imagination a little longer. Having rushed to the library in a panic to check for intruders after the bell rang, she saw the book you'd placed untidily on her desk. And in the same panic, she tried to put it back in its correct place. Just as you knew she would because, I assume, Miss Lonsdale had told you that she'd disciplined several of the girls for playing exactly the same mean trick. And, of course, the book came from the very top shelf. But Mrs Wadsworth never reached that shelf.'

Hepple grunted. 'And why was that?'

Eleanor glanced at the shotgun and hurried on. 'You see, I originally thought that vermillion paint had something to do with Miss Small's death, but then I realised it didn't. It did, however, give me the clue to Mrs Wadsworth's death instead. My butler informed me that royal seals used to be coloured with vermillion and my Holly House girls reminded me that royal seals were made from wax. The same wax you'd coated the top steps of Mrs Wadsworth's ladder with. Only you used wax without colouring so it was all but invisible. I realised just how invisible – and slippy – wax is when I almost took a tumble myself recently due to someone spilling wax from the candles in the chapel.'

Hepple smiled grimly. 'Actually, Miss Smarty, I used a mixture of shellac and wax. Much more slippery. And effective.'

Eleanor shrugged. 'Whatever it was, Mrs Wadsworth slipped and fell to her death as you intended. But the steps never fell. They probably wobbled a lot – I tested them before you arrived – but they didn't fall. So you see, Clifford and I were wrong all along.'

Eleanor smiled at the glowering head groundsman, aware of a movement in the shadows. 'Now, I know you called me Miss Smarty, but I do have a question to which I don't know the answer.

Which poison did you use to kill Miss Small? Cyanide, was it? Clifford checked and you keep both cyanide and strychnine to deal with pests. In the locked outbuilding nearest to your bungalow, actually. Which is what, I assume, you were really sneaking in there to get when we saw you. I know that cyanide can only be detected for a short time after death, or so my butler tells me, and looks like a particularly nasty heart attack, so I figure you used that?'

Hepple snorted. 'And why would I have wanted to murder Miss Small?'

'Ah, that took Clifford and I ages to work out as well. Then I remembered she mentioned that she had an acute sense of smell. Of course, after Mrs Wadsworth's death you'd gone back to the library while the police were being fetched and cleaned the wax, and shellac it would seem, off the step. But maybe a little fell on your clothing? I can't be certain, but I suspect Miss Small noticed the unusual smell when she discovered Mrs Wadsworth's body but thought nothing of it. She was also distraught, obviously. And then, she smelt it on your jacket, maybe? Did she make an innocent remark about how pungent it can be? Either way, you couldn't risk her eventually putting two and two together. So, I repeat my question. Was it strychnine or cyanide?'

Hepple grunted. 'Cyanide, actually. Effective at killing pests. All sorts. Some of them human varieties, as well.'

With unexpected speed he swung his shotgun around, but not quick enough as Clifford emerged from the end bookcase with a pistol and fired. Eleanor instinctively closed her eyes, but the expected shot never came. She opened them again and swallowed hard. *Act as if this is all part of the plan, Ellie.*

'Hello, Clifford.'

He bowed, his face and voice as inscrutable as ever.

'My lady, I do apologise. It seems my pistol jammed. Most unusual. I cleaned it only last week.'

Hepple's face, which a moment before had been one of fear and alarm, now relaxed into one of evil smugness.

'A mighty pity, Mr Clifford.' He waved the shotgun towards Eleanor. 'Now get over there with your mistress.'

With Hepple's gun trained on him, Clifford slowly inched around to the steps. Eleanor dared not do anything in case Hepple reacted by firing, so she kept perfectly still, her mind racing.

Before she could work out her next move, she felt a presence at her shoulder again.

'Well,' she said loudly, 'that clears that up, Mr Hepple. I think the only thing that remains is for you to give yourself up.'

Hepple shook his head slowly.

'I don't think so, Lady Swift. You are about to relive your precious childhood memory of climbing that elderflower tree in that there copse again. Only this time, rather than a sprained ankle – *he knows about that, Ellie!* – you're going to fall and break your neck. Such a tragedy.'

Eleanor smiled. 'Well, you'll have to get me off this ladder first, won't you? I'm pretty sure a shotgun going off would attract a crowd. And what about Clifford?'

Another evil smile played around the head groundsman's lips.

'Oh, I'll deal with him once I've dealt with you.'

'I don't think so,' a calm, deep voice said.

Hugh, Ellie! The secret passageway to the library in mother's book! He must have realised when he arrived with the uproar in the hall what I was up to and found one of the Holly House girls and told them I was in danger!

Hepple now had the shotgun trained on Seldon's chest.

'You'd better put your gun down, Mr Inspector, and join your friends.'

Seldon shook his head. 'Can't, I'm afraid. For one thing, I'm not carrying a gun. Nasty things. Don't believe in them. Saw far too much of what they can do during the war.'

And he never expected to need one today, Ellie, for whatever reason he came back.

Seldon looked coolly at Hepple. 'So, are you going to give yourself up and come quietly, as Lady Swift very sensibly suggested?' He nodded almost imperceptibly to Eleanor and Clifford.

Hepple gritted his teeth. 'I think, Inspector, I'm still the only one with a gun.'

'Really?' Seldon nodded again and swiftly sidestepped. At that moment Eleanor slid down the ladder, knocking Hepple forward. The gun went off where Seldon had been standing only a fraction of a second before. He stepped forward and nimbly extracted the shotgun from the astonished man's hands. For a split second Hepple stared at him and then charged. Seldon bent at the waist and flipped the groundsman over his shoulder and onto the floor, where Clifford was waiting. He grabbed the man's arms and held them while Seldon produced a set of handcuffs and slapped them on.

Seldon straightened up and looked over at Eleanor.

'You're hurt!'

Despite the pain in her ankle, she laughed and shook her head.

'I'm fine, Hugh. But why… why did you come back to St Mary's? You said if you even set foot on the premises again, you'd almost certainly be sacked.'

He glanced at Hepple handcuffed on the floor and then back at Eleanor and shrugged.

'I was driving up north and a voice whispered in my ear that you were in danger.' He looked her in the eye. 'And that I was putting my job before justice.'

As Seldon and Clifford dragged Hepple to his feet, she sensed a presence at her shoulder again.

'Thank you, Mother,' she mouthed.

CHAPTER 40

Eleanor was enjoying the moment more than any other she could remember in all her years at St Mary's. She cheered lustily and indecorously for the Holly House girls without worrying about Clifford having an actual heart attack over her impropriety. Mainly because no one could hear her over the enthusiastic applause from the parents and staff, and the whoops of encouragement from the girls in the other year groups.

Fingers crossed, Ellie. It's going well.

She held her breath as Morton and Elsbury pushed a wooden carriage on to the stage with Gladstone riding inside, resplendent in a union jack waistcoat. Parents several rows back stood up to see better before joining in the applause and discreet chuckles.

She bit her lip as her naughty litter of kittens took their final bow. 'They might still not win, Clifford, and it means so much to them. And to me.' She nudged his elbow. 'And don't bother to deny it. To you too, you closet softy. Conjuring up Gladstone's waistcoat and a carriage yesterday was beyond kind. Look! Lydia Goldsworthy is deliberating with her panel of sixth formers. Oh dash it! The other houses did a splendid job, too. It's far from a foregone conclusion.' She held the handkerchief over her eyes, sneakily wiping the quiet tears she couldn't stop from flowing. 'I can't watch.'

A moment later, Clifford tapped her shoulder gently, having to lean in again for her to hear him over the loud applause. 'I'd say it's probably safe to look now, my lady, but you'll likely require another handkerchief.'

She opened one eye and then yelled with delight at the sight of Duffy and Morton holding the silver house competition cup high above their heads. They stood with one hand each on the handles and the other round Elsbury's shoulders where she stood shyly in front of them.

'Miss! Miss!'

'We won!'

The Holly House girls and Gladstone bowled her over as they scurried up.

'I know! But that's because you were amazing and you worked so hard. And you too, Gladstone.'

Duffy grinned. 'And because our secret weapon made us pluckier than we could ever be.'

'Oh no. That's not quite right. Girls.' She beckoned them around her with a conspiratorial finger. 'I have a confession. I didn't make you plucky, at all.'

'Huh?' Morton said, staring around at the others. 'But then what just happened up on stage?'

'You simply let yourselves be the plucky girls you always were.'

'Thank you, miss,' they chorused.

'No, thank you. For breaking your precious rules once again and telling my friend about the' – she lowered her voice – 'secret passageway into the library!'

'He told us you might be in trouble, miss,' said Duffy.

'I know. But it was still good of you to break your rules. Oh, and speaking of rules, one word of advice.' She leaned in conspiratorially again. 'Best not to mention to the new headmistress some of the... er, "minor infractions" of the boarding house rules I may, or may not, have accidentally led you to break.'

As they scampered away, still giggling, she turned to Clifford and wrinkled her nose. 'Come on, I tried to toe the St Mary's line at the end there.'

His eyes twinkled. 'Poorly, my lady, but I think St Mary's will survive.'

'Thank you. Well, we'd better go pack our things once again. Then—'

'Miss?'

Eleanor spun round. 'Elsbury, yes, what is it?'

'I wanted you to meet someone.'

'Wonderful. Who am I going to meet?' She looked up to see the man who had been so loudly cheering the Holly House girls on from the front row.

The young girl's eyes welled up as she tugged on the corner of his jacket.

'It's my father, miss. He came!'

Eleanor's heart skipped. 'Which means he saw you win with all your friends.' She held her hand out. 'Mr Elsbury, it is a pleasure to meet you. You have a truly wonderful daughter. She is going to go on to great things.'

'I have never doubted that, Lady Swift.' He shook her hand and then placed his arm around his daughter's shoulders. 'She wishes to pursue science, it seems. I always thought she loved geography, but for some reason, she's been talking about nothing else except science projects. Oh, and fingerprinting or some such to do with the field of criminology, of all things!' He looked at Eleanor as if for an explanation.

'Really? I… I'm not sure where she would have—'

She was saved as he continued.

'It doesn't matter. Whatever field she wants to study, I'll give her my full support.'

'Of course you will. Sadly now, I must be going. Goodbye, Elsbury.'

Elsbury gave Eleanor a shy wave as her father led her away. As he did so, he half turned and mouthed, 'Thank you so much.'

Once they'd gone, Eleanor shook her head.

'Gracious, Clifford. I fear any more emotion and I shall disgrace myself. And, I confess now, my ankle is killing me.'

'Fear not, my lady. The Rolls is ready and Miss Munn has captured the errant Master Gladstone, I see.'

Mrs Jupe caught her as Clifford relieved Miss Munn of the overexcited bulldog, who had somehow slipped his lead.

'Lady Swift, I wanted to say goodbye. You've been a surprising hurricane of fresh air.'

Eleanor knew that Mrs Coulson hadn't mentioned exactly what had happened in the library. All they'd been told was that Miss Lonsdale was leaving and she had stepped up from deputy, to acting head for the moment.

Eleanor laughed. 'Thank you. I think.'

Miss Munn bounded over.

'It's been interesting on my part too. Interesting, delightful and humbling. You're a remarkable woman you know, Lady Swift.'

'My lady,' Clifford whispered. 'I'm afraid there is a jar of horse-radish marching in your direction.'

'Oh, botheration!'

The two teachers gave her a commiserating look and vanished. She slapped on a smile.

'Mrs Coulson, we're leaving now. Really.'

'Naturally.' Her grim expression softened. 'But not before I have the chance to say a heartfelt thank you. I am only acting headmistress at this point, but I believe the board of governors may appoint me permanently.' She leaned in and lowered her voice. 'Even though I understand from the chief inspector that Miss Lonsdale had no idea of the dreadful things that man Hepple did, she naturally felt it right to resign and leave immediately. There will, of course, be a full review of her… behaviour, but not until after Hepple's trial.'

Eleanor sighed. 'I believe Mr Hepple really does love Miss Lonsdale. I know he was worried about losing his job. I mean, at his age having been dismissed from his job, he had few prospects but poverty, but he did what he did mostly to protect her. He knew her career was everything to her.' She shook her head. 'But nothing can excuse what he did. And I understand Miss Lonsdale is leaving immediately. Poor woman, she must be devastated.'

Mrs Coulson pursed her lips. 'Perhaps, Lady Swift, we've all learned some lessons. Even me.'

Eleanor looked at her quizzically.

Mrs Coulson shrugged. 'If I am asked to take over permanently as headmistress, I might carry on a few of my predecessor's "progressive" ideas.' She straightened her shoulders. 'Not all of them, I hasten to add. However, I admit I might have been wrong to some extent about some "modern" ideas and "modern women". Modern women such as yourself, Lady Swift.'

Well, there's a turn up, Ellie!

'Thank you, Mrs Coulson. I wish you every success. There's probably nothing I can do to help, but—'

'Oh, but there is, Lady Swift.'

'There is? Oh, wonderful. Er… how exactly?'

'You see, just before they went on stage, the Holly House girls came to me with a request. A request which, as acting headmistress, I was pleased to agree to. One, in fact, I will extend to all the houses if I am appointed permanently. However, I need your permission for Holly House first.'

Eleanor shook her head. 'I'm so intrigued. What would you like my permission to do?'

'Well, Lady Swift, the girls asked if they could rename their house. Instead of being named after a fern as they are now, they asked for it to be named after an inspirational woman.'

Eleanor blinked in surprise. 'Really? That's such a fabulous idea.'

'I agree… now. And I need your permission as the girls have asked to change their house name from "Holly House" to "Henley House."'

Oh, Ellie! For a moment she was lost for words. Then a thought struck her.

'Of course you can have my permission. But why… why Henley?'

Mrs Coulson tutted. 'Even children can be detectives, Lady Swift. The girls confessed to me that they had wondered why their temporary housemistress had been the guest of honour on Speech Day. So they looked you up in the library copy of *Who's Who*. And found the name "Henley" listed as—'

'My mother.'

Mrs Coulson nodded. 'Exactly.'

Eleanor smiled. *So they knew all along, Ellie, but didn't say anything because I didn't.*

'And,' Mrs Coulson continued, 'they pointed out your mother's own entry in the same publication listed her, and your father's, achievements in pioneering educational programmes overseas. Before, that is, of course, their unfortunate disappearance.'

'Well, if my parents hadn't disappeared, I would never have been sent to St Mary's and I suppose I wouldn't be here now. So, maybe it's true. Maybe even the worst events do produce some good, somewhere along the line.'

'A very worthwhile tenet to hold, Lady Swift. You will, of course, be invited back for the official renaming ceremony. Now, if you'll excuse me, as acting headmistress I have to mingle with the parents. Have a safe trip.'

She walked off, leaving Eleanor shaking her head. *And you thought you'd had enough emotion for one day, Ellie.*

'Lady Swift!' a commanding male voice hailed her.

'Now what?' she muttered.

'Sir Oliver Goldsworthy, my lady,' Clifford whispered.

She turned and eyed the tall, grey moustached man standing legs apart, hands resting on a silver-topped cane in front of her. *Stay civil for the girls' sake, Ellie. It's their day. You don't want to make a scene.* She ignored her aching ankle that badly wanted her to sit and slapped on another smile.

'Sir Oswald. Good afternoon.'

'Hmm,' he grunted. 'That Coulson woman told me the basics of what happened. All credit to that inspector chap, I say. Made sure my daughter's safe, what? Can't say I agree with his methods, though. Involving women in detective work. What next? Pigeons?'

She heard Clifford's discreet cough and bit her tongue. *No need to point out that his precious daughter, Lydia, nor any of the other girls were ever in danger, Ellie. That's not going to help Seldon.*

Sir Oswald was still talking. 'Monstrous business. But the inspector managed to keep the whole thing under wraps, it seems. Not easy, especially once you start involving women. They do gossip so. Can't keep a secret to save their lives.' He tapped his nose with the top of his cane. 'Anyway, I shall call that detective chappie's superior again and let him know the man deserves a promotion.' He gave a curt nod and spun on his heel.

Eleanor took a deep breath. And then a smile slowly spread across her face.

CHAPTER 41

The muted rumble and stately sway of the Rolls were already soothing Eleanor's exhausted emotions, and her throbbing ankle, as Clifford drove through St Mary's gates for the last time. Gladstone's head lolled in her lap, his front paws either side of her legs.

'Are you sure there is nothing else you wish to do before we leave, my lady?'

She sighed. 'I don't think so, thank you. I'm equally happy and sad that this chapter is over.' She started. 'Oh no! Clifford, I forgot! The poor chaplain! We didn't—'

'All sorted, my lady. An old friend of his lordship's who has specialised in addictions for a great many years agreed to help most readily and with absolute discretion.'

'That's wonderful. That means the matron's job should be safe as well. She definitely learned a hard lesson she won't repeat.' She buried her face in the soft wrinkles of her bulldog's forehead. 'You know, it was such a comfort finding out about mother being at St Mary's. And now they'll name a school house after her. I have so much to think over. I can't wait for you to tell me the rest of her story. But at this moment, home is calling me. And so, I think, is my bed.'

'Only a minor emergency, my lady.' She tuned into Clifford's measured tone sometime later. How much later, she did not know, as she had fallen into a deep doze.

She struggled into an upright position, rubbing her eyes. 'What? Have we broken down?'

'If you would be so good as to alight a moment, my lady, I will attend to the problem.'

She ran a hand over her fiery curls, which were sticking out at all angles.

'Clifford. What the devil is going on?'

He climbed out and came round to open her door. Sliding her handbag under her arm, he helped her step out gingerly. She looked around.

'Clifford, we're in the middle of nowhere!'

'Everywhere is somewhere, my lady,' he said as he swiftly bundled Gladstone back into the car.

He went back round to the driver's door, climbed back in and calmly drove off.

'What the...?' She watched in utter disbelief as the Rolls slowly disappeared down the long straight road. 'Dash it, Clifford,' she called after the receding car. 'I'm too tired for jokes!'

The Rolls faded to a dot and then vanished as it rounded a bend. She looked up and down the now deserted road and shook her head. *The man's taken leave of his senses, Ellie! Must have been the strain of the last few days.* She threw her hands up.

'What on earth am I supposed to do?' she said out loud.

'Can I offer you a lift, madam?' A deep voice tickled her ear.

She spun around. For a moment she stared in disbelief. Then a look of comprehension dawned in her eyes. She folded her arms.

'Hmm, I'm rather more used to morning-suit tails in my chauffeurs than form-fitting blue wool overcoats and... distressingly flattering charcoal-grey suits. But' – she glanced down the road – 'as my usual chauffeur has obviously suffered some sort of mental seizure and abandoned his mistress in the middle of nowhere, I suppose I'll let it pass this one time.'

Seldon bowed and gestured to the bonnet of his car, poking out from behind a line of thick laurel hedging.

She tried unsuccessfully to keep a smile off her face.

'So, Chief Inspector, you just happened to be parked at the exact spot, Clifford—'

He held up a hand. 'Call me Hugh, always, Eleanor. I mean if we're alone. And I… I thought if we could manage a hundred miles together without arguing, just for once, then…' His lean cheeks coloured. 'I thought we might have the beginnings of a chance of…' He paused, his deep-brown eyes scanning hers anxiously.

'Of… Hugh?' she whispered, the cloud of butterflies in her stomach fluttering up into her chest.

Reaching out tentatively, he scooped her hands in his and pulled them to his burning cheeks. 'Of being more than just friends.'

She gave a mock wince. 'We may have a major hurdle to cross first then. I believe Henley Hall is well over a hundred miles from here.'

He leaned in and tucked one of her wilder straying curls behind her ear, smiling as it wilfully refused to stay.

'Good. I wish it were a thousand.'

HISTORICAL NOTES

First non-white teacher in Britain

Mrs Jupe is quite right when she says she is not the first non-white person to teach in Britain. In 1803 Tom Jenkins arrived in Britain from where no one is quite sure, possibly Sierra Leone or Liberia. By 1814 he was schoolmaster in Teviothead in Scotland and by 1820 he was teaching at a school in Pimlico, London.

He became well known enough for the Governor of Mauritius to ask him to run a school on the island. Tom agreed and in 1821, exactly one hundred years before Eleanor met Mrs Jupe at St Mary's, Tom left Britain to run his own school in Mauritius.

Tom's school finally opened in 1823 with only six pupils but soon grew to over one hundred. He carried on teaching in Mauritius for another thirty-seven years until his death in 1853. The school in Teviothead where he first taught still bears a plaque to 'The first black school teacher in Britain.'

First woman to cycle around the world

Eleanor tells her Holly House girls that she is not the first woman to cycle around the world and she is quite right. Annie Cohen Kopchovsky, known as Annie Londonderry, officially became the first woman to bicycle around the world in 1894–5. She was a Latvian immigrant to the United States and a mother of three. And, some say, slightly loose with the truth. How far she actually cycled in her fifteen months in the saddle may never be known, but however far it was, she was an amazing lady.

Northern Ireland

Miss Munn tells Eleanor that she's not quite sure whether she's supposed to be Irish or British. Northern Ireland was officially one of the four countries that made up the United Kingdom, although confusingly it is also described by some official sources as a 'province' or 'region'. It was created on 3rd May, 1921 a few weeks before Eleanor was due to give her speech at St Mary's. Even more confusingly, the rest of Ireland was known as Southern Ireland, but was superseded in 1922 by the Irish Free State which itself was superseded by the Irish Republic either in 1937 or 1949, opinion seems divided, I think.

'I think I have some ancestral Irish connection, you know.'

Eleanor says this to Miss Munn and she's right. In *A Witness To Murder*, she is able to stand for Parliament as a woman MP despite having an English title. Clifford explains this oddity better than I can:

'Nobility of the Irish Peerage have always been able to sit in the House of Commons. The 1801 Act of Union creating the United Kingdom did not give them the right to sit in the House of Lords, but did not exclude them from sitting in the Lower House. The well-known prime minister from the 1800s, Lord Palmerston, was such a titled Irish lord who sat in the House of Commons.'

Eleanor stared at her butler. Had he lost his senses? 'That's all very splendid, Clifford, but I don't happen to be Irish nobility.' She smiled apologetically at her visitor, who seemed suspiciously unmoved by the information.

Clifford coughed gently. 'Actually, my lady, your late uncle, Lord Henley, held a second title, which has also passed to you. That of a small baronetcy in West Ireland which would permit you to enter Parliament, although you may have to renounce your English title.'

Eleanor never does have to give up her English title, but that's another story.

Fingerprinting

As Elsbury tells Eleanor, fingerprints have been used on documents since ancient Babylonian times. They were first used in crime detection in the UK around 1858, but it wasn't until 1902 that the first person, Harry Jackson, was convicted on fingerprint evidence. His crime? Stealing a number of billiard balls.

Three fun facts about fingerprints.

1. It's actually a fallacy to say they are unique (there's no way to test this theory – it's based on sampling and probability).
2. You cannot convict someone nowadays on fingerprint evidence alone.
3. Identical twins do not have identical fingerprints.

South African hospital in Abbeville

While speaking to Matron, Eleanor is reminded of her time as a nurse in World War One. As she was living in South Africa when war broke out, she enlisted in the South African Nurses corps. There was, however, no direct fighting in South Africa, so the nurses were shipped to Europe where many of them served either in hospitals in Abbeville, France, as Eleanor did, or in Richmond, England.

Vermillion

Clifford gives his usual exhaustive explanation of how vermillion has been produced and used throughout the ages. In the first draft of *A Lesson in Murder*, I really wanted vermillion to be the murder weapon. Unfortunately, or fortunately depending on your viewpoint, no one has died directly from vermillion poisoning. Well, certainly not an art teacher in an English public school.

Flanking paths

Eleanor tells Miss Lonsdale that she is familiar with the idea of flanking paths as they allowed her to get away with mischief when she was at St Mary's. In truth, they did when I was at school as well. The library had a curved ceiling which meant, even though you were not supposed to talk (silence in the library!), if the teacher was in the middle of the room, you could stand facing the wall and whisper to your friend who was on the other side of the room and she could hear you, but the teacher could hear nothing!

Shellac

Hepple adds shellac to wax to make an even more slippery substance to coat the top couple of steps of Mrs Wadsworth's ladder. Modern shellac as used in nail care has little in common with the shellac Hepple would have used in the 1900s. Antique shellac was made from the resin secreted by the female lac bug in India and Thailand. It is processed and dissolved in alcohol and used as a wood finish and a food colourant! It was also used to manufacture gramophone records.

Double-helix staircase

There are several double-helix staircases in existence, probably the two most famous being the Bramante Staircase in the Vatican and the one Miss Lonsdale took for her inspiration, the one designed by Leonardo Da Vinci in the Château de Chambord in the Loire Valley, France. The staircase consists of two intertwining spirals, each a staircase in its own right, that allows visitors to the castle to ascend and descend without obstructing each other.

Victorian fern collecting

Eleanor's old headmistress was an avid fern collector, even naming the school boarding houses after English ferns. The craze, especially among women, became so widespread that a term was invented for it – pteridomania (*pterido* being Latin for ferns). Next time you eat a custard cream biscuit have a look at the pattern on it.

It's a fern, as custard creams were first introduced in 1830 at the height of the craze.

Who's Who
Who's Who is a reference book of the rich and famous, the good and the bad. First published in 1849, it purports to have an entry on anyone who is anyone. Last time I looked, I wasn't in it, so it's obviously not true. ☺

A LETTER FROM VERITY

Dear Reader,

I want to say a huge thank you for choosing to read *A Lesson in Murder*. If you did enjoy it, and want to keep up to date with all my latest releases, just sign up at the following link. Your email address will never be shared and you can unsubscribe at any time.

www.bookouture.com/verity-bright

I hope you loved *A Lesson in Murder* and, if you did, I would be very grateful if you could write a review. I'd love to hear what you think, and it makes such a difference helping new readers to discover one of my books for the first time.

I also love hearing from my readers – you can get in touch on my Facebook page, through Twitter, Goodreads or my website.

Thanks,
Verity

🐦 @BrightVerity

📘 veritybrightauthor

🖥 veritybright.com

ACKNOWLEDGEMENTS

Thanks, as always, to my amazing editor, Maisie, and the team at Bookouture without whom *A Lesson in Murder* would be so much the poorer.

Printed in Great Britain
by Amazon

37060455R00158